A Little Bit of Lust

by

Shirley Goldberg

Starting Over, Book 3

A Little Bit of Lust

Cover Art by *The Wild Rose Press, Inc.*

The Wild Rose Press, Inc.
PO Box 708
Adams Basin, NY 14410-0708
Visit us at www.thewildrosepress.com

Publishing History
First Edition, 2022
Trade Paperback ISBN 978-1-5092-4505-5
Digital ISBN 978-1-5092-4506-2

Starting Over, Book 3
Published in the United States of America

"Blimey," Lucy said out loud to the dressing room walls, channeling Eliza Doolittle. She turned her back and grinned over her pink shoulder. Then her best Queen Elizabeth straight from *The Crown*. "Philip? What do you reckon?"

She yanked off the top and slipped on the dress, clingy in all the right places.

"How is it?" Deon called from outside the dressing room. "Sashay on out here." She burst through the swinging door and twirled in front of him gripping the pink top in her hand.

"I love them both." She felt her own excitement transfer to Deon.

"Then take them both." He stared approvingly, broke into a smile when she caught him.

"Thanks, I will." *Which to wear on my Marcus date?*

"Just don't wear—" His eyes clouded. "Never mind."

"What?"

He didn't finish his thought, gazed past her. "It's perfect. Take it." He slid closer and hugged her, right there in the middle of the missy department. "You…look great."

Advanced Reader Reviews

"The characters are so spunky and real I wanted to join them for a glass of wine and share relationship advice!"

~*Marisa Mangani, ARC reader*
~*~

"My perfect evening is a hot bath, a glass of wine and this book."

~*Teri Moore, editor, ARC reader*
~*~

"An enjoyable read with engaging characters and more than *A LITTLE BIT OF LUST*."

~*Teresa Michaels, ARC reader, author*
~*~

"A hilarious depiction of commitment phobics on steroids."

~*James Hanna, ARC reader*
~*~

"Lucy and Deon are truly meant to be together in spite of everything!"

~*Elizabeth Brown, ARC reader*
~*~

"A story of romantic charm and self-realization that will rekindle the spontaneity and passions of youth we fear perish when seeking new love midway through life."

~*Gerard Bowlby, ARC reader*

Dedication

For my writing group. You know who you are.

Acknowledgements

I can't imagine writing in a vacuum, and thankfully, I don't have to. My Inky Links tribe of fellow authors know Lucy and Deon as if they lived with them: Teri, Marisa, Teresa, Lizzie, Jim, Rob thanks so much for your consistent support and feedback.

Many thanks to my readers, including newsletter subscribers, for kind words and funny stories. We can all start over and make changes in our lives at any age. This goes especially for my mom, who's ninety-seven, young-at-heart, and has been rolling along enjoying her reading and life in general, thanks to a positive attitude and inner strength. And thanks to my sisters, Barb and Sandi. You're always there for me.

Frances Sevilla, my editor at Wild Rose Press, knows how challenging this book turned out to be. We share a sense of humor that is priceless.

A big thank you to musician and harp player Peter Menta for the song lyrics. And Mark Mathes, for his editing savvy and catches on my final manuscript. Your expertise is much appreciated. Thanks to my fellow Roses, author friends, and the team at Wild Rose Press for their contributions along the path to publication. Special thanks to Lisa for her marketing skills and to RJ. Morris for the lively, colorful cover.

Chapter One

Dancing Funsday, Deon called it. Of course, he had names for everything, from movie stars to restaurant chains, friends' pets, politicians, and his favorite bad habits.

Lucy held the door against the March wind, gabbing with Travis the bandleader as he hauled in his sax and trombone. The smell of hops, french fries, and herbs drifted out from the kitchen. She glimpsed Rocky, one of the regulars, already perched in the corner of the bar by the wall with his entourage—Rita, Nancy, and Amy. Lucy waved to them and nabbed three seats at the bar.

She needed this. Where else could you go dancing on a Sunday afternoon? Only a smattering of folks in the restaurant so far, but that would change in the space of twenty minutes. Soon O'Donahue's would be rocking.

"Hi," said a guy two stools over. "Steve." He tapped his chest in a shorthand introduction. "You come here often?"

"Original line," Lucy teased. She eyeballed the restaurant. No sign of Deon or Phoebe. "Did you spend a lot of time coming up with that one?" She twerked her cheek in self-mockery. No point offending the guy since she didn't even know him. Maybe he wasn't a jerk.

"Sorry, meant to be a joke but it came out cheesy. I've seen you and your two friends here."

"So, you dance?" If she smoked, and it was the sixties, she'd have pulled out a Chesterfield or some European brand. Maybe Gauloise, one of those pungent cigarettes. "Dancing guys are at a premium, and O'Donahue's has a small floor."

"You get right to the point."

"I should have checked out your shoes. Now I'm forced to be obvious about it." She glanced down at his worn classics. "Hey, do you mind?"

"Mind what?"

She snatched her phone from her bag.

He chuffed and pulled back. "You're taking photos of feet?"

"Only dancing shoes." Lucy studied his well-loved footwear. "I'll bet those could tell stories. Blue shoelaces are the bomb." Other than that, the guy dressed like a metrosexual.

"Are you a photographer?"

"Learning. Mostly food. This is a departure. I'm branching out."

"Branch away." He gave a mocking nod.

"Thanks." She snapped off a couple of shots.

"Those sneakers of yours pass for dance shoes?" he asked.

She stretched out a leg and pointed her toe. "Masking tape is the secret so they slide, even with beer spill on this floor." He had banter. Who knew, she might be able to talk to this man. "You going to ask me to dance?" She gave him the side eye. Cute, if a tad stiff. She'd loosen him up.

"Sure am. First dance of the evening."

Lucy bent over her phone and quick-shuffled through the photos she had snapped of Steve, deleting all but one. Perhaps he had a girlfriend. Well, she wasn't coming on to him, and it was a dance, not a sleepover. She looked up to find him watching her and put her phone away.

"You know," said Steve, "you and your friends are like The Three Musketeers. Always together."

Together indeed. Lucy loved their routine. Arrive early while the band set up, grab seats, and make the rounds among their dancing friends. The band quit at eight, and they went home and got up early the next day to wrestle with classrooms full of middle school kids.

Steve leaned an elbow on the bar. "I've been here half a dozen times—"

He jerked back as Lucy's best friend, Phoebe, trotted up and plonked her bag on the bar, startling them both. "Deon's late. I don't see him," she barked.

Lucy sniffed and cleared her throat in a loud ah hem. "Mrs. Interruptus why don't you?" she growled. "And hello to you, too. This is Steve. Where's my hug?"

"Sorry, darling." Phoebe bobbed her head in Steve's direction, said a quick "hi," and wrapped both arms around Lucy. "Better? By the way, *interruptus* sounds sexual."

"I was trying to be snotty."

Steve stood and gave Phoebe his seat. "Thank you, very thoughtful." She shot Steve a quick smile and reached for her bag. "I'm stealing this dating idea from an ad for eight-minute dating. Some restaurant in Stamford." She opened her bag and peered into its depths. "Can't remember where I put that ad."

"Dibs on Deon for 'Chattanooga Choo Choo.'" Lucy raised a hand to signal the bartender. "I think Travis is impressed by my vast knowledge of Glenn Miller tunes."

"I'm certain he is." Phoebe, riffling through her handbag, gave Lucy a doubtful look. "You'd better alert Deon. He just came in. There'll be a ton of good dancers here today with this band. Competition."

Lucy glanced over at the stage where Deon stood talking to Travis, in Buddy Holly glasses and a porkpie hat.

"Got it." Phoebe brandished her phone and scrolled. "I forgot it was in my photos. Look." She thrust her phone at Lucy.

"Can't read it. The print's too tiny." Lucy flung her arm in the air and flapped it in Deon's direction, eventually catching his eye. He wandered over wearing his customary smirk, and Lucy handed him Phoebe's phone. "Read this, would you?"

Deon cleared his throat and launched into his favorite accent. Elvis. "Welcome, ladies and gentlemen—"

"Hah, it doesn't say that," Phoebe protested.

"Meet your dream gal or guy. Only eight minutes to your SoulMate IRL! Here's your chance. Ages forty-two to fifty-five. Follow the link for more information and your choice of evening.'"

"That sounds like torture," Deon said, dropping the Elvis. "IRL? What's IRL?" He cocked his head. "Code for I'm Really Likable?"

"It means In Real Life, Mr. Doofus," Phoebe said. "Don't make fun of those who are divorced and forced to date."

Deon hung his head in mock embarrassment.

"You're faking not knowing, aren't you?" Lucy patted Deon on the shoulder. *"I'm really likable. Seriously?"*

"Yes, but Phoebe called me Mr. Doofus." He turned and nodded at Steve. "In front of…sorry, didn't catch your name. Don't you think they treat me cruel?"

"Teasing you is what we live for." Lucy did a little flapper hand action, her fingers spread in front of her face.

Deon grabbed her hand, pulled her up and twirled her once, twice, and returned her to the bar stool.

"And you're dancing the Chattanooga Choo Choo with me no matter what," Lucy said.

Steve backed away from the bar with a little wave. "Time for a Guinness. Nice meeting you all. Catch you ladies later for a frolic on the dance floor." He disappeared into the crowd.

"A frolic? Who is that?" Deon turned to stare after him.

"Listen up, you guys." Phoebe leaned forward and dropped her voice, a teacher trick. "I want to do my own eight-minute dating thing. An event at my parents' restaurant. If I can convince them."

"Your parents?" said Lucy. "A dating…no, you maybe want to rethink that." *Didn't Phoebe know better?*

"It's all about ice cream. I'll keep it simple. Eight-minute ice cream dating. When the weather's a bit warmer." Phoebe pursed her lips. "Late May. What do you think?" She was dead serious. "Deon?"

Deon rubbed his shoulder. "You know how I feel about all that dating stuff."

"Oh, suck it up already." Lucy snorted. Thinking about Phoebe's stiff and proper Greek mom and dad hosting a singles activity, she burst out laughing just as drumbeats signaled the first notes of "Jailhouse Rock."

Phoebe shot her a dirty look, hooked Deon's shirt with her forefinger, and pulled him toward the band, leaving Lucy staring after her, partnerless. She looked around at the scattered crowd racing like lemmings onto the dance floor.

A voice behind her. "Dance?"

Steve. She lifted her chin. "Well, yes, don't mind if I do."

****

After the break, the band played four fast swings in a row. Lucy danced them with Steve and another guy who jerked his arms up and down in time to the beat. By the time the piano intro to "Can't Help Falling in Love" began, she was ready to rest.

Deon appeared in her path and held out his hand, palm up. He led Lucy to a spot near the band, his arms drawing her in. "Relax. Put your head on my chest."

"Very funny."

"Go ahead, you deserve it. You danced hard."

She eased into the unfamiliar closeness of a slow dance with Deon, and listened as he sang the lyrics along with Elvis.

"Am I annoying you, singing in your ear?"

"I didn't know you sang. What's with that?"

"What do you mean?"

"Me not knowing you sing. You have a great voice." Deep and smooth. What the heck, she sort of enjoyed Deon crooning to her. She snuggled against him, tentatively laying her head on his chest, feeling the beat of his heart.

"I haven't felt like singing for…a while anyway." He turned her gently and pulled her in again, sang about rivers flowing and fools rushing. "I am annoying you, aren't I?"

"Not at all." Dancing with Deon was…intimate. She lifted her head. His lips were six inches away, full lips. "You have Elvis lips," she said, and rested her head again on his chest.

"That a compliment?"

"I'd say so."

"My Elvis is credible, though, right?" He inclined toward her and lifted his upper lip in an Elvis sneer.

She giggled. "I try to *ignore* your imitations." What a lie. Why had she said that? She loved his imitations.

"Most people do."

"You don't usually like dancing slow…how come this one?"

"Shh. Feel the music."

Maybe this song was connected to Melinda. Whatever. She wouldn't think about it. She'd enjoy being held in Deon's arms for this one lovely song, and even pictured Deon singing it for real—he had a really good voice. Well, he wouldn't sing to her, of course. *If not me then who?* He wasn't dating anyone. She and Phoebe knew all his personal business.

He guided her into a turn and back into his arms. "You're a smooth dancer, and you've got great balance. Did you take ballet as a kid?"

"Are you kidding? I was a klutz. Totally unathletic."

As the song ended, Deon hugged her close and

bent down to kiss her on the cheek. "Thank you. I enjoyed that dance with you."

"Me too." She fluttered her hands as she pulled away. *Deon kissed me on the cheek.* What did that mean? Probably nothing. But it was a first. She closed her eyes, imagined kissing him, his familiar mouth pressing into hers, a light touch at first—

The mood in the room changed with the first telltale train whistle of "Chattanooga Choo Choo." Deon snatched Lucy's hand and swung her out, swaying to the music, the dance floor already jamming. Travis on trombone and a guy on trumpet made the band special. Not many bands on the Connecticut shoreline had the repertoire of this one.

Deon twirled Lucy, brought her in close and sent her out. Her leg collided with the foot of a heavyset man who stepped back onto her instep. "Ow," Lucy yelped. When Deon led her in a barrel roll jump—a turn followed by a jump-hop—she cannoned in front of an elderly couple who startled and backed up. The woman shot her a dirty look.

"Are you trying to kill those people, Goldbloom?" Lucy shouted over the horns, the sax, and the clarinet. "That could be your grandma and grandpa." She turned to apologize to the couple, but they were walking off the floor.

"Sorry," Deon said.

"Come with me." Lucy grabbed his hand and pulled him from the dance floor.

"It's the middle of the song," he protested, allowing her to lead him over to the couple they'd bashed, seated at a hightop.

"We'd like to apologize." Lucy nudged Deon with

an elbow. "You shouldn't have to leave the dance floor because of us."

"I got a little too enthusiastic." Deon hung his head. "I'm so sorry."

"Thank you," said the man, who looked shaken. "Young people nowadays don't watch out for us oldies on the dance floor."

"Well, we'll watch out for you tonight. Both of us." He squeezed Lucy's hand. "These people need to dance small."

"You're fine, fine dancers, and a mighty attractive couple," the woman piped up, and Lucy yanked her hand from Deon's grip.

****

Deon, at the bar with Lucy and Phoebe during the break, wished the Steve guy would get lost so he, Deon the Great, could get on with his evening. Okay, so he was a tad full of himself, but they were his friends, and Steve was blabbing about nothing much, sucking up the air around them. Enough already and who appointed him mayor?

Steve didn't need to know they hung out a lot on weekends and whenever. They were the three, not the four musketeers. Three, the magic number, now that Melinda was gone.

Deon had only stopped wearing his wedding ring six months and four days ago. Four years after losing Melinda. He still couldn't say "since my wife died," and according to his grief group, that was normal. He'd taken the ring off at home one evening after a special dinner of Phoebe's homemade spinach pie and an arugula salad, Lucy's contribution. The three of them had planned the occasion. "Retiring the Ring," they called it.

"It's time," he'd said in a melancholy voice and slid the ring into a tiny red box Phoebe had bought for the occasion and presented to Deon. They all got a little teary when Deon went upstairs to nestle the ring in his sock drawer. "I'll remember Melinda every day when I get dressed."

That comment made Phoebe and Lucy laugh-cry, and after they all recovered. Deon got out the marshmallows and graham crackers and Hershey's chocolate. They made a mess with their s'mores on the stove, three burners going, but Deon didn't give a shit and unfortunately, Melinda wasn't there to yell at him.

Oh, they had fun together, the three of them. Three being the operative word. Who needed Steve?

Was it the guy's pants, his shirt molded to his body? A tad fitted for Deon's taste. No, it was everything. Pants, shirt, his moves on the dance floor, but especially the small talk. They always joked about how they hated small talk. He'd done riffs on the irritation factor of *tiny talk*, as he termed it.

"You're all teachers?" asked Steve, his voice low and mellow as if he were trying too hard for the cool factor.

Lucy pointed to herself in response to Steve's question. "Lucy Bernard, science. Phoebe Karis, reading coach, and this is our school psychologist, Deon Goldbloom. We all teach at the same middle school."

Steve shifted his attention to Deon. "Like the singer Dion? The 'Runaround Sue' guy?"

Deon blinked at the mention of his name.

"Different spelling," Lucy clarified.

"So you all met at work?" Steve slid closer to Phoebe. Deon couldn't decide if the guy was interested in Phoebe or Lucy. He sure was a nosy bastard.

Deon's thoughts flopped all over the place, creating scenarios. What if Steve asked Lucy out? What if Steve and Phoebe started dating? The idea of their threesome coming apart, of no more happy hours, filled him with dread. He chided himself to stop ruminating.

Deon signaled the bartender and ordered Stella, his favorite beer. While he waited, he gazed down at Lucy's white sneakers perched on the rung of the barstool. Keds, the brand a lot of swing dancers favored. If that Steve fellow asked Lucy out, he'd probably take her dancing. *My Lucy* flicked into his mind for a nanosecond. Ridiculous to even think it. He squeezed his abdominal muscles to excise the thought. Even so, the past few months, being around her made him uneasy in a good way.

"Deon," called a woman entering the restaurant. "How's the psychology game? Counting down the days until vacation?" Roberta, one of the Sunday regulars, was a school psychologist in Hamden.

He wheeled around and trundled over to chat with her. "Unfortunately, the paperwork crunch comes first," he said with an ironic laugh.

She raked a hand through her hair, gazed briefly toward the bar and back toward Deon. "Lookin' good, Deon. I almost forgot those deep browns."

He digested the compliment, odd because Roberta never flirted with him. Was that what she was doing? He'd read somewhere that widowers go through a period of mourning followed by a lot of meaningless sex. Whoever wrote that article didn't know shit about what it was like to lose your wife. Or maybe Deon was stunted in the sexual department.

Melinda used to tease him about his brown eyes. "So you think those deep brown eyes are enough, along with your innate charm? Well, it's not sufficient for me. Your turn to wash the dishes, Buster. I cooked."

"I'll wash the dishes if you don't call me Buster," he'd reply. It wasn't funny, but anything *Buster* always made them dissolve into silliness.

The air crackled in anticipation as the band launched into Stevie Ray Vaughan's "Pride and Joy," and he swung Roberta into his arms, making her laugh. Steve led Lucy onto the dance floor where they leaned into one another in sync, thighs touching, swaying in a sensuous bluesy move that made Deon want to punch him. The guy focused so hard, Deon imagined he counted each beat. When he dipped Lucy, his face tightened with concentration as if he had to get it right with no room for error. Without missing a step, Lucy slid a hand through her hair, lifting it from the back and letting it drop in a Rita Hayworth move. Deon bit down on his molars.

The song ended and the band regrouped. Deon reclaimed his seat at the bar, remnants of a comment Phoebe made a few days earlier at lunch in her office tickling his brain. What had he said to provoke her? *I'm not your average alpha male.* Yeah, that was it.

"We're not lovers of the alpha male, are we?"

"I should say not." Lucy had reached over to tweak his cheek. "I appreciate nerds with muscles. Like Deon."

"Wait," he'd protested. "What about all those bare-chested alphas on the covers of thousands of books on

Amazon?"

"Oh, sure, but that's different." Phoebe and Lucy had launched into a discussion of historical versus contemporary romance. Deon tuned out, remembering the evening Melinda called him over, pointed to a webpage, row after row of book covers featuring males with bare chests and perfect pecs.

"Honeybun, you've got great hair and you work out. Why don't you take off your shirt and puff out your chest like these guys? Show me what you've got."

Had it really been four years ago?

He'd hauled her out of the computer chair with one hand and swooped her up under her ass with the other, Rhett Butler style. Lugged her all the way into the bedroom where, sure, they'd done it. Slow and tender like the beta man he was at his core.

He missed her so much.

Now three rock and roll numbers unspooled, and Deon danced all of them with different women, Sunday afternoon regulars. He refused an offer for a fourth dance, returned to his bar stool and upended his beer glass. He stared vacantly toward the dance floor where Steve and Lucy swayed to "Texas Flood," another Stevie Ray Vaughan at his slow, sexy best.

Lucy's hand slid to the back of Steve's neck and Deon's skin tightened watching them.

Four years. I've known Lucy for over four years. What am I waiting for?

Chapter Two

A few weeks later, Deon wandered around Totally Wine wondering which of their happy hour restaurants was on the agenda for that Friday evening. Since it was a freakin' balmy day, even for the end of March when snowstorms could still hit the shoreline, a walk on the beach would be great.

He paused at a display of California cabernet sauvignons and pulled a bottle from the shelf. Aptly named Bright Girl, the label showed a picture of a ringleted redhead in a yellow top and red skirt. *Lucy,* his brain shouted, as if in recognition and surprise.

"Could you possibly help me pick out a good red wine?" A halting voice to his right jolted him out of his Bright Girl reverie, his mind scrambling to figure out why anyone would request his help. Totally Wine had excellent personnel for that purpose. A woman smiled up at him, a slightly chubby woman in her late forties. Straight brown hair with expensive blonde highlights. He mentally shook himself, dumbfounded at the blatant pick-up line.

"How much do you want to spend?" He pretended to take the question seriously.

"Around fifteen?" He walked her over to the zinfandels and located his favorite, the Zinphomaniac. It showed a sexy, old-fashioned forties, bathing beauty on the bottle, an image that always cheered him, no matter his mood.

"This is a good one." He pulled it from the shelf and handed it to her. A chance to invite her for coffee? He wasn't in the mood. He was never in the mood, mostly because the thought of starting over, getting to know a stranger, felt like…too much fuss. There would be strained widowerhood conversation, questions about children and jobs and sundries he didn't care to discuss.

His cell whistled in his pocket, and he glanced at it, bobbed his head in apology, glad he could make a run for it. "Sorry," he mumbled as the woman thanked him. He sped toward the back of the store so he wouldn't run into her again. He'd been kind, recommended his very favorite wine to a stranger. His finger hit the text and—crap. Phoebe was cancelling. One of her migraines.

On his own, yet again. Another dinner in front of the television. He needed a dog. He loved dogs, but after Cubby, he and Melinda never got around to adopting another dog. Not that any dog could replace their Cubby.

He slouched down the aisles, his mind on all the changes. *Nothing I can control.* He shook his head at all the gloom this sort of thinking brought on, grabbed a six-pack of Yuengling, and tucked the bottle of Bright Girl to his chest, hoping he'd love it and come back for more.

Deon hesitated by the window where the afternoon sun lingered. Wait. He didn't have to dine alone. Lucy. He and Lucy, well, why not? They'd be a twosome. Like when they cruised yard sales and Goodwill together, not one of Phoebe's favorite things. The weekend stretched out like a banquet of exotic delights. Nothing planned, so unlike him.

He pulled out his phone and called. After four years of friendship, why spend the evening alone with the television? He'd sell Lucy on the idea that wasting this glorious afternoon would be a shame. Five rings before she picked up.

"Guess what I made today," Lucy blabbed happily. "Phyllo dough stuffed with blueberries, a touch of lemon. Invented it myself," she bragged. A few words about her online Instagram course, the importance of hashtags to increase engagement, and two new recipes for brunch. Her enthusiasm was heartening, a great diversion.

Who am I kidding? I'm looking forward to this like it's a date. Unless she won't want to come out. His gut clenched.

His daughter Sara was right to nag him to get out more. *For crap sake, Dad, you sound so gloomy when I call.* She loved the word *crap* even more than he did.

"It's crazy warm today," he began. "What do you say to a walk on the beach and dinner?" *Beach. Was it warm enough for a beach thing?*

"But Phoebe has a migraine."

At that moment, he had no comeback. "I don't have a migraine," he said. "Do you have a migraine?"

"No, of course not. Why are you asking?"

"We don't gotta stay home, missy. Bring old sneakers. Wear your dancing duds." *Why not go dancing with Lucy?* "Bus leaves in fifteen minutes."

"Old sneakers? Dancing? Where are we going?"

A few seconds of dead air while thoughts whirled in Deon's head. "Our favorite place?"

"All righty then."

All righty then. Deon felt more alive, more himself

16

than he'd felt in a long time. And that was nothing more than the anticipation of a good time.

****

Freak, no, he's heading for the beach. Sure enough, Deon took the road that curved alongside the water and parked in the lot closest to the boardwalk.

"I thought you were kidding about the beach. I'm dressed for dinner," Lucy protested. "My new flats." *Is he kidding?*

"You don't need no lousy shoes, girly-girl. I'll carry you." He wrestled his shoes and socks off and scrambled out, scurried around to open her door. "Hop on board."

"Yeah, like you can carry me?"

"Never underestimate a school psychologist." He grinned, reminding Lucy of The Joker, that creepy subhuman Jack Nicholson played in one of the Batman movies. "Let's take a walk, live on the edge."

She glared at him. How could she be mean? Poor guy was trying to show her a good time. Besides, spontaneous was fun, and so was walking barefoot in the sand before dinner.

"Come on, where's my adventurous Lucy?" He glanced down at her turquoise flats. "You're one colorful gal. Throw your shoes in the car, and grab your phone, you Insta fiend. Let's stage some shots."

How did he always manage to make her laugh? She slid out, breathing in the magical balm of the salty, sea weedy air, her spirit rising with the reassuring sound of the waves. So what if her skirt billowed in the wind?

He crouched and rolled up his pants, exposing milky white feet and…yes, she quick-looked. Mmm hmm, well-cared-for toenails.

They wandered off, limping over the stones in the lot and up onto the boardwalk, past the now-shuttered food concessions, and down the stairs onto the sand. A breeze floated more of that familiar beachy odor, and gulls squawked and drifted overhead, occasionally dive-bombing and skimming the top of a wave. A few teenagers clustered farther up the beach where a man ran with his dog.

Deon gripped her hand. "I'm glad we're doing this. I've wanted to…"

"What?" she prompted, curious. Did Deon mean he wanted to come to the beach with her?

"Never mind." He pointed at the seaweed, shells, and sandpiper footprints. "You taking pictures?"

"Yes. Help me style, will you?"

"Sure." He stood waiting.

"Grab a few shells and let's place them so we get those footprints in the shot."

"All righty." He trudged in a bent-over position, taking his job as shell-gatherer seriously, while Lucy combed the sand for feathery greens she could spread out in a photo. They trotted up and down the beach, as the sun lowered into a fiery orange ball. She stood amid the seaweed, shells, and horseshoe crab carcasses, and despite the dampening chill, a fever of anticipation shook her.

Deon brought back two perfect sand dollars and a handful of fan-shaped shells. "You want your photos to have punctum."

"What?" The phone dangled from her neck. "I've heard that word before."

"It goes to emotion. It's individual. Everyone reacts differently. It's hard to explain."

"Punctum. Yes, I like how that sounds." She crouched, fiddling with the seaweed. "Punctum," she repeated.

"You're my punctum." He caught Lucy bending over draping seaweed into a pattern on the sand, and pulled her up for a hug, nuzzling her earlobe. "You smell so good."

"Oh."

Deon getting touchy-feely. His neck went crimson. *He's nervous.* She ducked under his arm and took a few shots of the objects, giving him time to gather himself. That nuzzle was as close to physical affection as Deon had ever come.

"So, when did you start taking pictures?"

"My ex-husband was into photography, the one thing we had in common."

"Your ex? You never talk about him."

"We weren't together long."

Deon made a little depression for the horseshoe crab and arranged the sand dollars around it, along with a few larger shells. He looked up. "I've always wanted to ask you…why did you get divorced anyway?"

"Oh, I never told you? Huh. I got pregnant at nineteen, and we thought we could make it work. We couldn't. We were too different. Way too young."

"I'm sorry. I didn't mean to pry."

"You're not prying, and it was a long time ago." Talking about her ex was not a subject she was fond of, not that it was a big deal. *Liar. It's a big, gigantic deal when your husband leaves you, in the middle of the night, three months after your infant daughter is born.* She hunkered down and grabbed seaweed in shades of green and brown, tossed it Deon's way. It landed on the

19

crab. "Would you make that look pretty?"

"Sure."

She avoided his gaze, and he kept his head down as he repositioned the shells and the crab and made a little mound of sand then added more green seaweed.

"I have Lily, so a good person came out of our marriage." *Not that her father sees her much.*

"I'd go crazy without Sara." He looked out at the water toward the horizon. "It's hard enough now that she's in grad school."

Lucy put a hand on his arm. "It's not easy." The distance of twenty-eight years didn't make talking about her ex-husband any more palatable. She trotted down to the water, Deon following, and gathered some of that funny seaweed stuff with the little knobs and added it to the design.

He rolled his pants legs higher and waded into the water. "Yeah, well, getting dumped with a kid at nineteen can't be a picnic."

She startled and straightened, eyes moistening behind her sunglasses. "How did you…you guessed I got dumped?"

"You never remarried. Lucy, I never understood why you, of all people, never found someone."

"Yeah? I thought that about you, too. A widower with a teenage daughter, that had to be rough. Especially the first year or two." She bent and grabbed more shells, and they trotted back to the display.

Lucy clicked off a few shots from different angles, her right arm quivering, forcing herself to concentrate by tensing her muscles. It wasn't Deon's fault he'd stumbled on the worst thing in her life. She kept Lily's father in a special box in her mind she seldom opened.

"Step into the picture," she urged. "I want to get your bare feet." For a moment, Deon said nothing, and she wondered if he'd pester her with more questions.

"No way my feet are going in your picture." Deon made a dorky face, and Lucy threw a glob of the knobby seaweed at him. He peeled it off and lobbed it back.

"We'll both get in the picture." Lucy tugged at his pants leg and ticked off a few more photos before reaching for a handful of sand.

"Don't even think about it," he backed away.

"Silly, come back. It's for the picture. Sand on our toes. I'll do a closeup and…"

He slid an arm around her, hugging her close then moved behind and wrapped his arms around her waist.

"This feels good." His voice low, husky, his breath quickening. Or was she imagining this response?

Lucy wriggled away from Deon and snapped a few shots, hoping he wouldn't notice her hand shaking. Thinking of Deon's reaction to touching her, the heat coming off him in spite of the chill as the sun lowered in the sky. He slid close again, dropped his chin onto her shoulder, and nuzzled her neck, his hair tickling her ear. "You smell good. I already told you that, didn't I?"

Lucy didn't put much faith in pretty words, never had, but this was different. Deon wasn't some random internet date. Deon was…Deon. Best friend and maybe more. Her chest squeezed as he tilted her backward onto her heels, his grip around her waist the only thing between her and falling onto the sand. Her arm formed an arc over her head.

"Next time we go dancing, we'll try this." He righted her and moved his hand up and down her arm slowly, making her skin prickle. She noticed a tiny pink speck on his cheek where he'd nicked himself shaving.

"Did I tell you how beautiful you look today?"

"Tell me more." Drinking in the compliment, craving more while the late afternoon chill crept up her legs.

It was a teaser, that first tentative kiss. She wrapped both hands around the back of his neck and stood on tiptoes. His lips probed gently, then with increasing pressure and oh, it was good, really good. They stood like that kissing until her legs turned to frigid blocks that threatened to collapse. She pulled back and looked up at him.

"Are you cold?" He shivered and ran his hands up her arms. "I can't feel my feet.

"Me either. I'm freezing." The chill had sneaked straight up her skirt to her crotch and belly. "How did it get so cold when I wasn't looking?"

"The car. Let's run. I'll put on the heat."

They held hands and lumbered back across the wood planks of the concession stands and across the boardwalk to the parking lot. Deon murmured, "Don't worry, I'll warm you up." He unlocked the car and opened the door. Once inside, shielded from the wind with the motor running, they thawed out.

"I've got towels and things on the floor by your feet. Hold on, I'll come around.

He opened her door and reached down, coming up with a hot water bottle and a plastic tub. "Look what I brought."

"So that's what I've been straddling in your no-trunk car."

"It's part of the special surprise package I ordered for you."

She lay back and stuck out her feet.

He unscrewed the cap, poured the water over her feet, soothing, a comfort liquid. "I didn't want you to be cold. I figured with a hot water bottle, the water would stay warm for a while."

"They still make those? Warm water. This is heavenly."

She giggled, thinking of him heating the water at home, preparing for this outing. *Planning to kiss me?* Warmth spread from her chest to her toes.

"Laughing, huh?" He glanced up, working the towel between her toes, massaging, concentrating on the task.

She lay back, not quite believing this was happening. "You're familiar with one of Phoebe's sayings, aren't you?"

"Tell me."

"A man who plans is a joy forever."

He shook his head, smiling. "She's smart, that Phoebs."

After he slipped her shoes on, she lay against the seat rest, while Deon shook out the towel, poured water over his feet, and dried them. Then he put on his socks and shoes.

This is really happening.

A little warning prickle, nothing more than a flutter. She brushed it away. *This is Deon. He'll never hurt me.*

"Excellent service," she said as he sat beside her and started the car then leaned in to kiss her cheek. His mouth traveled down to her lips, and she turned so they wouldn't bump noses. The kiss lasted a few centuries—a full-on make-out session—long enough for the car to heat up, or maybe it was Deon doing the warming.

"You better?"

"Oh, yeah." Whatever was happening, she didn't want to analyze it.

Deon nuzzled her neck. "I'd like to take you to dinner now at O'Donahue's."

She waited, her toes curling inside her shoes. *Dinner and maybe a slow dance at her favorite place.*

"Can we pick things up after dinner?"

"I'll consider it," Lucy teased, fluttered her eyelashes. *Deon, unsure of himself. Was that possible?*

He pulled her close, kissed her neck, planted one on her nose. "Argh, your nose is cold."

"Oh, please, yes. Dinner and picking things up after." *Especially the picking things up after part.*

****

Yeah, it surprised the shit out of Lucy to be at O'Donahue's with Deon on a Friday-night date. *They were on a date, weren't they? Beach kissing followed by a dinner invitation equaled a date in her book. In all the books.*

O'Donahue's, their go-to place. They knew the wait staff, the menu, the regulars, the bands.

Deon disappeared through the double doors to the main dining room after they were seated. Lucy opened the menu and there he was, a few minutes later, easing into the booth opposite her, grinning. "Calamari for an appetizer?"

"Sure, sounds good." Deon could have said fried liver and she would have agreed, since her thoughts twirled around and around like pinwheels. *Deon doesn't date. Is this a real date? Am I the exception? He kissed me, so it's a date.*

The server appeared with a bottle of wine. "How about this? A Kendall-Jackson Pinot Noir." She smiled, proud of herself. So Deon had consulted with the bartender about the wine, how enterprising.

Deon gave the wine a cursory glance. "Looks great, thank you." She took out her corkscrew.

It was all so natural talking about Anthony Lane, the movie critic for *The New Yorker,* Lucy's new dance shoe series on Instagram, and how Deon's daughter Sara monitored his sugar intake, which amused Lucy.

"I love that we went to the beach before coming here. That was fun." She hesitated, her voice softening. "You're a really good kisser."

"Thank you. I'm a grown man, I've had practice, but if you think I could use more…I'm ready when you are."

"Oh I—"

"Sorry. I'm prone to lame jokes." Deon was flustered. Even so, he slid his hand across the table to grip hers. "I'm not kidding around. Kissing you was…it was the best. And I want more…with you. I've been wanting to tell you that for a while now."

She swallowed. What did he mean by wanting more?

"What would you like?" Deon asked. "I'm having the sesame-seared Ahi tuna. Comes with whipped potatoes and mixed vegetables." He closed the menu. "They take the potatoes in the back and whip them. You?"

"Make it two." Because it was easier that way, and food wasn't all that important. She had better things to do. Like dancing and then a lotta making out. They hadn't had dinner yet, and she was already planning on running her fingers through Deon's hair. They clinked glasses and took a sip. Lucy regarded Deon over the rim, seeing him in a new and more-than-a-friend way.

"Lucy, you look lovely tonight."

"Um, thank you." She was collecting compliments like hard candies. And here she'd thought Deon with the great hair and the Alec Baldwin smirk wasn't interested. Not in her, not in anybody. Deon, the guy who rarely raised his voice, who wore bright shirts to work—orange or cobalt blue, for example—and shrugged off the good-natured ribbing from his students. At parent meetings, no one ever went ballistic.

Oh, and he hasn't gotten over the death of his wife Melinda. Until now. Otherwise, he wouldn't have kissed her, would he?

While they waited for the food, Deon told Lucy about his daughter Sara visiting her grandparents in Sausalito the previous summer. They knew each other's kids well enough that she'd written a recommendation for Sara's study abroad program a couple years back.

"She wangled a job walking dogs," he said. "Loves it. Wants to do it again next summer when she visits."

"Good for Sara." Lucy's stomach was making funny noises. "Sausalito is a primo neighborhood for walking dogs."

"And how's Lily?"

"Thrilled. She got a job off campus, working for a couple who do a podcast and feature stories for NPR. Right up her alley."

"Both our girls are getting to that age, the flying away age." Deon shook his head, stared down at his fork, and back up at Lucy. "It's difficult."

The server arrived with the appetizers, and they each forked a tentacle. "Hey, kids today have it easy," he said. "They don't date exactly. Pretty much hang out. Simple, huh?"

"Oh, they date. It's tougher for them out there in dating land. In your twenties, you don't know what you want." She dipped a morsel into the red sauce, chewed. "The whole process of meeting people, getting to know them. Exhausting."

"I can imagine."

"Didn't you and Melinda date? It's not like dating is a foreign country." Was she spoiling the mood, bringing up his dead wife in conversation?

"Oh, we hung out the first night we met. I never thought of it as dating. We were together. That was it." He gestured to Lucy's bag. "Where's your phone? Let's have a look at our pics."

She scrolled through the beach photos, pointing out the footprints in the sand, the horseshoe crab, all the while thinking how lucky Deon and Melinda were. A *fairytaleish* romance. She tapped one of the photos and held it up. "This is my fave, our bare feet with the seaweed and the horseshoe crab husk."

"The poor shell of a guy." Deon wiggled a finger. "I know you want to."

"What?" The wine slid down very nicely, producing a pleasant buzz of well-being.

"Post a couple pics on Instagram."

"Later, maybe." She didn't want to spoil the mood.

After the waiter brought the entrees, Deon slid a hand across the table and took Lucy's.

"I'm a little…wound up." His mouth tightened and

then broke into a half smile.

In the four years she'd known him, Deon never gave her the slightest hint attraction-wise. She always thought of him as off limits because of the widower thing, and Melinda being Phoebe's good friend. Lucy thought of her friend at home with a migraine. Would they have connected if Phoebe had been here tonight? Unlikely. She chunked a piece of tuna. "We're friends. What changed for you? Today?" She put down her fork. This wasn't a planned question. It popped out. Now that it was sitting on the table, she wanted the answer.

"Friends makes it even better." His eyes closed, and he leaned across the table. For a second, she thought he would kiss her, but it wasn't the time. The lights were too bright. The place was too noisy. Behind them the band was setting up.

"So, I have an idea about how we should proceed. Want to hear it?"

"Proceed? Sounds so sexy," she joked.

"We'll go slow," he said. "We'll do stuff together, pedestrian stuff like grocery shopping. Working out. We can cook together. Would you like that?"

A grin started and expanded. He was describing coupledom, and Lucy hadn't been part of a couple for over a year now, ever since her occasional pleasure buddy faded away into a real relationship. Phoebe named him, by the way. She called him PB. She'd said, "If anyone asks questions, we're talking about peanut butter."

"Would you come sit next to me?"

Lucy slid over to Deon's side of the booth and insinuated herself, so their legs touched. He stroked her thigh, or gave it a light reassuring squeeze, and that's how they stayed. Except when he buttered his bread or cut his tuna.

In a little while, the band started playing, and Lucy swayed a little to the music, a bluesy number. She closed her eyes, enjoying the moment.

"Dance the next one?"

They fit together like matching pieces of a puzzle. Slow dancing with Deon, so sweet. The band played three slows in a row, and she slid her hand into Deon's hair, relishing all that thick curliness between her fingers.

How would they end up tonight? And what would she tell Phoebe?

The evening was perfect, like in the songs. He drove home slowly, holding her hand the whole way, even pulling into his driveway one-handed.

He twisted around to face her, the light from the porch illuminating his face. "I didn't ask if you'd come over, and I hope it's all right. If it isn't—"

"Oh, it is."

He kissed Lucy's forehead, making his way to her mouth with little pecks. Teasing, his lips barely touched hers, then he added the smallest bit of pressure until he was kissing her for real. Holding back, though, she could tell. It was unbelievable, the feel of his mouth, soft and slow, so slow it hurt.

"Let's go in, shall we?" His hoarse voice vibrated inside her.

Chapter Three

It wasn't easy kissing his best friend.

Well, not true. Once they made it up the sidewalk and through the door, him fumbling with the key, it was easy, way too easy.

He guided her toward the couch, urging her to sit because he was afraid he'd tip over in delight and they'd both collide with the coffee table.

"Lucy," he exhaled, "I've...I don't..." On the tip of his tongue to tell her he didn't want to make a mistake by rushing her. "Let me put on some music." Fumbling, almost dropping his phone. "Diana Krall, do you know her Paris album? A classic." He sounded like a baboon. Sweat gathered under his arms. Where was Diana Krall hiding? His thumbs searched at warp speed. *Slow down.* There, there. He backtracked, pushed *play* and heaved an inward sigh of relief as Diana's mellow, velvety voice filled the room.

"Sit. Let's relax. Wine? I have a credible zin, but you know I'm the king of zin."

"Sounds...nice."

They sat side by side, touching at the hip, sipping the wine, the silence growing weird. He had to make a move. If he didn't act now, right now—

"Maybe you'd like to kiss me?"

His stomach flipped, and then he relaxed. This was Lucy. He exhaled. When he bent over her, his cheek close to hers, the scent of the beach rose from her hair, and he pictured them back there buffeted by the wind, or was he imagining the sea air smell? He drank in the reminder, pleased and a little thrilled, and brushed her lower lip with his thumb. He kissed her, wondering why he hadn't done this sooner. His lips explored her smooth neck, traveled down to the rise of her breast and up again. It felt so right, his heart swelling, other parts swelling…especially when she gave a little moan.

"You're really kissing me."

"I am." He wasn't the only one who was nervous, and he knew from his body's reaction everything was…well, wasn't lust a good sign? A great sign. A primal reaction he hadn't experienced in a long time. "You like it? Me kissing you?"

"Don't stop," she said, grinning at him, making him kiss her smiling face until they both started laughing. It went that way, kissing interrupted by a little talking, a sip of wine. When Diana's "Peel Me a Grape" came on they danced, oh, so slowly, her arms looped around his neck, pressing into him. She nibbled his ear, and the instant jolt that ran from the nibbled ear to his groin made him squeeze harder, his hands sliding to her butt.

"Deon?" Her voice faint.

"Yes?" he croaked.

"I don't know if that going slow thing you mentioned at dinner is going to pan out." Poking fun at him, her hands wandering under his shirt, stroking his back. "You said we'd do pedestrian things. Remember?"

"Uh." He turned her in a small circle, dipped her, brought her in close. "Ladies' choice."

They drank more wine and kissed, hours blowing by like nanoseconds. And all the while he tried not to think *This is Lucy. Lucy's kissing me. I'm touching her breast.* Trying to get thoughts out of his head, give in to the moment.

At some point, his voice hoarse with lust and the awkwardness of his phrasing, he whispered, "Let's go into the room with the bed, shall we?" They rose and slipped into his bedroom where he undressed her, lingering over each item of clothing, dropping it to the floor, going on to the next. He caressed her with the tips of his fingers, his hand smoothing her surfaces as if polishing. "Ahh," and he buried his mouth in her neck.

"Is it all right?" he whispered, feeling foolish. This was his Lucy, and he had to be sure.

"Better than all right. Keep touching me…like that…yes. How do you know that turns me on?"

He couldn't get enough, couldn't get close enough. His hands traveled down, and he briefly thought…*no, this isn't happening.* Lifting off her top, kissing that flat, smooth stomach, moving up to her breasts, he held his breath, wondering what came next.

Everything came next, unfolded slowly, and his head emptied of any wayward thoughts.

Except how right this felt. Friends made it better.

Light wound its way through Deon's heavy bedroom curtains before they fell asleep.

****

They woke early, way too early for a Saturday morning. Lucy opened one eye and sneaked a look at Deon. *Why is it that men look cute and scruffy in the morning while women have raccoon eyes and crusties?*

After a little making out without even brushing

their teeth, Lucy and Deon tumbled downstairs and into the kitchen to make breakfast, bleary and tired and hyper all at once. Fifties-style with a Formica booth and black and white tile floor. Phoebe called it the Happy Days kitchen. "Except for the modern, turbo appliances, of course," she'd say appreciatively whenever they visited Deon and cooked.

"Open the cabinet," Deon said, massaging her back. He couldn't help wanting to touch her, could he? When would he stop wanting to hang on to her?

Lucy peeled open the cabinet doors, rummaged inside and came out with a box of buttermilk pancake mix. "Pancakes, let's make pancakes."

"Sure, we're pancaking it. I have frozen blueberries. Will that be good? And real Vermont syrup." He let go of her and got out the butter, milk and an egg. She nearly conked him in the head when she opened the freezer door for the berries. He grabbed the mixing bowl and spray, wondering how long ago he'd last made pancakes. Years.

"I'll measure, you cook and do the dishes."

"You have a dishwasher."

"Right."

He cracked the egg and whisked the mixture together, as Lucy held the bowl steady. "Hey, you're the master baker. Why am I doing this?" he teased, showing off his one-handed egg-cracker skills and letting go of her so she could search the deep cabinet drawers for a pan.

She brandished a flat round griddle he'd forgotten he owned, sprayed it, and turned on the stove.

"Don't I do good work?" He dipped the whisk into the batter to show her. "No lumps."

Her arms encircled him. "I can't believe it," she said.

"What?" His stomach tightened as she pressed into him. Hah, he knew what she was thinking.

"We did *it*," she said, lingering on the *it* so long a stirring in his groin got him thinking how great they'd been together.

"We did, didn't we?" They both laughed, the air pungent with the aroma of cakes on the griddle.

Minutes later the sweet scent of pancakes filled the space, and Lucy flipped them onto a serving dish.

Deon poured the coffee, and they sat at the table. "When are we breaking the news to Phoebe?" He cut his stack of pancakes in half and then half again.

A mathematical eater. How had she not noticed this before now? She forked a healthy chunk and dipped it in a pool of syrup. She stuffed the wad into her mouth, chewing and talking. "I haven't thought about it." *If he was serious about telling Phoebe, this was a good thing.*

Deon laughed. "We can double date now with Phoebe and whoever she's dating. Although, on second thought, I want you all to myself." He did the rapid Groucho Marx eyebrow raise.

"Don't be selfish," Lucy chided him. "It's not healthy."

"You talking mental health?" Deon pointed to his chest. "I'm the expert."

"You're an expert kisser."

"Why, thank you." He reached across and took her sticky hand. "We're on our mini-honeymoon. Let's do whatever we want to do. Walk. Wander around downtown. Take me to one of your favorite places?"

"How romantic." Lucy pulled back her hand and wiped off a little syrupy residue.

"It's true. I'm a believer in all things romantic." Deon mopped his pancakes in the melted butter on his plate. His phone rang. He grabbed it and took a quick look then shut it off.

"What if it's your mom?"

"It is my mom. How did you know?" He looked genuinely surprised.

"Good guess. Don't mind me. Call her back."

"Thanks, that's sweet." He squeezed her hand. "She knows I love her. I couldn't…my mind is on other things."

She ate almost as many pancakes as he did, and then they went upstairs to shower together. At first, when she looked at him, her lashes wet, drops of water streaming over her breasts, he got hard. Showering at the end of a long day, before dinner, was one of his sweetest memories of his past life with Melinda. Something they'd finessed with Sara in the early days, once she was old enough to entertain herself in her room.

"Time to read your book, honey," his wife would say before he and Melinda toddled off to soap up together. Later, once he could afford it, Deon had the master bathroom remodeled, doubling the size of the shower with easy-to-clean folding doors and a whirlpool tub.

Now the reality of showering with a woman other than his late wife hit him as he slithered in beside Lucy, the water surging down his back. He shook his head to rid himself of the image as Lucy's hand with the giant sponge rub-a-dub-dubbed not only his chest. He sighed with a mixture of pleasure and contentment.

And lust.

After the shower Deon dried Lucy, taking his sweet time before wrapping her in his shortie bathrobe, which came charmingly to midthigh on her. He guided her into the bedroom where they crawled back into Deon's bed, and he pulled up the covers.

"Share my pillow. Come closer," he murmured, eyes closing. Delicious, the fragrance of her hair on his pillow, so delicious. Even better, the feel of her body as he spooned her. He slipped the bathrobe off her shoulders and ran his tongue down her back. He felt his limbs relax as her breath slowed. She was asleep.

They had time, the rest of the weekend. For now…it was enough to catch a little Saturday morning nappy time with Lucy.

Chapter Four

"Let's drive out to the beach." Deon rolled over and nuzzled Lucy. She lay awake, not believing she was in his bed, barely believing they'd gone back to bed.

He kissed her neck. "Revisit the scene of our first kiss."

"Our first kiss. Hah, a whole day ago?" *So much had happened in such a brief time.*

"Wouldn't you like a nice brisk walk? Do us good."

"Now? I think it's cold, like freezing." She stuck an arm out from under the covers. "Brr. Yesterday was freakishly warm. I have no winter clothes with me." An excuse. She didn't want to overstay her welcome. "What time is it? Where's your clock?"

"One fifteen. Why? You have an appointment? On a Saturday?"

"No." She stretched. "I haven't slept this late since…I don't know when."

They moved slowly, got up, dressed and chugged a little coffee then drove over to Lucy's where she changed into jeans and grabbed a heavy jacket. So, she wouldn't get to show Deon the Sterling Memorial Library, her favorite place in New Haven. Instead, they drove to the East Haven beach, deserted except for a man throwing a ball to his dog, and propelled themselves down the sidewalk to keep from turning into popsicles. The wind stung as it whipped her hair into her eyes.

"We should have worn dorky hats and gloves," Deon managed over the pounding of the surf. "My eyes are tearing." He laughed and nudged her.

"Those waves must be ten feet high," Lucy said, striding beside Deon. "Whose idea was this ridiculous walk at the beach?"

"It'll feel good when it's over." There was that familiar briny saltwater smell, and the seagulls picking through the trash didn't seem to mind the cold.

They lasted thirty minutes before race-walking back to the car. Deon fumbled with the keys, and Lucy shivered, her nose running. She grasped the door handle. "Justin used to love coming to the beach in winter," she called over the roof. "He said it got the blood circulating." *Oops.* Her non sequitur hung out on the invisible clothesline above their heads.

"Yeah?" The lock popped and they clambered into the car, rubbing their hands together. "Old boyfriend?"

"My last relationship."

He started the car. "I hope you're not tiptoeing around me. You don't have to be afraid to reveal stuff about your past misadventures." He swiveled around and reached out to frame her face with his hands.

She jerked back. "Cold, your hands are cold."

"Sorry."

"Who's says I had misadventures?"

"Your past." He grabbed her hands in his larger ones and rubbed them. A sweet gesture. "Funny. I never realized I know so little about your former relationships even though we've been friends for what? Four years?

Why did you guys break up?" The warmth from the heater began to penetrate and Deon turned up the fan. He waited a few seconds, his expression thoughtful.

"Now, Deon?" Her acerbic voice. "Are we going to have a discussion about my former boyfriend?"

He startled as if waking up. "Oh, sorry. Ah, totally inappropriate. What was I thinking? If you, well, you'll tell me some day if you want to talk about him. Sorry."

"Not today. I'm not mooning about him, if that's what worries you."

"Hey, I have an idea. Let's not cook tonight." Deon leaned in and kissed Lucy's cheek. "Who says I'm worried?"

On the highway, they were quiet. Why she'd dredged Justin up after Deon kissed her...she'd spoiled the mood. No wonder he wasn't talking.

She sneaked a look at Deon, the curve of his jaw, how the slant of the sun through the car window highlighted his manly beard.

Justin's face loomed in her mind, that cement block look he shot her the day she gave him the *You're a great guy* speech leading up to the breakup news. Since her husband had left all those years ago, she'd been in charge of her relationships, deciding how often to get together, controlling the level of intimacy. She'd never again lived with a man. Was this normal for a woman her age?

Maybe she needed a therapist.

"Let's stop for takeout," Deon said as they neared Niki's, a neighborhood deli and restaurant. "A little homemade Italian?"

"I'm still full of pancakes."

He pulled into a spot with a meter and killed the

engine. "Humor me."

They sat for several seconds. A young couple with a frizzy white dog walked by. "The relationship wasn't right for me," Lucy murmured.

"What?" Deon thumped his head with his fist. "Oh, you're talking former boyfriend? That's why you didn't entertain me with things Instagram on the ride back. Sorting things out in your head."

"I'm a sorter."

"And me? I'm a planner," he said. "Anything else you'd like to impart about Mr. Former Boyfriend before we pop into Niki's?"

"Nope." She made a lip-smacking sound on the "p".

"Even though I love cooking, the idea of us lolling around all Saturday afternoon, not fussing with meals is rather appealing." He smiled that disarming grin, thawing her out. "Wouldn't you agree?"

"Yup." Inside her head where he couldn't hear, she was mulling over how long to stay. This was all so new. And she'd pretty much kept her boyfriends to herself with strict instructions for Phoebe not to blab about any personal business.

"Allow me to order, Madame?" Deon ordered away, not waiting for an answer. Chicken parmigiana, chicken casertana, sausage, and broccoli rabe.

"Made with love and caramelized onions," said Tony, the owner's son. "Very good."

"And a little of the linguini puttanesca," Deon said, leaning over the counter to get a better look. "You like that, honey?"

"I do. Isn't it a lot of food?" *He called me honey.*

"No worries, leftovers are our friends."

Back at Deon's, after stowing the food, he pulled out Scrabble. He won the first game, and they started a second.

"You played a lotta Scrabble with Melinda, didn't you?" Lucy set her letters up on the little rack.

"Occasionally." His tone flat, his smirk telling her another story. "In the winter it was Scrabble at home and poker with our friends, a couple who've since moved. I miss them."

"You and Melinda…you were close."

"Very." His fingers found hers and squeezed. "I'm with you now. That's the past."

"Deon?" Lucy shifted away from the table. She didn't feel in a Scrabble mood.

"Talk to me." He didn't let go of her hand.

"My husband…left me. After Sara was born. A few months after she was born."

"Oh."

"I lied to you. By omission. He was never interested in making a go of our marriage. It's not something I tell people. I'm telling you."

"That must have been—what an asshole. I'm sorry that happened." Deon grasped her hand, squeezed it.

"Hey, thanks. I was lucky. We lived with my parents a few years while I got my degree. They were wonderful. Anyway…it was a long time ago. I wanted to…thought you should know." She studied her letters. "I go first?"

"Yeah."

She slapped "pregs" on the board. Funny how getting those letters had prompted her to tell Deon about Sara's father who occasionally asked his daughter to dinner and not much more.

"That's not a word."

"I suppose not."

"You don't feel like Scrabble." Deon dumped his letters in the box and Lucy followed suit. "Let's make a spinach salad." He reached down and offered her his hand. "Because we shouldn't neglect our greens, and we need our strength." In the kitchen, he opened a bottle of zinfandel. "I'm setting the mood for our romantic dinner."

He pulled two little tables from the hall closet. "You want to watch a movie?"

"You've got old school TV tables." She sipped the wine.

"I live alone. I watch TV and talk to it, too. Shout sometimes."

"Is eating in front of the TV romantic?"

"It depends." He arranged the tables in front of the couch.

"On the movie?"

"Everything depends on the movie." He slid open a cabinet against the wall and pulled out a stack of DVDs. "You've got choices." He spread them out on the floor. "Take a look."

"Seriously?" She read them aloud. "*When Harry Met Sally. You've Got Mail. Sleepless in Seattle.* Nora Ephron. So you love Nora as much as I do?"

"Well, it's more—"

"*An Affair to Remember.* That's romantic. *Heartburn,* not so much, but it's a great movie. Who doesn't love Meryl and Jack?"

"There's more," he said, gesturing inside the cabinet.

"Let's watch *You've Got Mail.* I always cry at the

end."

"So do I."

"You're a man. What are you doing with romantic—" She stopped in mid-sentence. "Sorry."

"Melinda loved them, yeah. We weren't big on vacations or fancy restaurants. She loved a plain old movie night. And men cry at the movies too, you know."

"Oh, of course." Lucy hugged him. "You cry at the movies. That is so, so romantic."

"Sit, relax. And by the way, my lips hurt from all that good kissing. Do yours?"

"Nope, because I'm tough and you're a wuss." And he kissed her a nice juicy one right when the opening credits started rolling.

Halfway through the movie, when Meg Ryan was losing her bookstore, Deon paused the movie. They opened the bags and inhaled all the oregano and basil and homemade tomato smells, and prepared the plates with all the delicious Italian from Niki's. Deon warmed the food and poured more wine, which contributed to their getting all misty-eyed at the end when Tom Hanks comes around the corner and Meg says, "I hoped it was you." Which is what Lucy remembered her saying when she thought back on this moment.

Then Deon found *Arsenic and Old Lace* and they took turns fast-forwarding to all the scenes with Peter Lorre and Raymond Massey. Deon did his Raymond Massey imitation, thrusting out his jaw, threatening the Cary Grant character. "Mortimer, just because you're my brother doesn't mean I won't kill you."

Lucy howled and they rolled on the couch and made out a little. And then it was time for bed. Lucy's new favorite time, since of course, she'd be staying over.

****

On Sunday morning they lounged around like contented slobs, drinking coffee and reading the Sunday *Times*, too stuffed from their Italian feast the previous night to eat breakfast. Almost like an old married couple except...Lucy didn't want to overstay her welcome.

"I'll trade the book section for sports."

"I don't want sports." She gave him her special get-with-the-program look, usually reserved for students.

"Aw, you can keep the book section. I'm just messin' witcha."

"Cute."

"Are you saying I'm cute?" He scooted closer, pursed his lips for a kiss. "After two nights of compliments on your loveliness and that's it? That's all you got? You think I'm cute? Cute is for emojis. And puppies." He rolled onto his hands and knees and waggled his rear end. Giggling, she wrestled him to the rug and climbed aboard, stretching out her feet behind, her hands steady in the air above his head. "Look, Superman, I'm doing a Superman."

"We ought to do this more often," he said, "you on top. Well, maybe leave out the Superman part."

She raspberried his neck.

"Stop. Uncle, uncle," his mock cries making her laugh harder. She crawled off, and he sat up, puffing in mock exhaustion.

"I...I should...." Lucy gazed around the room. It reflected Melinda, from the plump burgundy couch to the unmatched love seats and the huge Pollock-esque abstract on the opposite wall. And the frog collection. Frogs everywhere, an army of tiny frogs, a couple of sad-eyed bronze frogs.

"The frogs are Melinda's?"

He followed her gaze. "She got started and couldn't stop. I don't even notice the little buggers."

She leaned in to peck him on the cheek. "I should get going."

"No, no, baby, don't go."

He called her baby. Everything couple-ish was new, and they'd gone at warp speed. It was good, so good she didn't want to spoil it, but Monday now loomed. Monday was other people, crowded halls, business as usual. What was the name of that movie? *Reality Bites*?

"You just got here." He made a face.

"Very funny."

"I'm not trying for funny." He clasped his hands, looking down at them. "I'm dead serious."

"Deon, this has been…so, so nice." She creased the book review section in half. "I should probably go. You've got things to do. I have things to do."

"What, you're dumping me on a Sunday morning? When I was planning on us spending the whole day together."

"I just thought—not wanting to overstay. Maybe you need some alone time, time to prep for tomorrow?"

"I've had years of alone time." He folded his hands. "Do you need alone time? I'll understand. I'll cry, but I'll understand."

She crawled over to him on hands and knees, and he pulled her into his lap where they spent some quality time snuggling. With no more talk of her leaving.

"Come, I want to show you my office."

She stood. "Is it far?"

"Yes." He took her hand, walked her down the hall and into a sunny room with a view of the front yard. "I usually keep it locked. Otherwise, I tend to work too much."

A huge oak teacher's desk, refinished. The requisite couch, a modern, sleek version, more like a very comfortable hammock, and a bistro table and chairs in the corner. A stuffed elephant and a giraffe sat in the chairs as if waiting for the party to start.

He opened a door on the far side. "Separate entrance, Melinda's idea. More professional."

"Nice. Very."

"Time for walkies. Enough sitting around."

"Okay." She pulled on her jacket and Deon buttoned her up, kissed her chin. They trundled out and up the hill to Prospect and around to Edgerton Park, the afternoon air cold and bracing, the sun beaming its brilliance, as if approving their new status as a couple. Holding hands for a few minutes until they both gave up and put on their gloves.

Later, back at Deon's, they played Scrabble again and took a nap, spooning. *I'm so glad I didn't go home,* ran through Lucy's mind right before she dozed off.

By the time they woke, it was late afternoon and dark. For a second, she forgot where she was.

"What do you say to dinner at Mamoun's?" Deon massaged her scalp, his fingers working magic. *Hey, this couples thing has benefits I haven't considered.* "Or would you rather go somewhere fancy-schmancy?"

"I love Mamoun's, my favorite BYOB place."

Secretly, she hoped they wouldn't bump into anyone from school. Still, it was a possibility since Mamoun's, an old beloved institution in New Haven despite the plastic utensils, was super popular.

Mamoun's turned out to be a romantic dinner spot after all, with a little help from the secluded corner table Deon requested and his bottle of pinot noir. That and bringing along real forks and knives.

And then it was Sunday night. Deon didn't joke about Lucy deserting him this time, and her falafel-stuffed belly contracted thinking of Monday. Would people know just by looking at them? The fishbowl effect. Most important, would Phoebe guess their secret?

They were together. Best friends and more, so much more.

"I'll call you tomorrow," he said at her door, hugging and kissing her a long one, then another. "See you soon." Before sliding into his car, he turned around and waved, blew her a last kiss.

Drove away. Lucy didn't go back inside until his car disappeared around the corner.

Chapter Five

Back home Sunday night, Deon wandered through the house at a loss, almost expecting Lucy to appear around the corner. Strangely unsettling. He went into the hall closet and grabbed his sneakers. A run would do him good, get his blood moving, but once he'd dragged on his running gear, his mood changed.

In the study, he checked his schedule for Monday. The usual caseload, no parents or meetings, an easy day. He'd already prepped for the week. His phone rang, Sara's special ring. She hadn't forgotten him after all.

"Daddy." His heart caught since she so seldom used *Daddy* these days. Texted, yes, but called infrequently, busy with her Columbia friends, journalism classes. A demanding program.

"I was going through the old photo album Grandma and Grandpa gave me last summer and thinking about Mom."

His head spun as she highlighted her little expedition through old memories showcasing Melinda's childhood, from Girl Scouts to track competitions, camping, birthday parties, and high school graduation.

"Lots of pictures of Grandpa and Grandma and Mom camping. Sequoia National Park. Gorgeous." He heard her swallow. She needed a moment. "Let's go there you and me. For my birthday? I want to go to the place Mom loved. You know…with you."

The longing in her voice jerked him from his weekend-of-passion balloon. "Sleeping under the redwoods? Sounds like a great idea." His daughter, so undemanding like her mother, wanted this, and he would give it to her. Gladly. "We'll talk more when you're home. I hope you took notes."

"Oh, tons. I love you, Daddy."

He ended the call with a huge smile, thinking back to the time he and Melinda had gone camping. Once. The mosquitoes were bad, and they were unprepared, didn't sleep the whole night. Unprepared remained a joke forever in their repertoire. "Dinner is unprepared," Melinda would say if he ever asked what was for dinner, and he'd say he was unprepared if she asked why he hadn't mowed the lawn yet.

That memory prompted a search for old photo albums, Sara's baby album, and the wedding album Melinda had assembled so many years ago. "Martha Stewart has these lovely ideas," she'd said at the time, following Martha's example of a cut-out with a photo on the cover, quality paper so the photographs would age well. *Twenty-four years together until the accident.* He flipped through slowly. *Oh, we were so young.*

After a while, he got up to pour himself a glass of wine from the bottle of zin he'd shared with Lucy the previous night and took it into the living room. His forefinger probed the photo of Melinda with baby Sara, six or seven months old, smiling out at him, plump baby cheeks and arms and legs. He could almost smell that new baby fragrance.

All he could think at the time was how lucky they

were. Their good fortune as a couple. Never knowing they would end…this way. Without one another.

They'd considered having a second baby, somehow never got around to it. Sara was enough. They were a close unit of three.

And now, he and Sara were closer than ever.

Would things change with Lucy in the picture? How could they not change? He looked out at the dark, quiet street, everyone tucked in for the night. Sure, Lucy had met Sara a few times. They got on. A full-blown relationship, though, was another thing. What if Lucy kissed him in front of his daughter?

He hadn't thought this through. There at the beach, he'd acted in the moment. Kissed Lucy, so sure the timing was right. So sure of his feelings, which had been morphing from friend to more than a friend for a while now. Months. He'd ignored those…urges. That sounded dirty. Well, nothing wrong with dirty, and obviously the way she'd kissed him back—

He shivered and closed the albums, stood up, piling them together and returning them to the bookcase. The whole weekend had been freakin' fantastic. And now? He wrestled with a few doubts.

The therapist side of him whispered, "It's normal to have doubts. Everyone worries." His grief group would tell him everyone handled moving on differently, there was no correct time to start dating.

The doubtful side propelled him into the kitchen for more wine. He poured, picked it up and brought it to his nose. "A hint of raspberries and chocolate," he intoned. Lucy had laughed at this last night. She was easily amused, and sharing a sense of humor was big. Very. Not to be taken lightly.

So why the doubts?

Never a single doubt with Melinda. Funny. Four years and he and Lucy were still strangers in many ways.

He put the glass on the counter and went into the hallway. A run in the dark, he had to take that run, burn off this self-induced stress, the twitchiness that came from dread. He located his running shoes in the closet and pulled them on. Lucy pregnant at nineteen? How hadn't he known that? Too caught up in his grief to bother getting to know her beyond the superficial, he'd put up intimacy boundaries.

He zipped his key into his pants pocket, and pulled the door behind him. Trotted toward the park, his usual nighttime route, fewer icy patches.

Sure, he'd heard stories about a couple of old boyfriends, the few jokesters she'd met online. Even so, they'd never talked seriously about relationships, what she was looking for, what he was looking for.

Was he even looking? That thought chilled him.

What had he done?

****

Back home after his run, Deon ransacked the cabinet for crackers and stuffed one in his mouth. His half glass of wine sat on the kitchen counter, and he upended it then poured another glass. Next, he searched the fridge for anything edible, found some dried out cheddar, and seized it. He'd eat anything.

Flash frames of the weekend with Lucy ricocheted around his brain. Sleeping together in the big bed. Spending a lot of time in that bed over the past few days, much more time than he and Melinda…well, you couldn't compare a long-term marriage with a new dating relationship.

He chomped crackers and cheddar over the sink. What would things be like between them at school now that they were a couple?

Were they a couple?

Lucy. The constant picture taking, getting her students involved, the creative energy. How much was too much? Always dressing up, those bright, clashing colors. Blues and reds. Yellow and lime green, fearless when it came to color. Like him, he realized with a start.

The little science teacher who'd made him moan in bed.

He shook his head to clear it of the image. Everything would return to normal in the morning. Monday morning. The light of day and all that.

Finished with the zin, he fetched the corkscrew and reached for a California blend on the wine rack Melinda had discovered at a tag sale years earlier. "Best bargain I've found in eons," she'd said that day.

His phone rang. Lucy's ringtone.

He leveraged the corkscrew over the bottle, screwed it in place and popped the cork.

Three rings. What would he say to her? Four rings. Lucy would sense his discomfort and his tone of voice would be a giveaway. He'd let it go to voicemail. No. Yes, he'd let it go.

"Hello?" Friendly, casual. As if he had no monkey thoughts and every little thing was perfect.

"Hi, for a minute I thought you weren't home."

His mind jumped at the possibility she was calling him from outside his door, and he shrank from the kitchen window. *You idiot, she's not a stalker.*

"Opening a bottle of wine," he blurted, pouring a healthy splash in his glass.

"Oh? Do you often drink alone?" she teased.

"Hardly ever." He couldn't match her playful tone. What was his problem?

"Look, I just wanted to say…the weekend was wonderful. Thank you."

"My pleasure," he said, his nether regions warming and humming like starting a car in winter. *Say something else.*

"Okay, then," she said. "I won't keep you."

"See you tomorrow," he said, instantly regretting it.

****

He woke up, startled to find himself on the opposite side of the bed from his usual right side, the sheets tangled around his legs. He checked the clock, thinking he'd forgotten to set the alarm, relieved he'd slept a few hours. Thanks to the wine.

Five in the morning. He got up and went into his client office, unlocking the door and going back to the kitchen for a couple aspirins and orange juice. Back at his desk, he called the agency that handled teacher absences. No substitute necessary.

The thought of listening to students drone on about their teenage angsty concerns made his stomach roil. No, that wasn't fair. It wasn't about them. He loved working with students, even kids like Grover, who hung out on the fringes. Getting them to open up made his day.

Lucy. He couldn't face her today, pretend all was well. The therapist in him balked, but he was taking the avoidance approach and crap, the lump in his gut wasn't imaginary. One part of him wanted to text her…no, call her, tell her they'd play hooky. Go somewhere for the day, and never mind the weather. They'd bundle up, go to a museum, go to freakin' Mystic where they had that walrus who patted himself on the back. Who cared where they ended up?

As he slurped the juice, his mind unraveled, examining every nuance of the three wonderful days spent with Lucy. Sure, the sex was great. Stupendous. Partly because they knew each other, but mostly because they had that friendship and chemistry thing.

Not something to take for granted.

From the office, he went down the hall to the living room and into his bedroom, stopped at his closet and jerked open the door. Melinda and he…his knees weakened and he eased down to the rug staring into the half-empty space. Four years ago, Sara and he had folded and bagged everything, donated Melinda's clothes to charity. Three giant garbage bags, shoes in their original boxes because Melinda liked everything tidy.

After dropping everything off, they'd gone to the luncheonette on Orange Street and sat at the counter. They'd both ordered grilled cheese, not in the mood for anything more festive.

Sara had said, "Mom wasn't big into clothes."

"Thanks for helping." He'd dabbed his eyes. "Don't kid yourself about the clothes. Your mom shopped carefully. Loved everything she bought and always looked great. Beautiful."

Sara reached out and took his hand.

"I can't part with those silly glass frogs," he'd told her.

"You don't have to until…if you want to, later."

Now he rose, slammed the closet door, and went into the kitchen to make coffee. Funny, he rarely noticed the frogs anymore, a part of the landscape. Was that a sign he was moving on? Lucy hadn't said much, but he remembered her looking around, curious. Polite, too.

Funny, he missed Lucy. Her curiosity, fresh sense of humor, even the crabbiness.

Lucy and Melinda were so different. Lucy loved clothes and had an endless wardrobe, loved to shop, mostly with Phoebe. He hated shopping. This wasn't a big deal. Other things were a big deal, though. Goals, values, money management. Investments. Planning for retirement was important at their age. Plus, that baking business with the huge professional oven—Vesuvius? Vulcan? Expensive.

Her daughter Lily.

He was searching for excuses now. For crap sake, she had a job, an income. Was he afraid of being part of a couple? Of integrating two families?

The coffeepot gurgled to a stop, and Deon poured a cup, took a sip, and burned his tongue.

If I back away, she'll probably never speak to me again.

He hobbled back to his office, cranky, out of sorts, and with a pesky cramp in his calf. Ridiculous. Sketching out a new life as if…Lucy and he weren't a couple. Not yet. The thought brought him instant relief. But he needed another opinion.

Phoebe. He'd confess to Phoebe. What would he say?

"I have a crush on our best friend. We had a thing

over the weekend, and now I'm having second thoughts. Phoebe probably knew about Lucy's bad marriage and the relationships that went nowhere. Well, his relationship with Melinda didn't work out that well either, considering his wife was deceased.

Phoebe would be unsympathetic. She'd had a troublesome divorce from the dermatologist who'd hired a vindictive lawyer. And didn't she take kickboxing classes with Lucy?

Not Phoebe. He grabbed his phone, dialing Erwin, his therapist and friend, and left a message with the service. Without Melinda, his social director, his inner circle had shrunk down to his daughter Sara, Phoebe, and Lucy. The occasional jibber-jabber with Erwin at infrequent meetings hardly counted.

Yes, he needed to run this Lucy thing by Erwin, a trusted friend who understood his antisocial soul. Now sitting at his office desk, he put his head in his hands. Taking the day off, calling out sick was the right thing to do. He needed time to think. Wait, did he have meetings scheduled for today? Impossible to sort things out in his head. He needed his calendar.

A text from Lucy —*Lunch?*—

Crap. She hadn't checked the board in the office listing teacher absences. His hand shook. What could he offer Lucy other than excuses? *I'm not sure. I need time. Maybe we went too fast.*

Were they a mistake? Maybe. Maybe not.

Putting her on *ignore* would be worse than rude. Passive-aggressive in his book. *Unforgivable.*

He rose from behind the desk and wandered back into the bedroom, climbed into bed, and pulled the covers over his head. To hell with whatever he had on his calendar. He needed a day off to regroup.

Too fast, way too fast. What was that mumbo-jumbo about going slowly? *We'll do stuff together, pedestrian stuff like grocery shopping. Working out.* He'd meant every word at the time. Then they'd ended up at his house and in his bed. Melinda's bed.

Their matrimonial bed.

He threw off the covers and sat up, his mind relentless. He was a freakin' therapist, for crap sake. His doubts would disappear as he practiced the art of looking inside himself for the truth, the way Erwin always suggested.

He stumbled into the bathroom, washed his face, brushed his teeth, then pulled on a T-shirt.

Nine-thirty in the morning. How exactly would this regrouping thing play out?

Back in the kitchen, he poured more coffee, now thick as cement. A rumble from his stomach reminded him he hadn't eaten since the cracker fest. The all-night pizza place would do the trick, white clam with plenty of onions, the perfect breakfast. He speed-dialed and speed-ordered.

Erwin hadn't called yet. Didn't he keep regular office hours? Deon shut off the coffeepot and dialed Erwin's mobile. This time he left a more urgent message.

Doubts were normal, weren't they? An unnerving ache wound around his belly and down to his groin. Didn't he tell his clients guilt was a useless emotion?

Back in the living room, he cranked out twenty push-ups. His gaze wandered to the DVDs stacked on the table. That scene at the end of *When Harry Met Sally*. Believing their one-night stand was a mistake,

Harry developed doubts. But Harry and Sally finally came together.

Harry and Sally enjoyed a happy-ever-after ending, which was more than he'd ever get, the way he was going.

The doorbell twanged at the same time Erwin's quacking duck ringtone sang out, startling him. He opened the door to the pizza deliveryman, and greeted Erwin. Reaching for his wallet on the side table, he wrestled out the credit card and handed it to the guy.

"What's up?" Erwin barked. "I have fifteen minutes. Or Finley will have my head. We've got a plane to catch."

A plane? Erwin was leaving? Deon was well acquainted with Finley, Erwin's wife, and her temper as the three of them had been in the Ph.D. program together. He never understood why Erwin married her.

"Women troubles?" said Erwin, in a joking tone.

Deon held the phone tucked into his chin and neck, nearly dropping the pizza.

"How did you know?"

"I was kidding. Hey," he shouted, his voice muted as if he held a hand over the speaker. "Deon's having women troubles." Muffled laughter in the background.

Now Finley knew his business.

"Cut that out." Deon couldn't keep the irritation from his voice. "It's not a joke."

"Sorry. You mean this isn't just a friendly phone call?"

"I need help." Three desperate words.

Chapter Six

Monday morning. Lucy folded her arms and surveyed the groups at the workstations in her classroom lab. Twenty-five minutes until lunch and not even one lousy text from Deon.

"No one's supposed to touch the wirecutters," Cullen said, "except me." His voice rose above the classroom chatter, and everyone stopped talking.

In the middle of the bridge-building lesson, Cullen and Jim had faced off against one another.

Cullen held out his hand. Jim flipped the wirecutters from one hand to the other.

"Don't make me come over there," Lucy said in a *Don't mess with me* tone. She aimed her death stare at the corner group and raised her hand, fingers counting in the air. They knew the drill.

Three seconds while the class held a collective breath. Then Jim handed the tool to Cullen, the designated toothpick cutter for his group. Thank God for toothpick bridges and eighth graders acting up, the only thing between her and a new checking-the-phone-obsession.

"Stick to your job description," she called out, circulating and admiring the varieties of bridge design. "Your goal is to complete one side of your bridge as a team. Twenty minutes, people. Cut the chit-chat."

A hand in the air.

"Yes, what is it, Bryan?" She sucked in her stomach. *Deon has a hell of a nerve.*

"Why are you so crabby today, Ms. Bernard?"

There was a titter, as if a breeze entered the classroom, a sign of recognition that she'd turned into a bitch. She stopped short knowing every student in the classroom waited for her reaction.

"I don't mean to be rude, Ms. Bernard. Honest." The thing about Bryan? He never spoke out of turn, got straight A's in all his subjects, and read people with the skill of a mature kid.

"Personal problem." Lucy squeezed the bridge between her eyes where a headache formed. *Was it that obvious?* "I sincerely apologize. I'm waiting for an important call." As her students took in this bulletin about their teacher, the phone dinged. A text. *Deon, finallyfinallyfinally.*

She meandered over to the desk to sneak a look, nerves jangling with each step. "Thank you for calling me on my bad behavior." A forced smile in Bryan's direction. She glanced at the screen. A reminder text from the dentist.

Chatter resumed and tension floated away. How amazing that a simple explanation diffused so much. A little honesty—okay, she lied, but who wants to say they're expecting an important text?

Deon. It wasn't her imagination. He'd sounded weird on the phone last night. Like he didn't want to talk.

Mondays suck.

No text from Deon that evening either.

****

Tuesday morning Lucy checked for Deon's name

on the board in the office where teacher absences were posted. He wasn't listed. *So. He's in school.* His office was on the other side of the building, so she wouldn't necessarily bump into him. Days went by when they didn't see one another unless they met for lunch.

This was different. *He's avoiding me.*

Before class began, Lucy shut off her phone and stuck it in the top drawer. *No more checking for texts.*

Three minutes before lunch break, two girls performed a little prancing show while carrying their group's bridge project, swinging it and giggling. It went flying, hit the floor and collapsed like The Three Little Pigs' house of straw.

Instead of going ballistic, she rallied. "You'll have to stay after school, reglue and redo," she instructed. They looked at each other and shrugged. "Save what you can now, then call your parents."

****

Thank goodness it was lunchtime, not that she could relax. When she turned on the phone, a text from Phoebe popped up saying she was on her way. What for? Oh, lunch. Monkey thoughts leaped and jumped. *Was Deon coming too since they usually lunched together?* That familiar stomach cramp of anxiety…she'd be trying to read his mind simultaneously while hiding her thoughts from Phoebe.

In the back, she tidied the rows of bridges and picked up toothpicks from the floor. *See, I'm keeping everything together, not letting Deon throw me off my game.*

She wasn't hungry. More like a twitchy, lovelorn sad sack. *He has his nerve. Just wait until Phoebe hears that Deon is avoiding me. And why. She'll kill him for me. Wait. It's only Tuesday. He's my friend. He's busy. There is an explanation.*

When Phoebe trotted in with her lunch bag, she half expected Deon to follow as usual, carrying his thermos of juice and a yogurt.

"Hey, I checked Deon's office. He isn't there so maybe he has a meeting. Did he text you?"

They sat at the work counter in the front, and Lucy pulled out a plastic salad container. "No, nothing." She'd texted him yesterday and again today. Was Phoebe on *ignore* too? Impossible. They'd been friends forever.

Early that morning at home, Lucy had taken the time to make fresh tuna and added a hard-boiled egg, the way her grandmother made it when she was a kid. The trailer of their weekend repeated in her head as she grabbed the mayo, chopped the egg, added an olive. Laughing, spraying Deon while they fooled around washing the dishes. Happy thoughts. All the while thinking of his touch on her skin, the kissing. As if they couldn't get enough, the feel, the taste. His sweet words. "Kissing you is…it's the best. And I want more…with you. I've been wanting to tell you that for a while now."

She'd believed him.

****

On Friday, Lucy ran into Phoebe in the office getting the morning mail. The place buzzed with phones ringing, parents waiting, and two teachers struggling with the photocopy machine.

"Hey," Lucy said, mind calculating Deon's absences. He'd called out the day before, which meant he was absent Monday, Wednesday and now Friday.

"Look who's on the board again today," Phoebe observed. "Must have a bug." She leaned against the counter by the mailboxes, clutching a sheaf of papers and sidled closer to the trash bin. "Never mind Deon. Let's go somewhere for happy hour. The two of us." She shuffled through her mail, dumping a couple of envelopes into the trash. "Get all happy."

"Uh, sure." Lucy stuck her hand in the mailbox, head turned away, afraid Phoebe would pick up on her shifty look at the mention of his name.

"Lunch?" Phoebe wore a cute red straight skirt and flats.

"Okay." She didn't want to have lunch with Phoebe. What she wanted was to crawl into a cavity and hibernate for as long as it took every wiry nerve ending to stop twitching.

Deon was never sick. His iron constitution was legend. And here he was going to great lengths to avoid her. So, he had second thoughts, third thoughts...doubts? Why couldn't he man up and talk?

She trotted up the stairs to her classroom, mind clicking. How long would this continue? He had to return to school someday. A tremor of doubt. What if he was really sick?

Lucy stopped on the landing. *I've done nothing wrong.* This whole thing with Deon was messing with her head. "I'm not crazy," she said out loud and continued up the stairs.

"Lucy?" Phoebe mounted the stairs, and the urge to tell her everything seized Lucy like a bad cough. She'd spill the beans, and together they'd confront him, march into his classroom after hours. But he wasn't in school, was he? Better still, they'd stage an intervention, go over to his house tonight, bang on his door. Maybe when he opened it, she'd sucker punch him in the gut.

Well, that wasn't happening. Because their lost weekend was still a dirty little secret after Deon's big pull-back. Besides, how would she broach the subject?

Ignoring me for five days. Five, five, five days. Lucy paused at the top of the stairs, clenching the mail in her hands, wrinkling it, and forced a smile. One of those fake smiles that curdles your face. "I was talking to myself." She looked down at her black short-sleeved sweater and black trousers, an outfit she'd worn twice this week. Not a speck of jewelry either. *I haven't felt cute since Deon put me on ignore.*

"Humfrey's for happy hour, right?" Phoebe said. "Whoever gets there first grabs a table."

During homeroom, Lucy composed a text to Deon at the back of the classroom while listening to the morning announcements.

—Hey, what's going on? Are you feeling okay?—

She studied the text, grinding her teeth, remembering how her mom used to grind her teeth when Lucy acted up as a kid, the signal she'd gone too far.

Shouldn't Deon be the one asking how *she* was doing? She glanced around feeling a little guilty for texting during homeroom. *Oh, hell, I'm human.*

Now came the lunch specials followed by an announcement from the basketball coach and a reminder the debate club was meeting after school.

Lucy deleted the text and tapped out another. *—It would be nice if you were upfront since you've put me on ignore—*

She sounded like the shrewish wife. This situation

called for something less lecturey, more to the point.

—*WTF?*—

****

Humfrey's, the peanut bar place, noisy and crammed as usual with New Haven teachers, twenty- and thirty-somethings posturing, and a smattering of regulars and Yalies.

The WTF text? No response from Deon.

Lucy and Phoebe nabbed a table, a small miracle, and looked around. Sure enough, Noelle waved from across the bar where she and Sunny and Dana, teacher friends from the high school, perched in a cluster. They raised their glasses in a toast. Traditional Friday after school happy hour, the first in a long time without Deon.

They slouched watching the crowd, Phoebe sipping pinot grigio, Lucy glugging a Stella. Their phones dinged at the same time, and they exchanged looks and reached for them.

Lucy's was another dental appointment reminder.

Phoebe looked up as Lucy put her phone on the seat. "You have a funny look on your face. Is it Deon?" Phoebe sounded concerned. "I've barely heard from him this week."

"My dentist."

"Noelle texted to say we should join them." Phoebe gestured with her chin toward the bar where their friends waved.

Another text hit Lucy's phone and she looked down as it lit up. Deon. *Deon, finally,* her mind shouted.

"Go say hi if you want." If her voice shook, Phoebe didn't notice. "I'm fine here."

Phoebe stood, gripping her wine glass. "Watch my bag. Be right back."

—*Please forgive me. May I come over? I've got some s'plaining to do.*—

Lucy blinked, held back tears, and was relieved Phoebe wasn't sitting across from her. *Deon, you little shit.* From five days of nothing to a house call? Making like Ricky Ricardo after ignoring her all week.

Her gut instinct was to sprint outside and call him. Lob insults, overwhelm him, verbally kick him to the curb. What good was that? Outrage boiled for a quick second in her belly as a shout of laughter and table-pounding arose among the group of young studs seated nearby. The pungent aroma of beer, Humfrey's signature scent, floated in the air. Lucy was suddenly glad to be here amid the friendly chaos of Friday night drinkers bent on rockin' and rollin' after work and class.

She snorted, fingers curling around her phone. Deon, thinking he was cute with his *I've got some s'plaining to do* text. She'd show him. Tell Phoebe everything. Starting with the romantic beach visit, the way Deon slithered close and kissed her, and followed up their make-out session with dinner and dancing. The confidence, taking her back to his house without asking. Alpha tendencies were grand as long as they were backed up with sincerity and trustworthiness.

"What's Deon doing tonight anyway?" Phoebe slid into her seat. "You think he's still sick?" She gazed around the crammed bar. The noise from the crowd had reached a crescendo, everyone talking over everyone else. The smell of french fries and fish fry from the next table almost gagged her and Lucy reached for her beer, gulped a long drink.

Phoebe grabbed her phone. "I'll text him, see why he isn't here. It's Friday happy hour for freakin' sake."

"Okay." Lucy held the Stella mug in front of her face like a prop to hide the strained look, a giveaway to the inner turmoil. Struggling for casual, wondering if she'd be able to keep pretending things were normal.

The moment to spill those beans passed.

Phoebe lowered her head. "Maybe he needs some space." She was thinking out loud, her way of working through things. "Maybe he has a date. Imagine. Our Deon on a date." Her hand clapped over her mouth as if chastising herself. "I shouldn't joke."

"No, you shouldn't," Lucy said with force. A joke Phoebe didn't pick up on. Beer sloshed as she banged the glass down.

"We have to be supportive." Phoebe ran a finger through a splotch of beer and wiped it on a napkin. "I don't understand that much about the grieving process, but it can't be easy when your wife dies in an accident, totally unexpected. Plus, they had a fairytale marriage."

"Fairytale?" Lucy's mind buzzed imagining such a thing. "He told you that?"

"Not in so many words. Melinda was a close friend, so it's easy to read between the lines. None of that bickering. They were kind to one another. Don't you think that's amazing? Soulmates. Corny but true."

Lucy sat for a few seconds, her inner defenses repeating *fairy-tale, fairy-tale, fairy-tale*, while another part of her mind taunted she didn't stand a chance. Phoebe eyed her with a peculiar expression of sorrow and curiosity.

Recovering, Lucy blurted, "Of course I think it's

amazing, and…so few couples make it these days."

"So sad." Phoebe got a faraway look. "I miss Melinda."

"You were close. Sometimes I forget that." Melinda's death left a hole in Phoebe's life.

Not easy, losing a friend. Not easy dumping a friend either. But Deon wasn't treating her like a friend. Any trust was lost. She had to let him go.

Not a conversation Lucy looked forward to.

And she'd have to tell Phoebe why she hadn't confided in her.

****

Nothing prepared Lucy for the moment she pulled into her driveway that evening to find Deon parked in front of the neighbor's house. She slid out and trotted across the lawn, up the steps and reached for the screen door. "Please. Lucy, wait up," Deon called from the sidewalk. "A minute. Will you give me a minute to explain?"

She turned, gripping her keys. *No way is he coming in the house.* What could he possibly say to excuse not communicating with her for five days?

"Explain? Why now?" Lucy's hip braced open the screen door as she thrust the key in the lock. She had to pee.

"I needed time. I texted you yesterday to—"

"Yesterday? Yesterday was too late," she hissed. Her mind grappled to sort out why Deon thought a text would solve what was wrong between them.

"I…I understand." Deon stepped closer. "A couple of minutes. It wasn't your fault, none of it was—"

"My fault?" she said softly, while inside her head she jumped up and down. If she let go of the hand on the key, she'd bound down the steps and kick Deon in the shins. Then the crotch.

He must have realized he'd misspoken because his voice changed. "No, sorry, I didn't mean it that way. I should have called or texted or… It was like I was frozen. I didn't have the right words…to say…say it."

"Say *it*?" Lucy faced him, let the screen door slam. "What's *it*?" She sneered the word. "What are you talking about?"

He shifted, his shoulders slumping. "I'm not ready." He swallowed hard and there was a heavy space where neither one spoke before he continued. "It sounds ridiculous after four years. I should be ready, I thought I was ready. It was so great, and I was so happy. Last weekend with you was so great."

He panted with the effort of explaining and swallowed, which brought up a croak. He raised an elbow and coughed into the crook of his arm, what they taught the kids to do. "Sunday night. Sunday, I had all these…I got scared. Everything happened so fast. We skipped the…we didn't date. We went for it and we didn't get to know each other in a dating way." He stopped. "That sounds really lame."

Despite herself, she laughed. "You're a therapist and this is all you can come up with? That we weren't dating?" A nasty little cackle escaped. "Good night, Deon. You explained. I listened. We're done. Have a good life."

She turned the key and stepped onto the threshold before she heard it. A sound like an animal in agony. She paused, not believing the sound came from Deon.

"Please don't cut me off. Please." He tilted toward her, his hands raised in a plea. "I have my family, my daughter, and I have you…you and Phoebe. That's all I have. Nothing else…nothing counts. I'm a mess without you."

His words caught her by the throat, cutting off her breath. Killer words. True and straight from Deon's heart. Without Melinda, Deon was at a loss, unspooling. Worse off than she'd known.

"Come in." Lucy swung the door wide. "Just for a minute." He entered and sank into the chair nearest to the door, hands covering his face. She barreled past him, dropped her bag onto the counter, and stomped into the kitchen where she poured two glasses of water and crossed the room, handed a glass to Deon. In the bathroom, she peed and washed her hands, refusing to confront herself in the mirror. She thought she'd enjoy kicking Deon to the curb.

She took a stance across the room from where he slumped. "Here's how it'll work. I need some time, a few weeks at least. I'll make some excuse to Phoebe for not hanging out with you guys. When I'm ready to be a *friend*," she leaned on the word so he understood her use of it was ironic, "I'll text."

He looked out the window, and she followed his gaze. A couple of teenagers trotted by with a puppy on a leash, their encouraging laughter a reminder of better times.

"Tell her," he said. He wiped a hand across his eyes. "Tell Phoebe what I did. It's okay. I can handle it."

"No." It came out strong and hard. Lucy shook her head. "She'll ask a lot of questions and it'll be weird afterward." The three of us getting together as usual, going back to the way we were, made my mouth dry like cotton balls.

He stood. "Thank you. For forgiving me."

"We're just friends. And I haven't forgiven you, not yet."

"Uh, of course." If he wore a hat, it would be in his hand.

"No benefits, Deon." So he'd never again think of putting the moves on her.

"I would never do that. I don't see you that way."

"That's pretty obvious, isn't it? Except for last weekend." This popped out of her mouth in a burst of rancor. "Last weekend you saw me that way, didn't you?"

"No, no, I didn't mean it like that. I don't see us as just some friends with benefits thing. That's not us." He looked at the floor, as if hoping he'd turn into one of those mythical little people who live in the floorboards, invisible to the naked eye.

Lucy walked past him and yanked open the door so he could hustle his ass out of her house.

Chapter Seven

Lucy scrambled up the ladder, cell phone in hand for picture taking. Today was Ice Cream Dating Day. Lucy saw those four words capitalized in her head like the title of a book.

Dating, any sort of dating, even thinking about dating *crabified* her. Phoebe too. She and Phoebe had invented the word *crabify* together one happy hour evening at O'Donahue's to describe their mutual feelings on the subject.

Not that they didn't date.

Truthfully, Lucy hadn't given the ice cream thing much thought since Phoebe laid out the plan back in March or whenever. Back before her lost weekend with Deon. Hard to believe they were near the end of May.

Mayday, Mayday. A secret word could come in handy in case…in case what? Some guy played the sex card? It wouldn't be the first time. Besides, the event was being held in a public place. "There you go, dramatizing," Phoebe would say if Lucy brought up the idea of a secret word. She aimed her new iPhone and clicked off a few shots.

The doorbell rang. Phoebe? Impossible. Lucy tiptoed backwards down the ladder. Phoebe was at her family's restaurant setting up for the ice cream thing. Unless…

She galloped down the stairs. Even a half hour

would be enough. Phoebe would ask her to pick her three fave outfits and go from there, knowing Lucy was always a mess before a date. Eight-minute dating. Way too much stimulation for anyone with her temperament to handle.

She yanked open the front door and blinked rapidly. Deon, all rangy and wide-shouldered and looking better than she remembered. How long had it been? A month?

"What are you doing here?" Her chest squeezed. Why couldn't she control her inner workings a bit better?

"Nice to see you, too." His mouth twitched. "I came to rescue you. Phoebe's orders."

"So now you show up whenever? Unannounced?" She sounded like a brat. *Well good, I'm a brat. It's what he deserves.*

"What kind of announcement do you require? Want I should text you?"

Lucy breathed in the earthy smells of springtime, a combination of freshly mown grass, humidity, and the touch of something undefinable in the air. Pansies and petunias. Wasn't it planting time? Maybe a tad early. She'd check with her neighbor who knew such things. Lucy turned her attention back to Deon.

He looked…pleased with himself. How irritating.

"Texting would work. Anyway," she flicked her hair behind her ear, "I'm good. Busy though, so if you don't mind, and even if you do. By the way, I don't believe Phoebe sent you." She began closing the door, but he stuck a foot out, blocking her.

"Look, I'll go, no problem." He stared down at the stoop. "But remember, Phoebe doesn't know anything about…she thinks we're still friends. In fact, she's been pretty confused the past couple months. You've pretty much crossed us off your dance card."

Lucy studied him, trying to figure out if he was kidding around about Phoebe and her orders. True, she'd cut back on Sunday afternoon dancing at O'Donahue's and refused most happy hour invitations, making excuses and even pleading a headache, although not a migraine. She'd never lie about migraines when Phoebe suffered from the real thing.

She stared down pointedly and he moved his foot. Hah, it would be so easy to close the door on him. When had she last seen Deon? Three or four weeks ago, maybe more? It wasn't Phoebe's fault. And this was sort of Phoebe's special day with her ice cream social and all the attendant fussing.

Time to make nicer with Deon.

"We're friends, aren't we? Don't you miss me a little bit?" He gave a puppy dog whine.

Next thing, he'd roll over and display his belly. At that thought her chest squeezed again.

"Not really." A twitch of her mouth gave her away.

"Come on, let's hang out. We've got time, and if you're shooting, I'll help you style."

She threw him a suspicious look. "How did you know I'm shooting?"

"I know you, photo slut," he sang and pointed to her nifty phone pouch. "Not a moment wasted."

Lucy groaned but gave in. He was a part of Phoebe's ice cream event, and she couldn't avoid him forever at school. Plus, she'd sort of promised to take him back as a friend.

"Okay, hurry, though. While the light is good." No

small feat capturing the exact moment the afternoon light filtered in through the skylight.

Upstairs in her bedroom, Deon circled the flatlay, her arrangement of goodies, on the floor. "Nice." He pointed a finger. "Maybe put the rose across the brownies? That way the design is—"

"They're blondies and I like it the way it is." Stubborn, resenting Deon's unerring sense of design. Pure instinct on his part. So irritating. Where he had an eye for the perfect shot, she jiggled and modified. Even after a year of posting on Instagram and three hundred and ninety-eight photos later, she struggled. Anyway, shooting a few Instagram photos helped her take her mind off the eight-minute dating thing and regain her equilibrium.

Lucy aimed her phone at Deon's Patrick Dempsey hair. The young Patrick.

"Throw your head back. Run your hand through your hair."

"No way."

"Come on. Unbutton a few buttons." He'd been working out more, she could tell by the swell in his arms and chest. The nerd was looking good.

"Stop it." He held his hand up blocking her view.

"You're all gussied up for this eight-minute dating thing. I just wanted to mark the occasion." She climbed up the ladder. No fun teasing Deon if he wouldn't play.

"You tried on this crap already?" He gestured to the bed where her dress, jeans, and tops lay splayed like scarecrows minus the stuffing.

"Pardon?" She shot him her most stern teacher look. "Deon Goldbloom, it isn't crap. You're supposed to be my calming influence."

"Relax, Ms. Bernard. I'm here, aren't I?"

True. Irritatingly present, like a fungus.

"What happened? Did Noelle cancel?" Noelle was their friend who taught at the high school.

Lucy took a few shots and climbed down to reposition the ladder. "Yeah. Phoebe needed help."

"You're saying I'm your last resort?" He looked genuinely hurt.

"Of course. You're a guy." Lucy smirked. "I didn't even know you were coming."

"Not just any guy. A guy with sensitivity and extraordinary taste."

"Sensitivity, my ass."

"Are you bickering?" called a voice from the hall, and Lucy's daughter, Lily, flew into the room to say goodbye. Lucy wobbled on the ladder, almost dropping her phone. Lily was on her way out for dinner with her grandparents, who lived one town over, in Hamden. She shot them an amused glare. "Play nice, you two."

"Hey, Lily, nice to see you." Deon and Lily hugged. "When do you start the internship?" Lily, visiting for the weekend from grad school, had snagged a much-coveted internship at the NPR Boston station.

"I'm so excited I can't stand myself," she snorted and ran a hand through her wild mane. "Staying with my besties. It'll be a blast."

Lily and Deon caught up for a few minutes while Lucy took more photos and rearranged the flatlay.

"So," Lily said, eyeing her mother on the ladder, "ice cream dating is a thing now?"

"Crap, I hope not," Deon laughed.

Lucy was glad Lily barged in with her freshness and humor, and her white jeans shorts and tiny, blue, raggedy-cool top. Her daughter disappeared a moment later, and Lucy got off the ladder.

She should stop raking on Deon. A tad sick that getting under his skin had become a game. Forty-seven years old, and she's playing games. Pitiful.

What she'd like to do is punch him in the mouth. Since she kick-boxed Mondays and Wednesdays, this wasn't an idle threat, even way inside her head.

Not so long ago, her legs had turned to marshmallow when he touched her. Now she'd happily crush his thumb in a vise. Or stomp on his big toe with her hiking boots and ask him, "How does that feel, dear?"

Resentment didn't disappear in a day. Not a thing she'd admit, even to her good friend Phoebe, who sometimes looked at her sideways, like when Lucy was cranky with Deon.

"Do you think this works?" she asked him now. They studied the blush-pink scarf and the turquoise plate stacked with blondies, the scattered seashells, and a long-stemmed white rose.

Instead of answering, Deon reached down, lifted the rose, and positioned it across the plate. He trailed the seashells in a circle.

"Perfect." Lucy curled her lip and climbed back up the ladder to reshoot. "You like my beach theme? Someday I'll be able to afford a Nikon or a Canon in the $1,500 range." Yeah. When she had a real following with affiliate links on her website, when her baked sweeties were in more local stores and restaurants.

"I love your beach theme." He scratched his chin. "Let's go to the beach one of these days. Do a photo shoot there." His gaze shifted to the plate of blondies.

"My favorites." He inhaled with a loud exaggerated sniff. "Pecan, white chocolate. When you're done, can I have one?"

"Sure." She aimed a condescending smile at him. "You're such a girl in some ways." Deon had a couple male friends from back in the day, but he preferred the company of women.

"I'm well aware I'm a beta male." A look of loss crossed his face. "Melinda teased me all the time about..." His voice dropped off and he checked his watch. "Phoebe's thing. Starts in an hour, doesn't it?"

"Yeah. So? We've got time." They were so different. TWT. Totally Wrong Together. Their friendship would always be edgy.

"You're obsessed, aren't you?" Deon observed.

Lucy picked up the plate, the shells, and stuck the silk rose into its vase on the bureau. "Yeah."

So far, no money with her little hobby. Her greatest accomplishment was her middle-schoolers' projects, with hundreds of likes and comments on their classroom Insta account from as far away as Hong Kong, Burkina Faso, and Australia.

"So," Deon said, "what are you trying on first?"

She swallowed and grabbed a dress and a few tops, wishing for the whole ice cream thingy to be over.

"I don't want to send the wrong message," she called over her shoulder and closed the closet door. How lame that sounded. Deon's last date was probably Melinda, his wife. How could he relate? He was coming along for the ride, and to support their friend Phoebe.

"Wrong message?" he called out. "I thought this was an old-fashioned speed-dating thing. You dress nice, you leave the house."

"Goldbloom, are you obtuse?" Lucy shouted through the door. "I don't want to be *overtly* sexy."

Am I letting my insecurities show? She slipped on the halter dress, emerged barefoot.

"Nice, really nice," he said and hesitated. Deon had an uncanny sense of style, especially for a heterosexual male. Maybe it was the therapist in him.

"Too much? Is it over the top?" Lucy's chin dropped as she attempted to determine the *sexy quotient* of her dress. She and Phoebe often discussed this very matter when they shopped together.

Deon gave her a look that answered her question. "That dress is *overt*."

"You know, at my age—"

"At your age?" He jerked his head. *At my age* was one of their running jokes since these days seventy-year-olds dressed like forty-somethings, especially now that the weather was warmer.

"Ha ha." Her gaze fixed on his new skinny black jeans and white shirt, the ones she and Phoebe bullied him into buying. "You're dressed pretty casual." She waggled her finger. "You look like a waiter."

His hand smoothed the stitched detail all down the front of his shirt. "It's designed to be worn outside the pants. Besides, sex appeal as you get older, well, some of us never lose it."

"Better hang on to that hair, Deon." Lucy grabbed the skinny white capris and silver-hammered top she'd found at the mall earlier in the week, and stepped back into the closet. "You're fifty-three." He deserved every jab she could throw his way. Last Christmas at the teachers union party, a thirty-something told him he looked like the actor James Marsden, and he puffed up like a blowfish. She and Phoebe pledged to make him suffer ever after.

The white capri jeans were fitted, ultra-fitted, surely a mistake, and a struggle to zip. But they didn't bind at the crotch or the waist.

Lucy stepped out of the closet to find Deon munching on a blondie, one hand cupped under his mouth to catch crumbs. He grinned, caught in the act.

The jeans showcased her legs and narrow hips and she twisted to check the rear view in the mirror. Not so bad. Her ass, not her best feature, looked perkier than usual.

Lucy wished Phoebe were here with her acerbic wit to lighten the mood. With Phoebe she could say anything, even "I'm hapless at dressing for speed dating, or any kind of dating, without feeling like a loser."

"Take a picture." She elbowed Deon.

Deon, still chewing, roused himself. *Wait, did he just gaze with longing at her ass, or was she imagining things?*

"You wearing *that*?" He clapped a hand over his mouth. "Sorry."

"Too young?" Instantly mortification. What if she's seen as desperate? Bought yesterday along with the silver top, they're going back. "Take a photo anyway. I want Phoebe's opinion. Then I'll try on the black capris, much more conservative."

"You look hot. For an older broad." His expression was matter of fact, not at all leering or mocking.

She tilted toward him, hand in a fist. "Older broad?" If she smashed him in the nose, all the

80

resentment of the past month would fly out the skylight with one right hook.

"Don't even think about hitting me."

"I'd never do that. I'm not a violent person."

"You're a violent person," he said, tapping her forehead. "Inside your head where you think I can't hear you."

"You're supposed to be supportive."

"Stand still." He clicked off two or three photos and sent them.

In the closet, her chest fluttered and she told herself Deon didn't mean anything with his teasing, calling her hot. He wasn't stepping over the friendship line.

"Don't change," Deon called. "Phoebe texted back you look great."

Looking great, one less thing to worry about.

Deon joined her in the closet, head moving as he surveyed the double racks of clothes. "Quite the collection. I think I'll keep this photo of you. Is that all right?"

"What for?" They stood so close she breathed in the scent of him, a mixture of aftershave and man.

"You look…well, you look great." He swallowed audibly, stepped closer, and kissed her, a lingering cheek kiss. When his lips moved to the corner of her mouth, she closed her eyes, a reminder of slow kisses, a weekend of kisses, and so much more. She wanted that again. The warmth of his body had taken her backward in time, and…the kiss was a more-than-friends kiss.

Shit. Lucy jerked her eyes open and stepped back. She collided with the wall of hanging sweaters and jackets.

"Deon, what the hell?"

"I'm—"

She shoved him away and stalked out of the closet, began gathering clothing from the bed. "Help me clean this stuff up." Her body had responded and well, she'd fight these...feelings for Deon. No more styling sessions and hanging out unless it was the three of them. *I won't let him slither into my life again.* He followed behind, and she grabbed up hangers and thrust them at him.

"Two more blondies and I'll do it."

"You're pushing it." She made a face, but his joke eased the tension.

"I'm not apologizing," he said, and she let it go. They worked in silence the three or four minutes it took to hang everything up.

"Ready?"

"Ready," she said. "Don't do it again. No kissy face." She wasn't imagining his lips lingered near her mouth.

"Okay. Unless you want me to," he added. "Kiss you, I mean."

"Shut up." Her mind whirled. *Definitely kissed me. Would he have continued if...no, I won't think about that.*

"I'll drive," he said. "We'll go together."

She nodded and collected the plate of blondies. Why not have a designated driver since Deon wasn't a big drinker? Lucy planned to enjoy herself tonight, get Phoebe to slip her a glass of wine to start the evening properly. A booster.

Deon trailed her into the kitchen where she wrapped three blondies in a tidy package with pink ribbon, her trademark, and handed it to him. The rest went into the giant ceramic panda cookie jar.

"Thanks. Hope I'm not depriving one of your clients."

"My clients are not deprived."

They tripped down the porch, cooled by a faint breeze that carried the scent of the neighbor's lilac bushes. "So you're doing this dating thing to keep us company?" Lucy said as they folded themselves into Deon's car. "Since you're not into dating at this juncture."

"Watching out for you and Phoebe," he said in a matter-of-fact voice. "At this juncture." Another joke.

What he's watching out for, Lucy didn't have a clue. Never mind. With twenty men and twenty women, there had to be one datable guy in the pack.

If I can't find one lousy man tonight, there's something wrong.

****

How much Deon enjoyed their conversations, which weren't so much actual interaction as Lucy talking, him listening and interjecting the occasional comment. As they flew down the highway, she pursed her lips in that way she had, signaling a story to come.

"I was at Stop and Shop, checking out the melons. Is it early in the season for them? Anyway, this guy asks me to help him pick one out. I look up and it's Dirk. One date last year. He didn't even remember me at first."

"How is that possible?" Deon laughed. "You're unforgettable." He tightened his grip on the steering wheel. The kiss in the closet was all he could think about. Should he apologize? He'd acted cocky, unlike him. His intestines were a mass of spiky prickles, trying to figure out what to do. Lucy had already given him a second chance.

What if she told Phoebe?

"He asked me to go for coffee." Lucy ignored the compliment, probably her coping mechanism to get him back on track. On the friend track, where he belonged.

Kissing her cheek was like breathing in the scent of peach and mango, like perfume found in nature. When he bit into a peach he thought of her, although he hadn't ever examined that thought or spoken it out loud. Kissing her caused all sorts of thoughts to surface. Possibilities of a future he'd forced himself to dismiss years earlier. A longing he'd buried after Melinda died. Kissing the corner of her mouth…no, he wouldn't think about it, not now with her beside him on the way to meet male strangers. Women too, his mind amended. Not that he cared to meet these women. *I would prefer not to.* Wasn't that the line from "Bartleby the Scrivener"? Yes, that's it. He's Bartleby. He can't remember another detail about that story other than that line. *I would prefer not to.*

"Wait, pull in here." Lucy gestured to the right.

"What? Where?"

"I need a glass of wine before this thing." She pointed to a dilapidated building with an old, rotting sign.

"The Beer Shack? That's nuts, we're late already."

"I don't care. Pull over."

He jerked right onto a gravely, weed-infested lot with three of four other cars scattered near the side. From the look of the dumpy facade, drinks would be cheap. He expected pool tables and decent beer.

Sure enough, a bell dinged over the door when they

entered. "Hi folks, here for Happy Hour? We have a margarita special tonight. Half price."

The guy knew how to make a margarita? Deon gazed around, mildly surprised at the homey atmosphere. No sign of animal heads on the wall.

"Yes, I want a margarita. Definitely. Not for my driver. He can't have one."

"I'll have a beer, thanks."

"Sure. What would you like?"

"Surprise me." *Why did he say that?*

They took seats at the bar, and Deon inclined his head toward Lucy. "Hope you know what you're doing. Phoebe gets nervous."

"We won't be that late." She shot him a look. "I'll blame it on you."

Deon gave a harumph, hoping that would satisfy her.

"Aren't you nervous? How can you be so calm?"

"I have no expectations."

"Me neither. I've never done this eight-minute dating." She tapped her finger on her chin.

The bartender brought over their drinks.

"Never done it either." Deon took a sip. "Good choice, thanks," he told the bartender, who nodded.

"Very funny. Except for Melinda, you've never dated. All dating is hard. Online dating is torture. You're lucky you never—" She cut herself off. "I'm sorry, that came out wrong." She squeezed his forearm and then his bicep. "Geez, you're solid. Have you been working out more?" She took a few sips of the margarita. "Thanks for stopping. I'm not usually this weirded out."

"Don't be so worried about this ice cream thing.

Just be yourself. Besides, I'll be there too."

"Never mind me. This is a good thing you're doing finally. Dating. Contrived social occasions tax most people."

"Count me as one of the taxed ones."

Lucy slid off the stool. "We'd better get going. Pay the man, would you? And leave a nice tip." Lucy wavered out the door and Deon threw a few bills on the bar and caught up with her. He hadn't planned on drinking more than a few sips of his beer anyway.

Back in the car, Lucy stared out at the shops and restaurants as they approached the city limits. Was it true he had no expectations? Pretty much. What exactly he wanted was the bigger question.

A foggy memory of the Dirk guy she'd mentioned earlier, the Bobs and Franks, Williams and Johns, part of the lore that made up Lucy's and Phoebe's dating history. Discussed for hours over wine or beer, the three of them, usually on a Friday happy hour.

Who was he kidding? Here she sat right next to him in all her forty-seven-year-old splendor. He honestly didn't understand some men's hankering for a younger woman.

Too late for him, though. He'd already made a mess of everything.

He needed a plan, a life plan. He couldn't keep going on the way he was, although it was better now than in the beginning. His grief group, the phone calls, the sharing. But until now, he hadn't wanted to…

Deon gulped and wondered how this dating thing worked, and who would end up with his Lucy.

Chapter Eight

"Hurry up and park," Lucy instructed, knowing Deon didn't like orders. Plus, he couldn't be rushed since he was almost famous for taking an extraordinary chunk of time finding the perfect parking spot for his 1963 split-window Stingray.

He wrinkled his nose at her. "Go, darlin'. There's nothin' around here," he drawled, "so I'll park and meet you inside."

"Your Elvis needs a Cadillac," she quipped. She swung her legs out of the car thinking Deon only did his Elvis imitation when he was in a good mood. Maybe stopping for a quick drink had bolstered him.

Before climbing the stairs to the deck of Zorbaki, Lucy paused and gazed around. Phoebe's parents owned the Greek taverna. It overlooked a cozy inlet facing a small beach with a dock for real fishermen, a dreamscape of a setting. Romantic yet family-friendly, an unusual combination. Gulls squawked overhead, and one brave guy dive-bombed the dock, alighting near a suspicious pile of what was likely fish guts. Lucy smelled the scattered remains from where she stood, mixed with the briny scent of the sea and the sound of the waves gently lapping on the rocks framing the beach below. This was her favorite spot in Branford.

As she mounted the steps, the chatter became louder and her stomach twisted. The restaurant deck was deserted, umbrellas closed. Phoebe, in a sundress the color of a poppy field, chatted in the doorway with their friend Noelle, who taught at the high school. Phoebe darted a glance toward Lucy for an instant then looked back at Noelle and squeezed her hands together as if she were begging.

"Please, I need you to sit in. Otherwise, I'll have an extra guy…" Her voice trailed off and Lucy strained to hear Noelle's reply. Something was up, and Lucy considered going around the back and slipping into the building from the kitchen to give her friends time to work things out. Instead, she leaned on the railing to consider her options and try to rein in any expectations.

She squinted inside at the café tables crowded together. Was meeting someone new today too big, too hopeful, too taunting the gods? And was this the best way, strangers, dozens of them, chairs crammed back-to-back, the atmosphere strained, a little forced. The opposite of party-like. Five o'clock in the afternoon, and all she had to look forward to was ice cream—the good part—and ice breakers. Over a dozen ice breakers, one for each stranger.

Nothing going on yet and Phoebe was already rattled. "I'm scared this whole ice cream thing will be a flop," she'd lamented on the phone earlier. "Is it ridiculous for me to think there's someone for everyone? Connecting is random, but it happens."

After a few minutes, Noelle disappeared inside and Phoebe stood at the entrance alone, holding a clipboard. Time to face the ice cream crowd.

"Hey," she greeted Lucy.

"Everything okay?" Phoebe panicked easily, but handled it better once a project got underway.

"Someone canceled at the last minute. Thank God Noelle is here. She didn't want to sit in, believe me." Phoebe's face was pink from exertion and stress. "And Artemis," she breathed, "came down for a long weekend, so she'll be helping. Bell ringing and whatever needs doing." Phoebe peered into the restaurant. "We're about to start. I'm scared this whole ice cream thing will be a flop."

This wouldn't do. Lucy threw her arms around Phoebe in a rough hug meant to instill a little courage. "I'm thrilled Artemis is visiting and everything will be fine. You're not in this alone, silly." Phoebe's daughter Artemis. What could be better?

Lucy leaned toward Phoebe, dying to tell her about Deon's kiss, but it would only confuse her. It confused the crap out of Lucy.

"I need a glass of wine," she blurted. "Sneak me a glass, will you?"

"Follow me." Phoebe led the way to the bar at the rear. "Everyone is here and the ice cream is melting." Pulling Lucy behind the bar, she grabbed a bottle of the house merlot and poured a glass. "Drink it now. Otherwise everyone will want wine, and I've got to start this…this thing."

"You mean like gulp it down?"

Phoebe glanced around at the chattering crowd. "My mom doesn't understand the concept of hot fudge and nuts and cherries. M&Ms as a topping? Completely lost on her."

Lucy took two quick gulps and shivered as the wine hit going down. Oh, she craved that. Her thoughts wound around how Deon would fare in this scramble of personalities. Likely he would meet someone and move on, and their little group of three would dissolve. She finished the wine. What Lucy needed was to expand her friendship base. *Friendship base.* Yes. What an odd expression. Why was she always uneasy when it came to putting herself out there with strangers? She couldn't spend the rest of her life hanging out with Phoebe and Deon.

A clanging from the kitchen. Phoebe winced. "My parents have been bickering all day." Her mom and dad reminded Lucy of the parents in *My Big Fat Greek Wedding*, one of her favorite all time movies.

"Where's Deon?"

"Parking his precious Corvette. Sorry we're so late, Phoebs. My fault."

Phoebe lowered her voice. "Deon's okay with this?" Her gaze swept the crowd. "This will be good for him. I swear he hasn't dated since the…maybe he's coming out of it, finally dealing with stuff." She blinked and attempted a smile, and Lucy remembered that Deon's wife was Phoebe's good friend. "He hasn't been himself since Melinda died."

"Yeah, it's been tough."

"Deon and that silly Corvette," Phoebe muttered. She regarded the crowd, growing restless. "One other woman is a no-show or she's running late." Phoebe's jaw stiffened, her shoulders hunched close to her ears. "Hope you meet a nice guy. You deserve it." She headed for the entrance, her daughter Artemis holding the bell. Phoebe turned to face the expectant gaggle of daters. "Hello, everyone. Welcome to Zorbaki. When you hear the bell, ladies only will switch. Eight minutes is all you have so take a few notes and enjoy."

Lucy scanned the room and the entrance. Still no

Deon.

She hoped Phoebe would meet a great guy. She deserved it. Whoever she found would have to get past that anxious exterior. Lucy should know all about anxious exteriors. For a second, she imagined jumping up and racing down to the beach across the street where a wealth of photo ops awaited her. Instead, she slipped into an empty seat and gave a half-baked smile to her tablemate.

Artemis rang the bell as Deon finally bounded into the restaurant, a blonde woman in wobbly, strappy sandals at his side.

"Sorry I'm late," they said in unison then looked at each other and burst out laughing.

Deon, the little shit, met a woman *on his way* to the ice cream social.

****

Deon and the blonde woman wandered out of the sun into the dining room where café tables sat crunched together, like houses in an overcrowded suburb. Voices melded in a meaningless din.

Artemis, as tall as Phoebe, and thin in a strong, competent way, greeted him with a hug. Her dark hair smelled of honey, and her eyelashes curled upward in thicket-like elegance.

"Nothing pedestrian about this party, huh?" Deon's gaze swept the room, searching for Lucy.

"Uh huh." Artemis hiked her shoulders in a little impromptu dance movement. "My mom outdid herself in the topping department." She gestured toward the tables. "Find a seat. You have a few minutes before we switch."

Colorful paper bowls of ice cream smothered in

candy and nuts and crunchy bits populated every table. Yummy. Chocolate and peanut butter, caramel and hot fudge, Deon was a sucker for anything decadent. He salivated, anticipating the first bite, imagined the chocolate coating his tongue. A mistake, skipping lunch.

He slid his sunglasses to the top of his head. Snatches of conversation surrounded him in a cacophony of meaningless small talk, the blonde woman he'd met a few moments earlier nowhere in sight.

"Your first time eight-minute dating?" a woman in a green-flowered dress asked a man in white shorts and a red shirt.

"What I need is a drink. You wanna get outta here?"

"Get out of here? I just got here." The woman punched him in the arm and the man laughed.

Deon wrinkled his nose. What was that smell? Sweat mixed with perfume, the odor of anxiety. Springtime on the Connecticut shoreline with the wide doors open, what could be more perfect? If only he were somewhere else.

The din of twenty couples bounced off the wall. Deon played the odd man out, the guy who's always late to the party. Melinda would have told him to suck it up. He smiled inside his head at the thought and gazed around. On a table by the bar, five restaurant-size tubs of ice cream nestled in trays like walruses on ice caps. He wondered at the flavor selections.

No ice cream for him; he's supposed to be giving up sugar. His daughter Sara, the health nut, is staying with her grandparents—his in-laws—in San Fran for the summer and has been on his case. "At your age, diabetes is common. You know Mom thought sugar was like poison." Yet here he was at an ice cream social. His little adventure was a secret from everyone in his family. This was the first time in four years he's done anything like this.

Phoebe walked over carrying a cup of deep chocolate. "Come on, you've already lost three minutes. Where's your new friend?"

"What friend?" Did she mean the blonde woman?

"Never mind." Phoebe guided him over to the tubs of ice cream where Artemis stood ready to cart everything away. "Come on, you're late. Get a move on already."

Artemis wagged the scooper, smiling. "What flavor would you like?"

"Give him the Chocolate Volcano." Phoebe nudged him with an elbow. "Fudgy dark chocolate bits, your favorite. And all the toppings. You'll love it."

Deon's mouth watered as she filled his cup, the ice cream fast-melting the way he liked it. His taste buds tingled. Let Sara eat Toffuti or whatever that fake ice cream was called.

"Now, follow me." They wound around the maze of chairs sticking out, blocking the aisles. "By the way," Phoebe shouted over the din of talkers, "what sorts of things do you like doing?"

"Like doing?" he repeated, scooping up a little chocolate and fudge. The question came out of nowhere.

"Outside of work."

"What are you talking about? You know what I do." He crunched the nuts between his molars.

"I'm practicing on you," she clarified. "Is that a good ice breaker question?"

"Oh, yeah. Suitably boring." He gave an exaggerated yawn and covered his mouth. The bowl of ice cream tilted and Phoebe reached out to rescue it. "You can do better than that, Phoebs, can't you?"

She wrinkled her nose at him. "Stinker." She handed him back his ice cream.

One of life's delights, teasing Phoebe. He squinted to view her as a stranger might. Leaning forward, he breathed in the foresty scent of her freshly-washed hair. "You look lovely, Phoebs. You don't need no lousy ice breakers."

She pointed to a single empty table in the corner, and they threaded their way through the crowd, balancing on their toes to squeeze between chairs of unmoving couples, catching tidbits of conversation.

"I want companionship. But sex is still important to me. Is it important to you?" Voices raised against one another, snippets of dialogue launching like missiles.

Deon and Phoebe smirked, and Deon quirked his eyebrows up and down. A woman in an orange low-necked blouse that revealed two fleshy, freckled breasts asked her table companion if he owned or rented. Deon averted his gaze and caught Phoebe doing the same.

"My son lives at home for the moment," said a woman as they flattened themselves past more chairs. "He's thinking of graduate school."

"How old is your son?" asked her table mate.

"Thirty-nine."

When they finally sat, Deon examined Phoebe's tense face. "So, what's going on?"

"My parents aren't ice cream people, and my father

likes to be in control." She huffed out an exasperated sigh. "Besides, my mom feels sorry for people." Phoebe waved her finger at the room in explanation.

"Sorry? How?"

"Divorced people. Older and still looking. It's a Greek tragedy, at least in her eyes."

"I'm not divorced. Although my story is a tragedy." He shot her a wan smile to lighten his comment.

"Hah," Phoebe honked. "Remember, I had to twist your arm to come. Anything that smacks of dating and you bolt."

Phoebe the nag. Always nudging him to move on. *I would prefer not to.* Moving on was overrated. Except maybe with Lucy. *Too late for that.* His chest did a mini flip-flop. Lucy wasn't interested. Although, in the closet… His eyes rested briefly on the guy at the next table wearing a tan jacket.

The guy pulled out a flask and offered it to a woman in a green off-the-shoulder dress. Clever. Deon pointed with his chin and Phoebe turned around in time to catch the woman taking a slug from the flask. "His secret weapon," Deon said. "The jacket has big pockets."

Artemis rang the bell. All around them women switched tables, confused about the unclear traffic pattern. *Where is Lucy?* Deon swung his head around, locating her at a table to his right, partially blocked by a big guy who rose and gestured with a flourish to the vacant chair. Lucy threw her head back and laughed as she slid opposite him.

"At least Lucy's making friends." Phoebe stood and patted him on the shoulder. "Sit there and look pretty. The women will flock over."

He wrinkled his face in fake hilarity after her retreating back. There's only one woman he wanted to *flock over*. It was time to up his game.

If only he had game.

Chapter Nine

Every eight minutes when the bell sounded, the room erupted in chatter and strained laughter as if everyone were enjoying themselves to the max. Lucy not so much.

Her last match, number six, had kept glancing at a woman with big boobs and short Betty Boop curls at the next table. Lucy scrawled a zero next to his name on her rating chart.

The kitchen door swung open and the scent of onion and tomato sauce with a touch of cinnamon permeated the room. Lucy cast around for a vacant chair.

Across the room Phoebe was talking to a big blond man who glanced at Lucy and winked before turning back to Phoebe. Lucy dropped into a seat opposite a guy who flashed her a 200-watt smile. (Nametag: Adventurer. Curiosity will do me in.)

"Lucy, nice to meet you." He leaned in to read her nametag. White hair and plenty of it, and he wasn't as old as the white hair would indicate. His skin was tanned and unlined.

"I'm Wyatt McArthur, so glad I came here today. Blue skies, a great restaurant on the beach, and a lovely eight-minute companion. What more could a man want?"

"I'm thinking about that question," she retorted.

"I'll get back to you." Wyatt's *lovely companion* comment sounded like he practiced it.

The kitchen door swung open again and they both caught a whiff of freshly baked pastry. Lucy's mouth watered. Homemade *spanakopita.* "Smell that taste of heaven? Spinach pie. The owner makes the phyllo dough from scratch." An effort to match Wyatt's level of enthusiasm. "A dying skill, I'm told." Her factoidy ice breaker.

His eyes met hers and didn't look away, and then he laughed. "You are a genuine person, Miss Lucy, and now I'm really glad I came to this here, whatever it is. Fifty-nine years old, right on the cusp, and don't think I don't know it. Divorced ten years now and getting a little desperate."

Lucy's eyes widened in mock astonishment. "Don't advertise desperation. You won't get any ticks on your dance card." She sounded rehearsed, like a 1940s rerun.

"Kidding," he said. "I have a weird sense of humor. And I can see you have a way with words, Lucy. You been divorced long?"

This wasn't where she wanted to go, down the personal history track, to be weighed and measured by her mistakes. "Long enough." She gestured around the room. "Have you done this before?"

He nodded as if agreeing not to interrogate further. "Never. Was in a long-term relationship until about six months ago. I thought we were getting married. I was wrong." The memory hung between them on his expression, a slice of melancholy and then he shook himself, like a dog after his bath. "But that's in the past, and I'm here with you." He made an elaborate show of picking up the tiny pencil, wagging it in the air. "Circling your name now because I'd like to see you again. I hope you want to see me too."

"All righty." She did the same to be polite. She liked Wyatt. Sort of. A few feet away, Deon was leaning across the table deep in conversation with a small woman in a green dress the color of freshly mown grass. A St. Patrick's Day dress. She nodded vigorously at something he said and a twinge of recognition hit Lucy between the eyes. *We talk like that, oblivious to everyone else, Deon and I.* And here he was talking intimately to a stranger. How did he manage that?

"Two grown sons and three grandkids."

Wyatt. She forgot him for a moment. It must be obvious because three fingers popped up in case she missed his point. "Own my own house. Have a fox terrier named Bongo, love to line dance and enjoy waltzing."

"Oh, well." That bell again.

"And I don't care what your hobbies are because I find you very entertaining."

"Entertaining?" She'd barely paid attention to the man and now, time to move on. She almost hugged Wyatt goodbye to make up for her neglect.

Transitioning was getting easier, and at the next table, a guy named Rob shook her hand, and as they said their hellos, she couldn't help overhearing Wyatt, her admirer.

"I'm Wyatt McArthur, so glad I came here today. Blue skies, a great restaurant on the beach, and a lovely companion for at least eight minutes. What more could a man want?"

She crossed out the little heart drawn next to his

name. *Will I really meet someone tonight?* What about Deon and Phoebe and her teacher-friend Noelle, who's here somewhere chatting up some guy who's probably trying to impress. Everyone's looking and hoping.

"You look festive," said Rob. (Nametag: Fun-loving, great dancer, musician.) "I guess we've got to talk fast. We only have seven minutes—"

"Six."

"Let's not waste them talking about minutes." He paused, studied her. "You're a pretty woman, but I guess I'm not the first to tell you."

What could she say to that? Lucy wished for a second glass of wine to better cope with such flagrant comments. Her gaze shifted to Deon, who had no one at his table. He looked lost, holding onto his empty ice cream cup like a life raft.

"Tell me about yourself." Rob was unfazed by her silence.

"Well, I'm...I'm a teacher. Science." A conversation killer for sure.

"I love science." Rob ducked his head and smiled. His teeth were bright and glowing like a row of spectators at a basketball game. "I'm a teacher too. Children's librarian, play guitar and use songs in my lessons."

"Oh, nice."

"Yes." He sat looking at her as if he was going to tell her a secret. The gap in the conversation grew and started to worry Lucy, and she was about to ask some dumb question about his favorite singer when he folded his hands and cleared his throat.

"Let's cut to the chase. We're all here for the same thing. Give me your phone number and we'll go out dancing, get to know one another a little better. What do you think? Eliminate the middle man."

Would this man be fun to live with? What would a life with any of these men be like? Strange thought but since her short marriage over twenty years ago, Lucy hadn't lived with anyone.

The bell rang.

"I'm writing your name here, on the back," Rob said, determined. "I'd like to call you."

Deon appeared at her side. "Meet anyone?" He stood watching Rob, who looked up at him and gave a toothy grin.

"Go away," Lucy hissed but Deon hovered, taking up space. "Mind your own beeswax."

"That's real mature." He bent over and whispered in her ear. "I have to talk to you. After." He moved away, looking at her over his shoulder with a baleful expression.

"Think about my proposal," Rob said. "Dancing. I'm a pretty fun guy."

"Hey, fella." A man in a tan sports jacket at the next table called out and Rob and Lucy twisted around. "My turn. I'm next. Let the lady go, will you?"

She waved goodbye to Rob and jerked her eyebrows up as if to say, "What can I do?"

"Nice to meetcha, pretty lady," said Tan Jacket. "Want a hit?"

"Pardon?" (Nametag: Lloyd. Friendly, flexible, enjoy movies and restaurants.)

Flexible? Her brain dissected all the possible ways this man could be flexible.

"I've got a little rum here, in my pocket." A sly whisper. "Bring that ice cream cup over and I'll add a little punch." She didn't need encouragement to slide the empty cup over. Lloyd eased his flask open under the table.

"Thanks." She upended the container and drank, banged it down. "Hit me again."

He did, laughing.

"Thanks, just what I needed." This time she sipped more slowly.

"I aim to please." He put away the flask. "So, ever done this before? I've done it four or five times. Always meet someone special. Never fails. Hope you'll check me off on your list there. Here, hand me your paper and I'll do it for you. Give you my number, too."

The bell again.

Lucy stuck her tongue in the cup, catching a few rum dregs, and pushed the paper across the table. Let Lloyd with his flask supply his digits, his address, and his Social Security number, if that's what he wanted. She eyeballed the room, measuring out the men yet to be met. A well-built guy with blond hair looked promising. So did a shortish guy who resembled an older Milo Ventimiglia from the NBC series, *This Is Us*. She perked up and prepared to smile at the next guy. And the next.

The tables nearby were already occupied, so she searched for a single man. Someone in the corner signaled with a wave. She waved back and headed his way. *I will get through this.*

"Hey, Lucy." Noelle perched at a table in her path with a cute, lanky guy who shot her a quick look before turning back to Noelle. They clasped hands, squeezing, and smiled at one another before she moved on. "We'll talk," Noelle trilled. "I'll call you."

Lucy's skin prickled. She'd just witnessed Noelle's meet-cute. Even if Noelle didn't realize it yet, the attraction was undeniable. And mutual. The guy couldn't tear his eyes away. Imagine telling people you met each other at an ice cream social.

Eight minutes and you knew.

She was already jealous.

****

Deon, ice-creamed out, looked up at Peggy (Nametag: cat mother, gardening, closet romance reader) as she plopped into the seat, rooted her butt around until she was comfortable, and eyed Deon.

"You're divorced?" she asked, her hair swinging forward as if it, too, were happy to meet him. "Oh, sorry for the dumb question. We're all divorced, that's why we're here."

At first, Deon contemplated how to respond to this Peggy person. Then he shook his head. "I'm not—"

"You're still married?" Of the five women he's met so far, Peggy was the first to ask about his marital status. And misinterpreted his answer.

"Not at all. My wife…my wife passed away. All I meant was I'm not divorced. We'd still be together if she didn't…she had this—"

"Was it cancer? I'm so sorry." She tilted her head with that irritating sympathy look everyone gave, the look Deon would never get used to.

"No." Something clawed up Deon's throat like sour-tasting medication. Over four years afterward, and he still couldn't cope with the pity. Maybe this was why he never got into dating.

"Car. Car accident." As he mouthed the words, he realized he didn't have to tell anyone his business. Who was this over-curious woman with no boundaries?

He cleared his throat. "What's with the closet romance thing? By the way, I'm a closet ice cream eater." Changing the subject. A message that the window for additional sad widower talk had closed. And an attempt at humor. *Geez, Deon, Cary Grant you are not.*

"Oh, me too. I had a tiny scoop of vanilla. Trying to watch my weight." She crossed her legs, kicking Deon under the table. "Sorry. I'm bad at sitting still."

He gazed past her at the beach and the water beyond, where a sailboat, a one-man craft, rode out beyond the inlet. A chance bargain twenty-five years ago brought Phoebe's parents to purchase this old Branford restaurant, renovate, their loyal customers following them from New Haven and beyond. He and Phoebe had been friends for eleven years. He can't believe it.

Phoebe and his wife, Melinda, were friends. Close friends.

"What's your favorite flavor?" Peggy asked.

"Anything dark chocolate." He's immediately transported back to the time he and Melinda ordered the ten-dollar, ten flavors with ten toppings monstrosity at Ice Cream Heaven, on vacation in Rhode Island. Ordered it in place of dinner and got five minutes into it when they both stopped, sickened by the super sweetness. Drove to a movie theater in nearby Pawtucket to order popcorn.

"Not me," Peggy stated, interrupting his thoughts. "Not a chocolate person." She's restless, has a nervous, twitchy way about her that Deon found irritating and endearing.

He peered more closely at her nametag and reread it. "Romance reader, I get," he said. "Tell me about the closet part."

"I don't think most people consider romance to be worthwhile reading. They think it's all formula and nothing of substance." She leaned in, as if to share a confidence. "Not true. Besides…" and she lowered her head, dropping her voice to a whisper, "I love erotic romance."

He perked up, neurons on alert, surprised to find this most unexpected tidbit captivating. Did he hear correctly? "Tell me more."

"Oh, no, I couldn't."

"You can."

She waffled. "I don't let everyone in on my…predilection, shall we say?" She put a hand to her throat. "Men make judgments, don't you agree?"

A witty, sly, smile from Miss Peggy prompted a tentative grin from Deon. Yes, he decided, a smile can be witty. *Wait till Lucy hears this.*

"Yeah, erotic romance. Nice to know it's a thing," he said, judging her in a good way. The bell sounded. "I'd like to see you again." Deon pointed to her paper as she stood. There were two checkmarks indicating her interest in two of the men she'd met. *She's doing better than I am.*

"Nice meeting you." Peggy paused, one hand on her chest as if talking about her favorite genre caused her heartache. "Maybe I'd like to see you, too. I'll think about it."

Deon didn't know how to interpret that little zinger. Sparring with Peggy wasn't so bad, even gave his ego a little boost. Lucy was not a sure thing, not even close. His mind was in the closet again where he could almost smell her skin, the fragrance emanating from her…and…who was he kidding? He'd already had his second chance.

He scratched a question mark next to Peggy's name on his rating sheet and wrote the letter E next to it. E for erotic.

He'd probably forget what it stood for.

A woman in a polka-dot dress threw herself into the chair, glaring at Deon. "Before you ask questions, I'm not divorced," she announced.

He jerked himself up from a slouch and squeezed his hands into fists in his lap. "All righty, then." He attempted a smile.

"I'm a widow. Being a widow is very different from a divorced person. No one here seems to understand that."

Deon took a few seconds before responding. The woman, Melanie (Nametag: Love, romance, happy thoughts) checked her paper and clicked her pen as if she'd already made her mind up about Deon and was ready to cross him off her list. Her round face made her younger looking than she probably was, judging by the gray threading her hair.

Deon kept his voice flat so as not to startle her. "I'm also a widow. Widower."

With that, she straightened up, eyes boring into Deon's. "Have you done any internet dating? I met my late husband the old-fashioned way. Waitressing, my summer job. I was twenty and he was the short-order cook in the restaurant where I was working."

"Internet dating?" Deon's mouth twerked.

"What a crock, huh?"

Deon's mind traveled back to a dating discussion the previous winter. Phoebe and Lucy at O'Donahue's on their usual Sunday afternoon. His friends, haranguing him about not dating.

"I'm not talking about going out with anyone," Phoebe said. "You don't have to act on anything."

"That's right," said Lucy, taking a swig of her beer. "You're not ready."

Deon never knew how to take these occasional head-butts into his personal life from his women friends. Especially not from Lucy, who could drink him under the table.

"Just be more open," Phoebe said. "Like bump into a couple of women."

"Bump?" *Geez, this was ridiculous.*

"Chat with anyone you meet in natural situations. IRL."

"That IRL thing again."

Phoebe reached over to ruffle his hair as he ducked, blocking her hand with his own.

"So I'm not your average alpha male," he protested. "Doesn't mean I don't have healthy alpha tendencies."

"That's why we love you so much," Phoebe said, with a quick look at Lucy. "We're not alpha lovers, are we?"

"Yeah, we're not," Lucy agreed, dismissing all the alphas on the planet. "We appreciate a sensitive man."

The woman's voice jerked him back to the present. "How did you meet your wife?"

"My wife? She was president of the debate club senior year in college. Argued rings around me. Never could resist her brain."

"Uh oh." She patted his hand.

"What?"

"You haven't moved on yet, have you? Emotionally, you're still attached."

Deon smiled, despite himself, thinking this woman could substitute for Phoebe any day. She didn't miss a thing. "How about you?" he asked. "Still attached? Emotionally?"

"Trying to turn the discussion around?" Her eyes bored into him. "Focusing on me?"

"Sure."

She reached into her bag and handed him a card. "Text me. Seriously. You get the whole widowhood thing."

The bell again. He pocketed the card. *Well, why not? Maybe.*

Melanie waved a quick goodbye and Deon's gaze drifted around the room in search of Lucy. He needed to think things through, needed to gird his loins, one of his favorite movie lines of all times. Stanley Tucci playing a guy taking dancing lessons to meet women.

The way Deon saw things, he'd cemented himself in Lucy's mind as the guy who put her on *ignore* after sleeping with her.

He had to fix that pronto, and he needed a grand gesture, like in the movies.

Especially since that cheek kiss spooked her. A mistake, bordering on creepy. The heat from his chest rose up his neck to his face. He needed help. He'd confide in Phoebe. He could tell her anything.

No, that wouldn't work. Phoebe didn't know about the lost weekend, and he couldn't lie to Phoebe of all people.

The bell rang.

Deon lounged alone at his table like a man drifting in a canoe without oars, lost in his own thoughts.

"Hi Deon." The unmistakable scent of everything Lucy wafted up as she plopped down opposite him, her curls swinging, that shiny top highlighting her spectacular boobs.

Deon startled, his hand riffling his hair, probably making it stand up in front. Had he said something out loud?

"You weren't expecting me? How are you holding up? Let me see your notes." Lucy lunged for his paper folded in half under his hand, but he snatched it away and held it over his head.

"Stop it. This is private."

"Private? I just want to see if you have any checks. Made a connection. Show me."

"You're getting as nosy as Phoebe."

"I'm watching out for you. Like you said you're watching out for us. Me and Phoebe."

"I'm always watching out for you guys. I'm the designated driver, your dancing partner, and all-around handyman."

"You're not that handy."

Deon's face mock crumpled. "You hurt my feelings. I'm pretty handy. Change light bulbs. I'm there when you need me."

"No. You're not."

They stared at one another.

"That's mean." He cringed at her words. She was right. He hadn't been there for her. "Won't you ever forgive me?" he shot back. His insides curled with remorse. He had to make things right. But how?

Lucy blinked twice at the velocity of his response. It had popped out, surprising her.

She studied him for a moment. "Someday." Irritation marred her expression. "Let's not talk about this now."

The bell. Lucy unfolded from the seat, slung her bag over her shoulder.

"Let's go to the beach on the weekend," said Deon in a rush to get her attention before some other guy sidled up. "We'll take photos and I'll help you style. Driftwood, horseshoe crabs. Dinner."

"I don't think so," she said, and floated away.

Chapter Ten

"I've been hoping you'd come join me." Marcus wore a shit-eating, lopsided grin. "Holding my breath."

Blond, with a pinkish complexion and wide shoulders, the only man wearing blue jeans and a fitted T-shirt. Black.

Lucy shifted into the seat across from him. *What opening lines*. An unladylike snort sneaked out, but no clever retorts. Nothing.

He looked down, wagged his head, sheepish. "Sorry, I'm coming on too strong."

Lucy remembered the Chris Rock joke about how everyone sends their representative when meeting someone for the first time. Well, her representative sat up straight, and sucked in her stomach, hoping her mascara hadn't drifted to the corner of her eye.

Marcus was hot, like athletic hot, like rock-me-all-night hot. *Stop*! her mind shouted.

"Wait." Her representative excused herself and Lucy took over. She wasn't letting him get away with teasing, not without a fight. "Didn't you wink at me across a crowded room?

"Why yes, yes I did."

His smile dragged her in. See, that was her problem—glib, flirty guys with broad shoulders. Guys who made promises with little follow-through.

To grab control of the conversation, Lucy read his

nametag out loud. "Outdoor guy, loves dogs, books. Seriously looking." She let loose a sly, teasing grin. "Seriously looking? You were sitting with another woman, winking at me like a pickup artist."

He reached across the table and took her hand for a moment. "My turn to read. Okay?"

She nodded.

"Lucy, baby," he purred, working the whole playful thing while reading the tag. "Love working with teens, Insta stories, baking. Kindness." He eased back in his seat, crossed a leg as if preparing for a long session on his therapist's couch. "You bake, I'll eat."

"Deal. I'm known to feed my friends."

"Known? What's your specialty?" His eyes danced. *This guy is lethal.*

"Healthy desserts packed with fiber. Fiber is our friend." As soon as it left her mouth, she winced.

He laughed, an unexpected chortle that turned his expression from cute to irresistible when a dimple appeared on his left cheek. "Fiber, huh? And Insta stories?" He leaned closer, invading her space. "What's that?"

"Instagram. I bake and take pictures. Tell stories."

"Never paid much attention. Show me?"

"Sure." Lucy whipped out her phone. In six seconds he was scrolling her Insta feed, nodding and smiling, but she could tell he didn't get it. The magic wasn't there for him.

He handed back the phone. "Impressive, but I'm here to talk to you." Elbows on the table, so close she breathed in his scent, a mixture of aftershave and soap. "Here's a thought. Do you have a pen?"

Thick, dark lashes. *I'm jealous.*

She reached into her handbag and handed him a pen.

"Give me your number. Please." He posed holding his arm in front of him on the table, writing on it as she whispered her phone number, smiling at the silliness. They're back in the eighth grade when writing on your arm was a thing. "What would you like to do on our first date?" he asked.

She hesitated. The flip banter wasn't the problem, more likely the direct approach that floored her. After all, this was a free-for-all flirt fest that everyone paid to attend.

He waited for Lucy to respond, a little wary now. A quick check around the room assured her this ice cream socializing couldn't last much longer. She'd met almost everyone.

"A walk on the beach?"

Deon, a few tables away, chatted with a woman wearing pink peep-toe heels tied at the ankles with bows. He sat with arms folded, meaning lack of interest. *Not interested*, another of their jokes. Stolen from an old movie the three of them watched one rainy vacation afternoon at Phoebe's. He glanced their way. Marcus took her hand again. *Will Deon notice?* A tiny quiver racked her, a response to Marcus' intimacy, perhaps? Or nervousness.

"Perfect. The classic walk on the beach," Marcus smiled in agreement. "Corny but simple."

"Corny?" Pretending to be offended.

"When we're done here," said Marcus, interrupted by the bell, "let's catch a drink."

"Catch?" His way of inviting her for a drink without paying?

113

"Have a glass of wine with me." That dimple again. "Here or somewhere."

She drew a heart next to Marcus's name. "Sounds good."

"See you later," he said, and sure enough, another woman stood waiting for her to vacate her place.

She got up and took a sideways glance in Deon's direction. He waved his arm in great circles and Lucy half-smiled back, mind racing. He'd been acting a bit peculiar, not like Deon at all. And what did he want to talk to her about? This whole ice cream thing was crazy with personalities. Originals every one. The guy with his flask, the overdressed women, hot Marcus flirting and inviting her for wine, now Deon flapping his hand, waving, over-the-top. Had he been drinking? In a daze, she wandered over to the nearest available seat where a guy with long brown (obviously dyed) hair in a ponytail that crept halfway down his back bowed from the waist, his forehead nearly touching the table.

"Hello, doll," he said. "Nice to meetcha."

Doll?

"You're one of the best-looking ladies I've met in this damn ice cream social." He leaned closer and muttered, "Good thing I had a beer next door before this thing started."

The margarita and the hastily consumed wine had worn off. Lucy wanted—no, needed—another glass of wine. She'd get one, too. As soon as the bell rang, she'd sprint over behind the bar. Let Phoebe try to get in her way, she'd mow her down.

"I'm available," Ponytail said deliberately, drawing the word out. "How about you?"

Maybe if she kept her mouth shut, he'd keep

talking, the bell would ring, and she'd escape.

"You turned up here so I'm guessing you're up for a date. How about it? Do you like opera?" His eyelids half closed.

"Um. I don't know much about opera."

"I drive in to attend rehearsals in New York once a month. They're free. This month they're doing *Carmen*. What a show! You won't want to miss it. Plus, you've got me. You know, to explain the story." He turned sideways and put an elbow on the table. "But I've got a question."

When would that freakin' bell ring? Why wasn't there a clock in here? Where was Artemis when Lucy needed her? Any second...come on, come on, ring, ring.

"Sex is important to me," Ponytail said. "Not to be blunt but some women aren't interested. Therefore, before committing, I need to know. Is sex on the table? I don't know how to put this..." His voice tapered off and he stopped speaking as Lucy sweated into her new metallic top.

"Sex? You want to do it on the table? We're at an *ice cream social*. Are you a freakin' freak?" blasted out of her mouth like projectile vomit.

He cleared his throat and ended up coughing, a raspy, hacker of a cough, covering his mouth with one hand and reaching into his pocket with the other for a tissue.

The effort of keeping her voice low made the scream in Lucy's head louder.

"Heck, you offended?" Ponytail glared up at her.

"You're a dick." Lucy jerked out of her seat bumping into Deon as the bell sounded.

"Isn't it normal to like sex?" Ponytail snarled. "Darlin', I'm not lookin' for a gal pal."

Deon glared at the man, who instantly pulled out his phone. "Suit yourself."

"Are you okay? You want me to punch him for you?"

"What?" Deon couldn't be serious.

"I was on the boxing team in college." He threw a dirty look at Ponytail. "I'm not bad."

"Yes, Deon, I do want you to punch him. Right now." She stood on her toes, huffed, "Don't be ridiculous," into his ear as Deon moved closer to Ponytail. The man bent backward and held his hands in front of his face. Lucy tugged on Deon's shirt, dragging him away. "Sit down. Where's your table? We're not messing up Phoebe's party."

He slumped into his seat and wrapped an arm around Lucy. "I would have done it. I was eavesdropping on your conversation. Nasty bit of business, that guy." He jolted, as if remembering. "I'm proud of you. Calling him on his behavior."

They both glanced in the direction of Ponytail. His table was empty.

"Good riddance," Lucy said.

"You're tough."

"Yeah, that's me." She looked down at him. "I'd better switch."

"Soft too. I should know," Deon said, his face coloring instantly.

"Shut up, smartass." She twisted away, calling over her shoulder. "I'm not riding home with you tonight."

****

Strappy Sandals, the woman Deon met before the

event, sat opposite him.

"Hey, didn't we meet in the street before? Ever try running from the parking lot in heels? No, of course not, you're a man. Anyway, I couldn't get a space. Almost broke a bone. Shouldn't have worn these." She waved a leg in the air, pointed her toe. "Three-inchers. I'm still recovering." She sighed and stretched her legs out to the side, flashed a wide grin.

With those heels she must be six feet tall.

"Sometimes I go to my cousin's." She lifted her hand, pointed vaguely out the door, "down the road in Guilford. They're almost on the water. Any closer…"

Deon sketched a tiny high heel on his paper as she droned on. He wanted a beer. Lucy enjoyed a beer from time to time. The first thing he would do when he got out of here involved a beer, maybe two. He glanced a few tables over where she sat talking to a guy in white shorts and sandals with socks. Like she'd go for a guy who wore socks with sandals.

He leaned his chin on his hand, pretend-listening to Strappy Sandals. So Lucy was pissed. He'd fix that with his grand gesture. *We're going to the beach, the two of us. Perfect setting to tell her…whatever he's going to tell her.*

At last the bell rang, and Deon waved goodbye as Phoebe sat down, thank God. Deon had the urge to hug her and he leaned over the table and squeezed her cheek to his.

"What is going on?" Her voice muffled against his jaw.

"Nothing. I'm glad to see you."

"I can stay? Even though we already had our turn." She twisted around as if someone would catch her cheating. "I sneaked over to your table. Let me stay?"

"You're running this event, hell, stay." Deon, cheered not to have to make small talk with yet another stranger, swept an arm toward the empty chair, a magnanimous invitation. "Stay a whole nine minutes, live on the edge."

She sighed a giant sigh, heavy with angst. "It's been a tough week."

"It's almost over."

"Noelle's here. Have you talked to Noelle?"

"Like I've had the time? With this whirlwind tour you cooked up." He bumped a fist on the table top. "You're not trying to match us up, are you? She's nice but not my type."

Phoebe hesitated a few seconds and blushed. "How do you know she's not your type?"

"Stop it."

"Don't be crabby, Mr. Middle Aged With Hair. Middle aged men have all the advantages when it comes to dating."

"Look, it's a beautiful night, we can take a beach walk, the three of us." Deon shifted forward in the chair. Making plans for Phoebe and maybe Lucy, not a bad idea. Assuming they would all be at loose ends after this thing ended.

He didn't want to think about Lucy meeting anyone.

Outside, leaves whispered in the cooling breeze as the sun lowered. The whole party could be moved to the deck to watch the sunset. Behind Phoebe, Noelle waved and he waved back.

"You're having a crappy time, aren't you?" Phoebe waited for his reaction.

"What?"

Her eyes moved around the room as if on stalks, darting and measuring people's enjoyment quotient. He could almost hear her thoughts ticking. "It's awful, no one is having a good time."

"Well, I wouldn't say that, certainly not." Some people were having a laugh riot.

"An ice cream social, the worst idea ever. Maybe if I asked the waiters to take drink orders?" Phoebe closed her eyes for a moment and opened them, her words rushed, as if she needed to dump everything in her head onto the table before the bell sounded. "Noelle was not thrilled about sitting in but what could I do?" Her hand went to her throat.

"Who knew speed dating was such a pain in the ass?" Deon shifted back in his chair glad he had no part of event planning. "My dad would find this hilarious, but you know what? There's nothing funny about searching for a mate when you're over forty."

Phoebe ignored his attempt to humor her and whispered, her upper lip damp with perspiration. "Two of the waiters even complained about old people being bad tippers." Her eyes moistened. She took out a hanky, a real old fashioned, ironed hanky, and dabbed.

"Take a breath," Deon soothed in his most professional voice. He couldn't have her crying on her own turf, in front of strangers and possibly her future soulmate. "Phoebs." He laid a hand on her arm to calm her. "They're into it. Look around if you don't believe me."

She obeyed by turning in a complete circle, rising out of her chair for a moment so she could better view the crowd. A gasp escaped. "Yeah, yeah, that's good."

"Real good. You're a success."

"Oh." A smile appeared.

"Keep smiling, that's my Phoebs," he said with a burst of affection. "Collect any names?" An effort to divert her.

"Two, so far. A lawyer and some musician guy, a little short, but what the hell. You?"

Deon crossed his legs, tapped the spoon against his cup. "Not much."

"You should call Lucy." She said this casually, watched for his reaction.

"Sure. I always call Lucy. Why wouldn't I?" Deon, master of the laconic comeback. *What is she getting at?*

"It shows."

"What? What shows?" His kidneys lurched. *Does she mean what I think she means?*

Phoebe tilted toward him wearing her *this is serious* expression. "I can see it in your face whenever...never mind. I shouldn't have said anything."

When the bell rang, Deon's torso jerked, and Phoebe laughed at his reaction. "So twitchy. No worries, I'm wrapping this up in a few minutes." She patted his head like he was her pet, and he gave her a quick goodbye grin as she moved to the next table.

She had seen him through the worst time of his life, the aftermath of the accident. It occurred to him that Phoebe hadn't been in a relationship in quite a while. Maybe she, too, held secrets.

Without turning his head, Deon tracked Lucy. Was she connecting with any of these jokers? But how would he know? Lucy chatted easily with everyone although she called herself an introvert. When this thing was over, he'd mosey over and—his own thoughts intruded on his reverie. *You should call Lucy.* He wouldn't go there, wouldn't analyze Phoebe's words. What did she mean by the *it shows* comment? Were his feelings obvious? His kidneys lurched again.

A few tables away, some tall, buff dude in a turquoise shirt leaned across the table invading Lucy's space. Deon craned his neck and frowned in disapproval.

"Hello?"

Deon smiled as Noelle sat at his table. "Hey, sorry, didn't see you."

"Nice to sit with a guy I know. Relax for a few minutes." A tentative smile. "I'm worn out from talking with strangers. Hard work."

"Don't I know it." Deon experienced a lift hearing he wasn't the lone reluctant ice cream socializer.

"Yes." She crossed her legs and leaned forward. "But the online alternative is rough. Have you ever tried it?"

"Me?" Her question struck him as humorous. He realized she was waiting for him to finish his thought. "You're saying this is better?"

She hesitated as if reluctant to reply. "I hit it off with someone today, though."

"Great." His voice rang louder than he'd intended. All he could think was *what if?* What if Lucy met someone today? His gaze traveled from Noelle to Lucy to the buff dude, who was now showing her something on his phone. His hair hung over his forehead. *Yeah, like he doesn't train it to flop like that on purpose.*

"Hey, Deon. You okay?" Noelle tapped his hand gently with her forefinger.

"Sorry. I came with a friend. Lucy. You know her, right?" He pointed with his chin. Of course, Noelle knew Lucy. New Haven teachers were all connected, like some incestuous, gossipy cult. Deon's chest squeezed. He stopped, uncertain Noelle understood his point. "I'm a little surprised by her enthusiasm for this whole…" The right word eluded him.

"Enterprise?" Noelle supplied. They both looked over at Lucy and the dude, talking and gesticulating.

Noelle cleared her throat. "What's the best thing that's happened to you in the past week?" She slouched back and waited for him to answer the question, hurtled from outer space.

"What?" He could be having a heart attack. It happened. Fifty-year-olds having heart problems, happened all the time. He sighed deep inside, a private sigh that expressed oh, so many things. Deon had no doubt it was his heart. Had no doubt it wasn't a heart attack. His father was eighty and going strong along with his mother, at seventy-five.

"I'm taking a Masterclass—famous people teaching. Heard of it?"

"No."

"Anyway, David Sedaris despises small talk, and says people should ask interesting questions. I was asking an interesting question."

They sat like shy birds on a wire looking at each other.

"The best thing that's happened to me…" Deon's voice dropped, "is I realized I'm…I'm in heavy like with my best friend." He shifted away from Noelle and gazed down at his hands clasped together in his lap. Why did he blurt this out? They barely knew one another.

Noelle cocked her head to the side. "Heavy like? Do you mean you're in love with your best friend?" She looked at him steadily, her expression calm. "You don't have to tell me."

"I…I…" He'd already told her. Pretty much.

"Not Phoebe. You two go way back."

His head buzzed. Should he reply? He regretted saying anything. The buzz traveled to his ears. No, no, this was good, he should get it out there. Deal with it.

Before he could regroup, Noelle jerked a thumb in Lucy's direction. "Lucy?"

Deon's eyes followed the thumb, his torso twisting in the direction of Lucy's laughter, wide and full-bodied. The dude joined in, tilted the chair back on two legs. Deon hoped it tipped over.

Something curdled in his stomach. He wanted to hear that full-bodied belly laugh, be the cause of all that merriment.

"You need to tell her," Noelle murmured.

Now was the time to take it back, tell Noelle he was kidding, making conversation. He opened his mouth, but no words fell out.

The damn bell again.

"Nice seeing you," he said instead. "I mean it."

"Break a leg." She smiled. "I mean it, too. Metaphorically, of course."

"Of course," he said.

Chapter Eleven

The bell rang. "Mark your three choices," Phoebe yelled, cupping her hand over her mouth.

Deon studied his paper where a series of squiggles, triangles, and eyes with enlarged pupils placed beside names conveyed...what? Women he's found to be special in eight, lousy minutes?

"When in doubt," Phoebe chirped, "give a person a chance." She rolled her eyes upward as if glad she once gave someone a break. "You never know. Away from all this pressure, we're all different people."

Artemis wove her way among the tables, collecting papers. A guy at the next table rose and Deon heard, "Time to get hammered." The beer he'd promised himself beckoned. More fellows and a smattering of women headed for the bar, and soon everyone milled around the room chatting. Deon decided he'd find the snotty widow with the attitude since he had nothing better to do, but in a sea of nametags, he couldn't locate her.

A tap on his shoulder. "Deon?" A woman in an orange dress stood before him. "Sorry for interrupting. I meant to ask if you were named after Dion, the singer. Is that a misspelling?"

"No, that's correct. I was named for the singer."

"Dion, the singer?" came a male voice from over his shoulder. "Really? He wasn't that good."

"Who says?" The orange dress again. "I love 'Runaround Sue'. Great song."

"I give it a four out of ten."

"I give it twelve out of ten," another woman said.

Deon caught sight of Lucy near the doorway as the faint scent of vanilla and citrus wafted up.

"Hi, are you staying?" Peggy. Still wearing her nametag. *Erotic romance.* The label stuck in his mind, identifying her forever.

Across the room, the blond guy handed Lucy a glass of wine and she looked up at him. She looked so tiny…vulnerable next to him.

"Are you all right? Your face is white, maybe you should sit down." Peggy pointed Deon to an empty chair, and he sat. She rubbed his shoulder. He remembered telling this Peggy he wanted to see her again. What did that mean, *seeing* someone? He never understood that expression, always thought of it as lame.

"I think I'll stay," he said. "Why not?" He sneaked another sidelong glance in Lucy's direction, where she and the showy, muscular guy stood. From the way he leaned in, it's clear the guy was staking his claim, blocking anyone with a hint of interest. It would take a guy with big balls to interrupt the happy couple.

Deon considered their mutual interest in Lucy, his hands clenching in his lap. Now he felt an overpowering compulsion to stay, keep an eye on her. He shrugged away the warning twist in his gut. Lucy wouldn't desert him now that they'd gotten through the ice cream ordeal, would she?

"I'm going to see about a drink," Peggy said. "You look better. It was probably all that sugar." She headed in the direction of the bar.

Deon should offer her a glass of wine. Meanwhile, Phoebe's parents emerged from the kitchen and circulated, shaking hands and talking to the small groups of singles. They made a handsome pair, tall and imposing, her father with a full head of dark hair, her mother in a blue sleeveless dress, her arms toned and lightly tanned.

Phoebe banged a glass with a spoon, and everyone quieted. "Please feel free to stay for wine and cheese pie. Zorbaki's is offering half off to everyone as a thank you for participating today." Her eyes searched the crowd and stopped at Deon. A moment later, she came over carrying two glasses of wine.

"Hey." Phoebe handed him a glass. "Try this Agiorgitiko. It just came in. Dark cherry and espresso."

"Thanks." He sipped, savoring her choice. "Nice. Very."

"A bribe so you'll circulate. Chat someone up. Thank God this is almost over."

"I thought it went well." Deon arranged his expression to appear sincere and took a long sip of wine.

"I can't wait to see the results. Almost everyone stayed, isn't that great?" She upended her own glass. "Tell me who you're interested in. Her enthusiasm over the top, she thrust out her chin. "Point with your chin. Come on, look around." Tilting his way, she whispered, "The woman with the spectacular heels? Or the one in the flowered dress? She's definitely your type."

He spun away from her. "Nope. Not tattling. I need time to think." He didn't like this version of Phoebe, pushy and on edge.

She planted herself in his path. "Come on, tell me. There's got to be one woman you—"

"Hey, is the wine any good?" Peggy was back. "I didn't get over to the bar yet. Too crowded."

"I'll get you a glass." If Deon stuck with Peggy and used her as a buffer, he could fend off Phoebe's eagerness and everyone else's. Or he could get drunk. *Yeah, like I'd do that.*

The one exception to his dating detachment? Lucy.

His doubts after their perfect weekend had messed him up, but he wouldn't let *that* happen again.

Deon wanted another chance.

He delivered the wine to Peggy and refused to let her pay. They clinked glasses, and he eyeballed the room, hoping Phoebe wouldn't keep bugging him.

"Hey," Lucy appeared at his side, the blond guy in tow. He breathed in her perfume, the light scent of mango and musk. "Deon, this is Marcus. Marcus, my good friend Deon." She emphasized the *good friend* or was it his imagination? Two little words to demonstrate they were in the deadly friend zone for eternity.

"Good to meet you." Either Marcus emphasized the word *good,* or Deon was paranoid. It wasn't all good. Nothing was good.

He shook Marcus' hand. What else could he do? The urge to get Lucy alone, speak to her in private gnawed at him. "You staying on a while?" So much to say, but not here, not now. "Phoebe broke out some special Greek wine. I thought…"

Impossible to complete a sentence with Marcus looking at him as if he knew. *He knows I want what I can't have.* Marcus saw through Deon, the distress in the handshake, tone of voice, all fake casual, his insides roiling.

"I love this Greek wine." Peggy being her friendly self. "Have you guys tried it, the one Deon's talking about?"

"Peggy," Deon said with a chin wag. "This is Lucy." He paused before saying, "and Marcus." *They're not a couple.* His gaze floated over Marcus' prominent biceps and pectorals, on display in the fitted shirt. *This dude works out. Yeah? But does he read fiction?* Lucy and he sometimes read the same book and discussed it. *Take that, Marcus.*

"Marcus, what's your story?" Peggy asked. Deon could have kissed her.

"My story? Which one?" Marcus draped a hand on Peggy's shoulder. "Tell me." As Peggy and Marcus chatted, Deon nudged closer to Lucy.

"Look, how about we stop somewhere on the way—"

"We're taking a walk on the beach," said Lucy. "Don't worry, Marcus is giving me a ride home." This said in a rush, a wave of her arm, her voice breathless. *She really likes this guy.* Now he's lost what little appetite he had left.

He nodded tightly. No time to pull her to the side, talk to her. Marcus cupped a hand on Lucy's elbow as they left, the din in the room echoing in Deon's ears, making it impossible to think clearly. *This guy is a stranger,* he wanted to tell Lucy, even as she disappeared down the stairs and crossed the street to the beach. A light breeze fanned Lucy's silvery top, displaying her smooth back for an instant. She glowed in the fading light, even from a distance. *I stood in her closet and helped her pick out that top. I kissed her.*

Sort of kissed her. Take that, Marcus.

The lights on the deck switched on. Business as usual, the party atmosphere dissipating despite the faint romantic glow. Couples and a few families gathered for dinner, the waiters buzzing around them.

Deon was at a loss. He hadn't foreseen being deserted at the end of the evening. He scanned the crowd of at least ten or eleven leftovers, like him, who lingered at tables and at the bar. How did he not see it coming? Of course, Lucy met someone tonight. *She's on the beach. Right now. With him.* A bitter taste rose in his throat.

"Deon, are you staying for some appetizers and a glass of wine?"

Deon forced a smile and turned back to Peggy, a distraction against his thoughts.

"Of course," he beamed too brightly, raising his glass and saluting her.

What else was there to do?

****

Between spoonfuls of oatmeal, Lucy dictated her list of summer resolutions into the Reminders app on her phone. Like getting up early every day and going to the gym. Birds chirped outside the open kitchen window where the scent of freshly mown grass hung in the air.

A text blew in from Phoebe. *—Hot guy Marcus got my number and already asked me out. Let's talk later —*

—Great!— she texted back, thinking *ut oh.*

Her thumb hovered over the message icon. She and Phoebe going out with the same man? A lousy idea. Maybe she wouldn't go out with him. Then she remembered his biceps, his negative stomach in the black T-shirt, his full-on banter.

This will sort itself out, a phrase her mom was fond of and which she'd never for a moment believed. It roosted in her head conveniently as she moved on to more pleasant tasks than telling her best friend her hottie was keen on two women.

Only a few more weeks until heavenly June, the month all teachers appreciated since it led to summer vacation. Sure, the kids were antsy and a tad on the wild side. So what.

Lucy continued her list. Make two desserts a week. Post more often on Instagram. Get on dating app for ten minutes. Ugh. She added the pile of poo emoji.

At the sink, she texted Deon her list of resolutions along with a teaser.

—*Dude, take a look at how productive MY summer's gonna be. You?*—

On autopilot, she opened the cupboard to get out the ingredients for chocolate orange brownies, a favorite recipe, preheated the oven and grabbed an orange and the zester. Slopped a half cup of butter in the pan, stirred in the cocoa, and took it off the burner to cool. Marcus didn't waste time. Last night after their beach stroll, he'd dropped her home and asked for her number. No kissing but she knew. They hit it off. Everything was effortless, the banter, a little hand holding.

Except for the part where he'd asked out her best friend.

Lucy greased and floured the pan. Marcus probably had no idea which one of them he liked better.

Next, she beat the eggs and added the cocoa

mixture, turning Marcus over in her mind. Pretty clear he'd asked them both out to compare. Couldn't blame the guy.

"I'll blame if I want to," she sang out loud to the tune of an ancient Leslie Gore song. Instantly, her mood improved. She measured and threw in sugar, flour, walnuts, juice, zest and salt. Mixed, poured into the brownie pan, and shoved it in the oven.

When she'd spent weekends with Justin, the man she thought would be her Forever Guy, he begged her not to make the chocolate orange brownies, saying he had to work out forty-five minutes extra at the gym.

"I can't resist your brownies. Or your walnut pie," he'd say, putting his arms around her as she leaned into his solid chest.

"Can't resist me either, can you?"

"No resisting you," he'd respond, squeezing her hard.

Justin. The first man she'd trusted in a long time and yet…she couldn't relax. It was as if she played the waiting game with every man who entered her life, waiting for his exit in the middle of the night. Unwieldy baggage, a holdover from her brief marriage.

Sweet words. So why did they break up? Oh, yeah. She dumped him. Mostly she was the dumper. That way, no man had the chance to dump her first.

It's a miracle any relationship worked out these days.

She set the timer and wiped down the counters and stovetop. All was well when the kitchen gleamed and there was a goodie in the oven.

In the study at her computer, she checked the dating site for notifications. There were four lame attempts to grab her attention and she deleted them. Generic, canned invitations were a turn off. Why was online dating such a pain in the ass? Not that she'd made much of an effort. Hmm. Posting photos on Instagram or baking a new pie was more fun.

On Safari, she typed in fruit pies and 699,807,368 results popped up, including a fruit pie with a lattice crust that would photograph oh, so well for Instagram.

The doorbell rang, and she startled, peeked out the window. Deon. Deon? At nine am? She trotted down the stairs and swung open the door.

"Hey." His hair stood up cartoonishly. "I was out for a run and I ended up here. Smells like you got up early. Watcha makin'?" He rubbed his belly in a parody of a ravenous person. "Got any of those chocolate macaroons? You hiding 'em?" He jerked open the sliding door to the mini laundry room and shook his shoulders. "Those macaroons? I dream about them every so often."

"Coffee?" Lucy offered. He followed her into the kitchen and sat while she poured.

The brownie aroma permeated the kitchen and Deon sniffed in appreciation. "You're fulfilling those resolutions you texted way ahead of time. Good for you."

"You're working every day?"

"Not until the summer. A few more clients though. Young."

They sipped their coffee in a comfortable silence.

"You survived, I see." A reminder of the ice cream social, the one thing sure to vex Deon.

"What? Oh, the thing last night." He gazed out the window at a squirrel rustling around the bushes. Deon fixed Lucy with an unblinking look. "You're going out with him? That guy you walked on the beach with?"

"That's what you came over here to ask me at nine in the morning?"

"How did it go?"

"How did what go?"

"Walking on the beach with Godzilla. How did it go?"

"You think Marcus is cute, huh?" She shot him an evil grin. Sometimes she got such pleasure from irritating Deon.

"Did he…was he aggressive?" The intense look on his face told her his question was dead serious.

Concerned for her welfare? A stab of remorse for picking on Deon. "I'm not telling you any details. What's got into you?" *Sure, go on the attack. You're such a meanie,* taunted the little voice in her head.

"So he was pushy?" Deon's jaw tightened.

She's overheated as if she's baking along with the brownies. What's with all the questions? It's not as if she's never dated before.

"Phoebe wouldn't be thrilled about that." Deon gave her a hard stare.

"You mean the walking on the beach part?"

"She's all excited about going out with him. Does she know you guys had a little sunset walk?"

"I'm not sure." Lucy drained her coffee. Phoebe must have texted Deon too.

"And you have a date with him?"

They sat looking at one another. He hadn't shaved, going for the scruffy-sexy look. Despite Lucy's perma-irritation level when it came to all things Deon these days, she appreciated his cuteness factor.

"We're going on a triple date." She sprang up to hide her smile and pretend-checked the oven by turning on the light and peeking inside the window. "Phoebe adores my idea. A way for the three of us to get to know one another."

A glance at Deon showed he wasn't buying her ridiculous story. "Look, I just met him." Her tone was reasonable, convincing. "Phoebe just met him. We don't have to explain anything, not at this point. We don't—"

"I think you should at least tell her you're going out with him. She should be armed."

"Armed?"

"With the information. Unfair advantage."

She heaved a dramatic sigh and took the coffee cups to the sink, ran the water. Deon leaned on the counter. "Look, I'm not trying to badger you."

Lucy finished rinsing the cups, not looking at him. "I'll tell her, of course I'll tell her. When I deliver the pies to Zorbaki. She's probably working there today."

"I should get going." He put a hand on her back, and she wheeled around to give him an awkward hug. *That kiss in the closet.* Lucy pushed the memory away.

The residue of confusion that colored her thoughts about Deon came and went in waves ever since their lost weekend. The closet kiss only made things more confusing. Something was off.

"I didn't get your number last night," he joked. "Didn't put it on my paper." Trying to lighten the awkwardness.

She pulled back and pressed her wet hands together. "Silly." He had that intense look again.

"Thanks for coming over yesterday. Helping me

with the flatlays. I'll look at the photos today." She dried her hands on the dishtowel and wound it up, preparing to snap it at him. "My needs are simple."

"Nothing about you is simple," he snorted and caught the towel before she attacked, stopping to study her. Strange. "I'd better get going, do another mile. I have a client at eleven."

"Okay." She grabbed the towel and dried the counter, an excuse to keep busy. "Hey, did you ask that...Peggy, that's her name. You get her number?" Why was she asking Deon about other women? She didn't want to know about...how would they ever work out as friends if they were both prickly?

"Yeah." He had that look again as if he wanted to say something. "Never mind Peggy." He swallowed. "Maybe the beach some day?"

What was going on? "I...I don't know." Her palms squeezed together. Was he kidding around?

His expression changed, became guarded.

"Sorry. We've both gotta prep for school Monday and we'll be dancing Sunday anyway. Forget I mentioned it."

Awkward. He'd almost asked her out.

She walked him to the door.

"Keep in touch," he said, a quip from a mutual friend in Minnesota who called it the state mantra.

She had the urge to crawl back into bed to think about what this all meant. And she couldn't get that *nothing much* closet kiss out of her mind.

If it was nothing much, why did she keep going over it in her mind?

Chapter Twelve

Sunday afternoon, Deon meandered around O'Donahue's greeting friends and regulars while the band was on break. Doing his best to avoid that guy Steve, who hovered near Lucy and Phoebe like a groupie.

Eventually, he landed back at the bar where his friends sat hunched together, chatting in low voices about the ice cream social.

"Did the guy with the flask offer you rum?" Lucy beckoned the bartender.

"Yeah, I even asked for seconds. How many names did you get?"

"Four."

"Anyone you actually like?" quizzed Phoebe.

"Sort of. You?"

"One guy. The one I texted you about."

Steve slid closer and quirked an eyebrow, looking back and forth between the two women.

Deon frowned. The Godzilla guy, that's who Phoebe was talking about. They were *in like* with the same guy. What a mess in so many ways. He couldn't gauge their reaction or ask any questions with Steve hanging around. Yup, the guy was getting up his craw.

But no matter what, tonight was the night.

Lucy twisted around on the barstool to face Steve. "You're a bit mystified, aren't you?" Playful, teasing the guy.

Steve grinned. "Ladies, you got some s'plainin' to do."

Deon almost choked on his beer. The guy did a believable Desi Arnaz.

"Oh, we did a meet and greet thing at my parents' restaurant." Phoebe expanded on the eight- minute ice cream social for Steve's benefit, and Deon *enough was enough of that Steve guy* wandered over to the band.

"Hey, man." Travis, the leader, sported his customary porkpie hat, which he usually discarded once he warmed up. He extended a hand and they shook. "It's been a little while."

"Yeah, well, you know." Deon ducked his head. Travis met Melinda over the years many times, and had attended the funeral. More recently at gigs, he'd invited Deon to sit in but never pressured him.

"Tonight, Dude. You wanna sit in? You got your harp handy?"

His harmonica…stuffed in his back pocket for the first time in a long while. "I'm mighty rusty." A prickle shot up his back. He'd play tonight. For real. *Thank God I've been practicing.* He'd really do it, get up in front of a crowd.

"No judgment." Travis was always cool. "Catch you later. Send me a signal."

During their first set, Deon danced with Phoebe and Lucy and Roberta and a few other regulars. The dance floor was crowded and tight, and when Deon needed a breather, he sneaked out the dining room door.

He took a walk down the side street, breathing in the sea air and thinking how Melinda would be thrilled he'd plucked up the courage to face an audience again.

Feeling comfortable with an audience was very much like being married to your special person. With time, practice and experience, you wouldn't have to make a special effort for your fans, knowing you were always accepted for who you were.

That was one of the things he loved about marriage, and he'd taken it for granted. Just as he'd taken his playing out with bands around town for granted. Never dreaming paralysis would hit him, prevent him from picking up his harp.

Back indoors, he squinted at the band from his barstool, impatient for the break to end. At last, Travis headed for the stage, the other band members following. He was hoping for a little Stevie Ray Vaughan, something he could sink his lips into, get lost in.

They played three in a row, and when the guitar solo introduced the first notes of "The Thrill is Gone," taking him back to an old recording by B.B. King and Eric Clapton, he knew this was it. Travis gave him a barely perceptible nod. Deon's hand reached for the harmonica in his back pocket.

He slid off the barstool, walked through the crowd on the dance floor ignoring the hammering in his chest, and hopped onto the stage.

****

Harmonica? On "Rock Me"? Since when did the band have a harmonica player? Lucy, dancing with Steve, craned her neck and twisted back to get a peek at the stage.

"It's Deon," Steve said, and twirled her in a loop so she faced the stage. Right there. Deon onstage playing the harmonica as if it extended from his hand. Lucy stopped, transfixed, the hair on the back of her neck rising. *Who is this man? Do I know him?*

"Awesome," said Steve. One by one the dancers gathered to watch. A ripple of excitement passed through the crowd.

"Oh, my God, I don't believe it," Phoebe yelled.

Lucy gripped Phoebe's shoulder, gaping at the spectacle. "Deon plays harmonica?"

"He used to...but he hasn't in a...since Melinda." Phoebe's eyes moistened. "It's a breakthrough," she whispered. "And it requires a lot of skill with the lips and tongue." Phoebe shot her a long, meaningful smirk and something deep and low in Lucy's gut vibrated, aching with the music.

Deon leaned toward the guitar player, slanting his shoulders, shaping the melody, the magic flowing as they riffed off one another with Deon adopting the refrain, making it his own. He moved in a sinuous bluesy crouch, the harp full and rich and textured. Electric. The hottest guy on stage.

At the bridge, the tempo sped up, and couples began to dance again, the sound, mellow and haunting, playful with a touch of melancholy. Lucy stepped away from Phoebe. She remembered seeing a little black case in one of the cubbies at Deon's house and asking him about it. They'd gotten distracted and he never answered. It was a harmonica case.

Steve moved in close, and they swayed and bent to the slow, sexy blues number. Up on stage, Deon was all coolness, singing with no self-conscious gestures or awkwardness—full-on flirting with the audience.

When I make my harp flutter,
it will thrill you from head to toe.

When I make those notes moan
it will rock your love-starved soul.
When I make my harp flutter,
it will thrill you from head to toe.

After the song ended, everyone clapped madly. Phoebe and Lucy retreated to their bar stools as the band began the guitar lead into "Stormy Monday." Slow and bluesy, Deon bending into the notes as if he invented *sexy harmonica player*, the phrase that repeated over and over in Lucy's head. She woke from her trance only when the bandleader broke the mood at the end, after the applause died down.

"Deon Goldbloom, everyone," Travis announced. "He'll be joining us again later on, so stick around."

A few hoots and hollers. Deon left the stage and was instantly surrounded by well-wishers.

"He's a hit," Lucy said. "Our Deon. We knew him when."

"He used to play a lot," Phoebe gushed. "All my musician boyfriends loved jamming with him."

"You ran out of musicians a while ago, didn't you?" Phoebe was a little famous for dating music guys, and Lucy got a lot of mileage teasing her about them. "What about way back? Did he play with your ex-husband, the dermatologist?"

Phoebe rolled her eyes. "I have one and only one ex-husband. Why do you insist on calling him my ex-husband, the dermatologist?"

On a roll, Lucy couldn't stop. "It's funny imagining you with a dermatologist. Way beyond my scope of what's right with the world."

"That is a ridiculous thing to say. Without him, I wouldn't have Artemis. Remember that when you're making jokes about the people in my life."

"I'm not making jokes, I'm being snappy. Who am I to make fun of anyone's choices in men? With my man history."

"True." She put a hand to Lucy's cheek, a typical Phoebe gesture of tenderness. "Our exes had a small part in that. I have Artemis. And you have Lily."

Lucy took a few seconds to reflect on her short marriage to the guy who didn't want to be married and Phoebe's to a classic workaholic. "We don't see our girls much these days, do we? Which reminds me, Lily is coming home tomorrow, and we're doing a cookout with my parents. I can't wait to see her."

"You doing your traditional movie binge?" Phoebe and Artemis joined Lucy and Lily on a few of those occasions. Their custom was to watch at least one trashy romantic comedy and stuff themselves with chips and guacamole and their beverage of choice, wine for Lucy, iced tea for Lily. Or maybe a little wine, now that she's grown up.

"Yup." Lucy didn't issue an invitation, not wanting to share Lily when she saw her so seldom.

Deon slid into his seat, radiating happiness.

Phoebe leaned in and tapped Deon's arm, her voice low and teasing. "You did good out there. Plus, you've got your edge back."

Deon quirked his lip. "My edge? Seriously?" He got up to go to the men's room, and Lucy figured this was the moment to mention the Marcus date.

Phoebe straightened in her seat. "There's something I've been wanting to talk to you about."

"What?" Lucy didn't like the sound of that, plus Phoebe wore her interrogation face.

"Are you flirting with Steve for real? Like trying to make Deon jealous?"

"Are you kidding?" Lucy made a clucking noise. "I never flirt with Steve or any of these guys for real." There. That was true. She took another sip of beer.

"It's not that exactly." Phoebe stared at her glass. Whatever she needed to tell Lucy was troubling her. "How can I say this?"

"Spit it out."

"All righty then. I think Deon likes you. You're special to him." She peered closer at Lucy as if gauging a possible response then spat out, "And you're so damn mean to him."

Lucy blanched, taken aback by Phoebe's bluntness.

"It's been going on for a couple months." Phoebe brushed her hair over her shoulder. "Did something happen? Um, between you guys?"

"I've…not really," Lucy huffed. "He says things that…he looks at me like…" She should have told Phoebe about their lost weekend months ago. Now everything was complicated, with too much to explain. How could she justify her outrage and attraction—competing forces—to Deon when she didn't understand them herself?

The bartender brought Lucy's beer.

"We've got to talk fast. Deon'll be back any second. Look, I'm not imagining this. It's like you get pissed off at him for no reason."

"He kissed me before your shindig. In the closet."

Phoebe stiffened. "Was that a bad thing?"

"It wasn't a real kiss, just a cheek kiss. Oh, and near my lips."

"Is that so awful?"

"He lingered."

"Lingered? What do you mean?"

"His lips. It was…intimate like maybe he was thinking about going for the real thing."

Deon returned from the men's room, Roberta trotting beside him.

"I still don't get why you're so…never mind. Later," Phoebe whispered.

"First dance of the second set?" Roberta asked Deon, who nodded.

"Deon, honey." Phoebe's smile was wide and a little fake. "Tell us. Did you collect a couple names at the ice cream thingy?"

Nothing like putting the poor guy on the spot. He shifted from one foot to the other and surveyed the line of bar sitters. "Yes, but I forget her name. She's sweet."

Phoebe poked Lucy in case she'd missed the subtext.

Sweet, she got it. As for telling Phoebe that Marcus was going out with both of them, well, she wasn't in the mood to spoil this evening. That news would wait.

Chapter Thirteen

Deon doodled on a pad as Chip Weinstein, his second client of the day, crossed his knee on his leg and wiggled his foot. Good things must be happening in *Chipsville.*

"I've lost fifteen pounds. Fifteen pounds." Chip pulled and snapped the waistband of his trousers, adding an exclamation point. "Fifteen pounds. I'm at my fighting weight."

Deon shifted in his chair. After only a month of therapy, Chip's attitude had improved exponentially from his initial visit. That day he'd announced he would never date and wanted nothing to do with women.

"Last week I went for coffee with a woman I see at the gym almost every day. We had plenty to talk about." Chip's expression turned sour. "I could have walked her to her car. I didn't. Turned chicken and couldn't ask her out."

He gave Deon a look that said it all, a *Help me* look. Deon needed to live up to the faith Chip had in him as a practitioner of shrinkage.

"Divorced two years, it's about time." Chip's statement was more of a question. "Don't you think, doc?"

Deon took his time answering, offered a calm, level gaze instead of words. Chip was a forty-five-year-old Yale physics professor with a sixteen-year-old son at Choate, a smart guy. Unfortunately, he wore dorky pants that grazed his ankles and colorful, short-sleeved dress shirts that made his arms look like pasty noodles.

Deon hadn't yet expanded his practice to offer the client a complete makeover along with therapy. And some would question Deon's taste. Today he wore an orange shirt and cobalt blue tie, one of Melinda's old favorites.

"Doc, give me some advice here. Don't you think it's about time?" Chip banged a fist on the arm of the chair. "I've got to get out there."

Why come to me with these questions? Deon wondered. How could he keep taking this man's money when he had no idea what to tell him? His mind clawed for an idea.

"Look, Chip, I have the same problem." He scratched the back of his neck. Maybe admitting his own dilemma wasn't the best therapeutic approach. He had loved being married and the idea of dating filled him with subdued hysteria. He craved instant understanding and acceptance, wanted to lay his head in Melinda's lap and laugh at one of her stupid rom coms.

He'd give anything to go back to those days. Both nuts and an arm.

"You do?" Chip gazed at Deon sideways, like a curious horse. "You're the therapist. Aren't you married?"

"My wife—we're not here to talk about me. All I'm saying is that relationships are a universal problem. A challenge. Keep talking to this woman. You like her?"

Chip nodded.

"Go slowly. Ask her if you can work out together.

That way you'll learn a few things about her, no muss, no fuss."

"What does that mean?"

"Oh, don't complicate things by proceeding...uh, by going too quickly. Get to know her."

Too bad his father's old *No muss, no fuss* didn't go over that well. Nothing wrong with appropriating an occasional cliché for the benefit of his client.

Chip's face lit up suddenly. "I get it, doc."

"Here's another suggestion," Deon said after they set up the next appointment. "Go shopping. Get your son to tag along, help you out."

"Shopping? Usually, his mom takes him. Why?"

"He's young, he's cool. Get him to help you pick out a couple of trousers, shirts, and workout duds." Deon stopped, wondering if he'd gone too far with the advice-giving.

Chip peered down at his shirt, limp and baggy. When he looked up, it was as if a buzzer went off in his brain. "Doc, that's a stroke of brilliance, a stroke of brilliance." His wide smile reflected his appreciation of Deon's idea. As he moved toward the door, he spoke to Deon over his shoulder, his enthusiasm unchecked. "We'll go to the mall, eat there for a change, suss out a few stores. Maybe I'll buy him new jeans." A quick wave and he was gone.

Deon couldn't help thinking he got lucky, struck exactly the right note with Chip.

He checked his calendar. A mother and daughter coming in a half-hour. Later, a single guy in his thirties, complaining of getting cold feet before his wedding. The guy's second session. His fiancée, astounded by his attitude, made the appointment for him.

"She's appalled because I have doubts. Appalled. That's what she said. I'm human. I'm being honest and look what I get for it. A pissed-off fiancée. You gotta help me."

Deon stared at the calendar for a moment. He was meeting Peggy from the ice cream social that evening. Why in hell had he made a date with Peggy?

More clients on the book for the months ahead, referrals through fellow practitioners, a couple friends, his former therapist. He planned eventually to retire from teaching and practice full-time, liked the idea of specializing in a marriage and family practice.

He lifted the pot from the coffeemaker and went to the sink to fill it, then decided against more coffee. With his little problem, he didn't need the jitters.

Lucy. He's been thinking of her nonstop, ever since the arrival on the scene of Godzilla. Crap, he shouldn't call the guy names.

No? He would call him whatever he liked in the privacy of his head. Why did he always have to be the nice guy? Nice guys didn't make an impression. Marcus made an impression. Marcus, after all, was a real specimen of manhood.

Forget Marcus.

Phoebe. He'd tell Phoebe.

What would he say?

I have a crush on our best friend. We had a thing over the weekend a little while ago and now I know I made a mistake putting her on *ignore*. Insecurities and guilt, I guess. How do I get her back?

Phoebe was the only one in his school he had allowed to visit him—besides his family and one childhood friend—after the accident that left him a widower. *I'm a widower and a wallower.* He'd known Phoebe for eleven years, Lucy for four.

He grabbed his phone and called Erwin, his therapist and friend, left a message with the service then shuffled through a few papers on his desk, checking notes before the mother and daughter arrived.

A few hours later, after the reluctant bridegroom left, Deon finished making notes for the next day and locked up. An attempt to force himself not to work until two in the morning.

Work kept him from ruminating about Melinda.

About now they'd be opening a bottle of zinfandel and planning dinner together on the couch. He'd sneak a kiss, happy to pull her close, her legs slung over his thighs. Or they'd FaceTime with Sara, depending on her schedule. His life with Melinda was mundane and normal.

This life was not normal.

He checked the clock, got up and opened the drawer in the wall-to-wall built-ins. Melinda stared out at him, a photo of the two of them in London, taken before Sara was born. He needed a shower. He closed the drawer.

Countdown to meeting Peggy forty-five minutes.

Melinda would give him a kick in the ass. Tell him to stop wallowing. Tell him to move on already. Melinda wasn't a pushover, but she was the most understanding person ever to grace his life. God, he missed her. Twenty-four years and he'd never wanted anyone else.

****

"You have a private practice and you work full-time? Amazing." Peggy's chin-length hair bobbed as she talked, giving her the air of a pert chipmunk. Chattering couples surrounded them, making him lean in to listen. He should have picked a quieter place for dinner.

Why had he called Peggy? A lapse in judgment. Answering a few friendly questions was beyond him. *I'm becoming a curmudgeon.*

"How do you organize your day? Shop for food? That's a lot on your plate."

He raised the wine to his lips, looked over the glass at Peggy, thinking of Lucy. How effortless it was hanging out with her, how…entertaining, yes, the perfect word. What popped out of her mouth was often a surprise. Even irritating, Insta-obsessed Lucy styling her photographs, and messing up on the dance floor was more fun than anyone else. *Flatlays*, he tossed the word in his brain, remembering her correcting him.

"I have more clients in the summer. Don't take a lot on during the school year." He tossed down more wine, wondering if the other diners, the daters at other tables, had to wade through a series of question-and-answer hoops. Peggy now knew he had a daughter and lived on Cottage Street in New Haven.

She chatted about her ex-husband while Deon separated the couples into groups of smug-married and new relationshippers, a game. How to tell? He guessed, gauging by how close they leaned into one another. It wasn't true that married people didn't talk. He and Melinda never ran out of things to say.

"By the way, about my favorite movies," he said as the waiter placed their plates in front of them. Lamb chops with parsley pesto for Peggy, and Asian salmon patties for Deon. "I'm not a total idiot when it comes to movies. A sucker for those rom coms, though, for sure." He's cheered to note the healthy portion of rice, laced with vegetables.

"Looks great." Peggy reached for her wine.

White. She'd made a face when he suggested ordering a bottle of pinot noir or a zinfandel. He rarely drank white wine.

"You're a rom com kind of a guy?" She made a funny sound in her throat. "Interesting. Didn't peg you as a sentimental romantic."

He took offense at her comment. Rom coms, where would the world be without them?

She sliced into a chop. "On the other hand, you must learn people's secrets, listening to them all day. Their rom coms." She honked at her own joke. "My dinner is delicious. Thank you for asking me out."

"You are very welcome." He marveled at her graciousness even though he represented a perfect example of social ineptitude. He needed to get out more often with people other than Lucy and Phoebe. Expand his conversational menu. The last time he got out was fooling around at Lucy's, taking photos before the ice cream social.

"I told you my secret," Peggy chirped. "My erotic reading habit. Your turn. I want something juicy. One of your clients, give me some dirt. No names, of course."

"Of course." He chunked off a piece of salmon and chewed. In his head, Deon tore through his client list.

"Take your time," she said. A glob of mascara sat at the corner of her eye near her nose. Should he mention it to her?

"There's a couple who first came to me six months

ago. They have an open marriage, and it's worked for them for three years. Now, however..." Deon's voice trailed off while Peggy leaned in listening as if he was Scheherazade in short sleeves.

"They have rules. They set up the rules from the beginning. When, where, how often they can see..." Deon hesitated, searching for the correct word. "The outside party, let's call it. See, the wife met someone and has continued to see this outside party and only him, and the husband is angry because she's violating their agreement. They couldn't resolve the issue, so they came to me." Deon sat back to see Peggy's reaction to his story.

"The husband is jealous. Did the wife give up the guy?"

"Not yet."

"It's been six months?"

"Yes, it has." Deon forked some rice. He's hardly eaten anything all day and he's hungry. Peggy finished her glass of wine. "Would you like another glass of wine?" Maybe she got more gabby the more she drank.

"Yes, please." She studied him. "Six months and you haven't gotten anywhere with them?"

"They're both very stubborn. He's at the point where he doesn't want to continue in an open marriage. This is after threatening to find someone special for himself. Violate their rules."

Peggy shifted forward, chewed, sliced another morsel of lamb chop. "What will you do?" Her eyes sparked with interest, and a warmth spread through Deon, starting in his chest and working down. He's no social misfit, in fact, he's quite the entertainer.

"I'm leaning toward helping them understand how

they're both contributing to the demise of their marriage." He helped himself to more salmon cake, rice, and took another sip of wine. "How about you, Peggy. Done a lot of dating?"

"Just think." The waiter brought her second glass of wine. "All around us, people are talking. And every one of them has a secret. I wonder how many are having sex with someone besides the person they're here with?" Peggy's eyes glittered.

Deon's phone vibrated in his pocket. He checked the caller ID. "I'm sorry, will you excuse me?"

He strode out to the lobby, glad for a break. "Lucy? Aren't you out with Marcus tonight?"

"Tonight? No. Phoebe and I are both going out with him next weekend."

"Oh."

"I'm out with Rob tonight. From the ice cream thingy."

Deon couldn't speak. In the background, the unmistakable sound of a toilet flushing. "Is that what I think?"

"I'm calling you from the toilet."

"You're coming in loud and clear."

"He's pushy, this guy Rob. It's like he's planning the next month of my life."

She doesn't like him. Relief hit Deon like a thunk. "It's only a date. Think of it that way and you'll get through it fine."

"He's buying me dinner. I feel guilty that I don't want to see him again."

"I'm buying Peggy dinner, and I don't want to see her again," he blurted before thinking.

"You're on a date with Peggy? Seriously?" Her

voice was almost shrill.

"My point is I'm paying for dinner. I invited her. No need for guilt."

A few seconds passed before Lucy spoke. "All righty then."

"You want guilt? I was so desperate to make conversation, I fabricated a whole story about my client just to get through dinner."

"You'll tell me? I want to hear the whole thing. Let's meet tonight. After our bad dates. Corner Bar. Can you get rid of her in an hour?"

Chapter Fourteen

Corner Bar was pretty much what it sounded like to Lucy, an alcove on Orange Street with the lingering scent of fish and chips mixed with beer. The perfect combination. The place was almost empty, except for a couple guys sitting at the bar, and two women at a corner table.

Deon saluted her with his Guinness and patted the seat beside him at the bar.

"A seltzer please," she called to the bartender. "I haven't told Phoebe I'm going out with Marcus."

"No wine?"

"I had two glasses, probably more."

"You got the guilts?" Deon leaned in and looked closely at Lucy. "It's not that big a deal. She'll be fine."

"You think?" A nudge from the little whisperer in her head. *What do men know about the nuances of women's friendships?* Her stomach gave a little flutter of warning. The sooner she confessed to Phoebe, the faster her insides would settle down.

The door swung open, and Phoebe trotted toward them with a "Hi guys," and a wide smile. "What's the occasion? I thought you both had dates."

"We did," Lucy and Deon said in unison, then looked at one another and laughed.

They moved to a table in the corner and the bartender shuffled over. Phoebe ordered a gin and tonic.

"I feel like celebrating." A brightness, almost eagerness in her voice. "I have a date tomorrow with someone I actually want to go out with for a change. Can't believe we met at the ice cream social. In front of my parents. Not that they noticed. I don't think they noticed, do you?"

"Nah," Deon assured her. "They were a little busy."

The drinks arrived. Phoebe sat back, her eyes half-closed. "What's going on?"

"Nothing." Deon studied his Guinness. "Why?"

"For one thing," she turned to Deon, "you looked surprised to see me and don't deny it. You didn't even know Lucy invited me."

"No big deal. She forgot to mention it."

Phoebe hesitated, studying them. "Something is…you two know something I don't."

Deon's mouth opened and Lucy's eyes darted around as she warned him silently not to say anything about Marcus, not yet. "As a matter of fact—"

"Don't tell me, let me guess. It's good news." She took a slug of her gin and tonic, her smile gigantic, as if she'd swallowed a big hit from a helium balloon. "I know what it is. You're together. You're dating. I'm thrilled for you both!"

Lucy's mouth flopped open, and she forced a grin. Deon's eyes zinged everywhere but on Lucy, his expression waxy, unmoving. For a long, silent moment no one spoke.

Phoebe, aware of her mistake, slid her eyes toward Deon, but he busily chugged his beer, set down the glass with a clunk. "What gave you that idea?"

A hoarse laugh popped out of Lucy's mouth. "No,"

she drawled. "Why would anything be different?" Another weird silence followed. Deon kicked Lucy's foot under the table, signaling her it was time. Why hadn't she told Phoebe the Marcus news on the phone? Or in text? No, text was all wrong.

Maybe the direct approach was best. Rip off the Band-Aid. "I do have something to tell you." She threw a pointed look in Deon's direction to warn him she needed backup, but he still refused to meet her gaze. "Marcus." *How best to frame this?*

"What about him?" Phoebe's back straightened against the chair.

"You need to know…he asked me out too. For next weekend." Her gut roiled. "I should have told you sooner."

"Why *didn't* you tell me?" Phoebe looked as if she just swallowed an apple, whole.

"You were so excited." Lucy's voice took on a sincere tone powered by guilt. "It wasn't the right time to bring it up and burst your bubble." *Was there a right time to burst her best friend's bubble?*

"And you?" Phoebe paused. "Are you excited?" Phoebe didn't take her eyes off Lucy.

Lucy cleared her throat. "The truth is I was excited too. Until I heard he asked us both out."

Deon watched as if they were all actors in a bad play. "Totally normal," he piped up, his voice sounding falsely peppy. His arms cut the air, as if the point he had to make was of world-shattering importance. "It was a dating event, for crap sake. What do you expect to happen?" Now he adopted his Bogart voice pitched two registers lower than normal. "Two gorgeous dames. Ice cream on the beach. A roomful of opportunity."

Deon's voice wavered and stopped. Another silence. "You know what we guys are like."

"Shut up, Deon." Phoebe directed a forced smile at the two of them and Lucy held her breath. "I'm not sure how much I like him anymore," she said, deflated.

"Me too," Lucy agreed.

"You don't want to go out with him now?"

"I didn't say that," Lucy stalled, confused. *Do I want to go out with Marcus?*

Phoebe gulped her gin and tonic.

"What are you saying?" Lucy quizzed her. "Changing your mind?" Her voice held a tight hoarseness fueled by frustration. "Because he's asked me out too?"

"I'm not sure," Phoebe said. "But I'm not losing my best friend over some guy I met once." She gestured, palm up. "You can have him."

"You take him. I think you like him more."

They turned to face Deon, who held up his hands in mock horror. "Don't look at me, I don't want him." They cracked up.

"A glass of wine. I need and want one." Lucy waved for the bartender, who shot over.

"How can I serve?" Humoring them.

"I'll take the house pinot noir, and my friend here would like another gin and tonic. Deon?"

"I'm good."

"I wasn't planning on another—"

"I'm buying." Lucy owed her friend a drink. At least that.

"You feel guilty?"

"Nope."

"You feel guilty for not telling me sooner," Phoebe

pressed. "Admit it." Her hands clenched together over her chest. Never before had they competed—if this counted as a competition—over a man. Strange and disquieting.

An older couple strolled in, holding hands. The man had white hair and a little potbelly, and the woman sported orange sandals. Cute together.

"I tried to figure out how to tell you. Kept putting it off. Then mistakenly had the idea our pal here—" Lucy jerked her chin Deon's way and curled her mouth in mockery— "would soften the news tonight with his boyish charm and a few choice remarks."

Deon stuck his lips out like a smirking chimpanzee. "Not coming between my lady friends."

The waiter appeared with the drinks on a small tray and put them down. He hesitated. "No pinot noir, miss. Will the house cabernet meet your taste requirements?"

"Thanks, that's fine." Lucy turned back to Phoebe. "This is a bit of a crappy situation we've found ourselves in," she muttered. "Has he kept in touch?" popped out of her mouth. *Should I be asking her this?*

Phoebe regarded Lucy over the rim of her gin and tonic.

"Are you texting him?" Lucy asked. The more Phoebe played it cool, the more Lucy wanted to know.

"Don't. Do. This." Deon's voice cut through the uncomfortable moment.

Lucy fought to conceal the tightness behind her eyes. "I'm sorry. I never should have asked."

Phoebe nodded. "It's okay."

"Both of you," Deon said. "Listen to yourselves."

Phoebe and Lucy looked at each other.

"Maybe this guy has Noelle's number too. Have

you considered that possibility?" Deon asked.

"Uh, no." Phoebe, dragged out the word. "Maybe he's got ten numbers," Phoebe cracked, and they hooted with laughter and reached for their glasses. Lucy turned toward Deon. "From a man's point of view, what should we do?"

Deon drained his mug and signaled the waiter for another beer. "Well, you can both cancel. One of you can cancel. Or you can both meet this peckerhead and see. I vote for both of you going on this date and ragging on his ass." The waiter dropped off the beer, and Deon took a long swallow. "There's something going on with that dude I don't like. He's not good enough for either one of you."

Phoebe tilted her glass in Lucy's direction. "It's settled. We'll both go out with him?"

"Agreed." Lucy clinked glasses with Phoebe.

Deon let loose a long sigh. "I'm glad that's over. No squabbles. Also want a full report."

"Like that'll happen," Phoebe smirked.

"Awkward," Lucy sang out.

"And no sleeping with Mr. Pecker on the first date." Deon flicked his index finger at Lucy. "Especially you." He stood and headed to the back of the bar.

"Is he saying I sleep around?"

Phoebe shot an exaggerated wink at Lucy. "Hmm."

"Hmm," echoed Lucy.

****

A few days later, Deon stood in front of the dressing room mirror while Lucy lounged on a mini sofa waiting for the verdict. Would Deon go for the items she'd handpicked?

159

They'd trekked out to Macy's at the mall in Meriden in the late afternoon because Deon begged her to take him shopping. Claiming his pants were all worn out and dated. Old man pants.

"Not bad," said Deon. He shoved his hands in the pockets. "Is this the new look? Not sure it's for me."

"Oh, don't we look snazzy," said Steve, who'd been lingering close by. The very same Steve Lucy had danced with at O'Donahue's. He'd helped her sort through the vast array of choices and pick from the stacks of folded shirts and pants, the confusion of brands. Yes, quite the coincidence. A dancer-slash-salesman. No wonder the guy was a flashy dresser.

"That particular trouser is perfectly cut," he now said, looking Deon over, arms folded.

Steve threw a look at Lucy, and the corner of his mouth lifted. Was he flirting? Good, she could use an ego boost. Hah. He wore the cousin to Deon's trousers in a subtle check and a yellow-gold shirt that picked up the gold flecks in his hair.

"Snazzy, huh? These pants are tight and clingy." Deon stared in the mirror, squatted and bounced a few times, testing the flexibility of the material.

He was pleased and didn't want to admit it. Lucy's theory was that he was afraid he'd call too much attention to himself.

"Are they supposed to be this clingy?" Deon faced the mirror, twirled in a full turn on one foot, knee up, arms spread. A showoff.

She'd glimpsed that cute little Deon butt naked once upon a time, proving all those sad-widower gym workouts paid off. Funny, when they were together that lost weekend, it was so natural, so relaxed...she got sucked in like one of those mysterious sinkholes that swallowed people if they got too close.

"Fitted, not clingy," Steve commented, jerking Lucy out of her reverie. "Just enough roominess, if you get my drift." Steve gave her a look hard to misinterpret, taking in her electric blue skirt and red top. Half-closed eyes, as if the two of them had a secret from Deon. "The material is supple," Steve added.

"Supple's what I'm after." Deon, energetic and hangover-free, was oblivious to the looks Steve and Lucy exchanged. Whereas the day after their outing to Corner Bar, her hangover was exactly that. Hanging over.

"These trousers? Can't make up my mind."

Lucy grabbed one of the shirts Steve hung on the rack for Deon to try on, a spike of flirt-fueled adrenalin hitting her. "Stop *whingeing*, mate." Her best Australian accent. If only she dared thump him upside the head.

In contrast, Steve followed her with his eyes as he folded and tidied, lugged over more shirts and trousers for her approval. An excuse to interact? He stood so close at one point, she tilted away wondering if Deon noticed.

"Whinge? Is that British for whining?" Deon asked.

Lucy sneaked another look at those trousers. Slim leg, definitely hip. *Admit it…Deon's hot.*

I hate him.

"We can't have whingeing in front of your lovely girlfriend, can we?" Steve piped up in the best British accent Lucy had heard in months. "It's simply not done."

Deon's head snapped around owl-like. Open-mouthed, Lucy waited for Deon to deny her status as his girlfriend, but nope, *nada*. His expression maintained its blankness.

"London accent?" she asked Steve. Of course, Lucy had no clue about discreet British accents, but she wasn't missing a chance to rib Deon. "Well done. Are you an actor?"

"We have some casual shirts you can pair with those trousers," Steve said, a great coverup to an awkward moment. He was a few inches from her, his Listerine breath on her neck.

"Get two pair. One gray, one camel. No, get three." Her voice traveled up and down to cover her nervousness before she turned toward Steve. "A good fit is everything, don't you agree?"

"Absolutely."

She looked back at Deon and followed Steve out of the dressing room. He stopped at a stack of dress shirts, the display rife with color, from butter-yellow to red. Statement shirts.

"Tangerine? Or is that way off the grid, shall I say, for your gentleman?" The London accent was back.

"He loves bright colors." In fact, Deon was famous for pairing crazy color combos. He'd be the unabashed fashion leader in his age group for the whole school district if he bought into this look.

"Good. Let's run a few of these by him then." Steve plucked three of the shirts and moved on toward a rack of pants. "I am an actor. I guess I was showing off. Haven't worked in two months."

He riffled through the rounder and came up with a dark green, khaki pair. "Got a gig in three weeks. New Haven and then Off-Broadway. A little dancing, a lotta

162

singing."

Lucy's interest level in Steve climbed from around a three to a seven, no, an eight. The accent helped plus his status as an employed actor, not just a salesman. *You're a snob.*

"So, what's the play?"

"Let me deliver these pants and I'll tell you." He reappeared a moment later. "We're doing a musical based on *Cloudy with a Chance of Meatballs*, the book for kids. A short run of the play."

"Love it. Used to read it to my—"

"Well, I'm ready to blow this pop stand." Deon, arms full, looked from Lucy to Steve.

They carried the shirts and pants up to the counter where Steve pulled out plastic hangers from underneath and arranged the pants on them. Deon handed over his credit card.

"It's a musical? Do they rain real hamburgers down? Or just plastic?" She giggled with the thought of meatballs and pancakes with syrup and soup coming from the clouds, plopping on the stage, splashing on patrons.

"Very cleverly done." Steve finished ringing up the sale, covered the pants in plastic, and handed everything over to Deon. "Stop by again and thanks for shopping with us."

"Thanks for the assistance," Deon said and started walking.

"Lucy, may I speak to you?" Steve said.

"Deon, give us a minute, will you?" she called.

Steve pulled out his wallet and handed her a card. "I'm inviting you to my play. That way, you'll see how it's done. The meatballs and such. Text me." He leaned both hands flat on the counter. "Enough pussyfooting around." The British accent was back. "Are you and Deon together?"

"Uh, no."

"In that case…would you mind awfully sharing your number? Sorry, I'll stop with the Brit speak," he said in his normal voice. "It's a defense mechanism."

"I don't mind." She gave him her number, but not her last name.

"I'll text you. Nag you to come to my play."

At this, the moment lost any awkwardness for Lucy, and she gave in and grinned at Steve. *I have an admirer. Even for one afternoon, it still counts.*

"Nice seeing you again," he said, as she backed away, waved.

Deon and Lucy wandered through the store to the missy department, jammed with displays and sale racks. What to wear on her Marcus date? A dress or jeans? She could use Deon's advice, but something told her he was in no mood for anything Marcus.

He stopped at a rounder of sleeveless, scoop neck tops in jewel colors. "Pink." He chose a top from the rack. "This is you."

She held it against her chest. "Good color for me?"

"That guy Steve was totally flirting."

"You think? Should I go for it?" Casual tone with an *ah-hah* on the inside. Her spine tingled realizing Deon noticed their flirtation. And he was irked. He had no right. She's the one who should be irked.

"Depends." He frowned. "He's an actor. How long's he in town for?" His hand scraped his cheek. "I know you're pissed at me. Ever since that weekend—"

"Me?" She flipped the price tag on the pink top and

her eyebrows shot up in exaggerated surprise. Pissed at Deon? Sure, but she wouldn't admit it, not to him. "You have good taste."

"I'm sorry about—"

"Expensive good taste." Whatever Deon felt he needed to say, she wasn't revisiting old wounds.

"Lucy, don't make me come over there." An attempt at humor, followed by a hangdog look of regret. "Look, I want to talk to you about…can we talk later? At dinner?"

"Of course. Why wouldn't we? We always talk at dinner."

"You maintain price is no object," Deon teased, deftly dropping the subject. "A good fit is everything, right?" He moved closer and cupped her chin. "I'm dead serious. About talking."

She twisted away. *So, this is how he wants to play it.* Seriously, a talk? After the *ignore* thing, what more could he possibly say? She wasn't sure she wanted dinner with Deon after all. "Did I say price is no object?" She pulled out a short black dress and danced it on the hanger. "This is cute."

"Nice. You don't wear much black. Try it on," he urged. "Try them both on."

In the dressing room, Lucy smiled in the mirror. Deon was acting ultra-nice, like he had an agenda. Weird. Close dancing at O'Donahue's and those long looks she'd caught him giving her in her kitchen the day she was baking, and he dropped by. Mixed messages, definitely.

The pink top showed off her shoulders. At $118.00, it was no bargain, but why did everything have to be on sale? She wasn't her mother, the ultimate bargain shopper. She wanted this sexy little top so Deon could picture her in it later. With Marcus.

The pink top has punctum.

The word came back to her, a surprise. Punctum, the word Deon used a while ago on the beach while they were taking photos. When he'd kissed her for the first time.

She and Deon together on the beach, fooling around. Best get rid of that image forever. She needed to move on, and ruminating wasn't helping.

"Blimey," Lucy said out loud to the dressing room walls, channeling Eliza Doolittle. She turned her back and grinned over her pink shoulder. Then her best Queen Elizabeth straight from *The Crown*. "Philip? What do you reckon?"

She yanked off the top and slipped on the dress, clingy in all the right places.

"How is it?" Deon called from outside the dressing room. "Sashay on out here." She burst through the swinging door and twirled in front of him gripping the pink top in her hand.

"I love them both." She felt her own excitement transfer to Deon.

"Then take them both." He stared approvingly, broke into a smile when she caught him.

"Thanks, I will." *Which to wear on my Marcus date?*

"Just don't wear—" His eyes clouded. "Never mind."

"What?"

He didn't finish his thought, gazed past her. "It's perfect. Take it." He slid closer and hugged her, right there in the middle of the missy department.

"You…look great."

"Thanks." She inhaled the familiar scent of Deon, soap and that unidentifiable man smell, a tad rattled by the closeness, Deon's obvious enjoyment of the mall experience. She and Phoebe usually needed a tractor to get Deon anywhere near a mall. What was with all the…enthusiasm?

"You hungry?" he asked. "I could eat a whole goat."

"Starving. Please, no goats." An attempt at humor as lame as his.

"And we've got to deliver your cheesecakes. Let's go to Branford for dinner."

"Fine. We can see if Phoebe is free when we drop off the desserts." Lucy headed into the dressing room.

"No. No Phoebe. Just the two of us," Deon called.

She paused, mid-zip. "I'll text her." Surely, she misheard him.

"No." His feet appeared outside her dressing room cubicle. "Don't invite Phoebe. Not tonight." His voice tight, controlled. "And by the way, I'm treating tonight."

"Well I—"

"A special dinner for the two of us."

Was she imagining an emphasis on *two of us*?

It didn't matter.

There was no *two of us*. Not anymore.

Chapter Fifteen

Deon snared a corner table on the deck, thanks to his reservation, made the moment Lucy agreed to the shopping spree he cooked up. Thank God his plan was still on, and that Steve guy had faded into the background. Who would have guessed he was an actor? What if he had her phone number? He wouldn't think about that, not tonight.

The rambunctious dinner crowd was in full swing—high-wattage garlic, onion and oregano goodness wafting from the various plates, carried by the faint wind. He loved Permutation, loved the way the deck hung over the shoreline, lights blinking for miles and miles, sailboats berthed a few hundred yards away.

Once they were seated, relief washed over him much as it did when Lucy and he had dropped off the pies and chatted briefly with Phoebe's mom in the clanging chaos of Zorbaki's kitchen. Chore done, no hanging around.

He took a longing look at Lucy, head bent scrolling on her phone, wavy hair with glints of natural red, tousled like curly fries. The evening morphing into the intimate, romantic outing he was hoping for.

Lucy raised her head from the phone and smiled, the glow from her red blouse reflecting on her face. "One sec while I find...it's here somewhere." Animated, electric, talking while she swiped. Miles away from his wife Melinda, who was more on the quiet side in temperament and in taste. For once, his thoughts didn't make him feel disloyal, and he sighed deeply, relieved at the lack of guilt. Melinda would welcome him moving on, he was sure of it.

He'd bet on it.

He wanted to stretch out a hand, cup Lucy's chin and refocus her attention from the phone to himself.

"Found it. All my students' projects will be on Instagram next fall." Excited, she slid the phone in his direction. "Videos of our experiments. The bridges."

He craned his neck to check out the photos. A short video played. "Great." He put energy behind his praise. "Good quality and you don't show anyone's face." He was dying to put aside Instagram, students, talk about *them*.

When the server arrived, he ordered a bottle of wine. Extra courage was indeed on the menu.

Lucy's nails matched her red blouse which matched her lipstick. *Flamboyance is her middle name.* He savored the sound of that sentence in his head and was about to tell her, but she rushed ahead of him. "I'm already planning lessons for this fall. Themed units."

"Lessons? You're kidding. We've barely been on vacation." His spirit deflated along with the belief that he could inject even a hint of romance into the conversation. Dancer Steve probably got her number. He's sure of it.

"I know it's annoying hearing Instagram stuff all the time. But see, I'm really into…it's the great motivator." Lucy broke off a piece of popover and smoothed butter on it, took an enthusiastic bite. She looked around the deck. "This place is lovely. You've brought me to a new-to-me place. Did you come here with Melinda?"

The question startled Deon, but he recovered, asked Lucy how she knew.

"I didn't really, but it's pretty romantic. When the three of us go out, we usually hit the down-home eateries, don't we?"

"Well, tonight I thought—" The waiter appeared with the wine, cutting off his response. Grateful for the generous pour, Deon tilted his glass toward Lucy and they took a long drink. A sense of well-being floated through him. A few more sips of wine as Lucy showed him the newly-loaded photos of three fruit pie slices, one raspberry, one strawberry, and one blueberry. "I had to use frozen blueberries," she explained. Each on a shiny, brightly colored plate of a contrasting color, the backgrounds all a pale lemon, rosy tulips for contrast. How did she find the time?

"Are those real tulips?"

Lucy didn't hear him, too immersed in her phone. He reminded himself to play it cool, enjoy their moment by the water in this *lovely* place, as Lucy called it. Flirt. What could be wrong with a subtle flirtation?

"Your photos are amazing." He slid a hand over hers for an instant only. He wanted badly to kiss that lipstick off.

"Thanks." She put her phone down, opened her menu. "I may have to take a couple pics," she said behind it. "Of our dinners. I like the texture of this wood table." Her head popped out. "Will that drive you crazy?"

"Sure, but I'll grin and endure." He needed to slow down with the wine. His stomach sloshed.

They sat for a moment and Lucy chewed on her popover. "You've gone quiet."

"I don't multitask the way you do. You're creative and you're learning a lot and you're excited by it all."

"Yes, I'm a little consumed."

He smiled at her, his indulgent smile. "I like what you're doing, plus it's a passion. Everyone needs a passion."

"So. What's your passion?" She sipped her water. "Can we order so I don't fill up on popovers?"

Again, he startled. *His passion*? His work? He worked to avoid thinking. "Sure, let's order." He waved over the waiter and asked Lucy what she was in the mood for. She selected the tuna steak with grilled eggplant, and Deon ordered the roast chicken with parsnips and swiss chard. Bland. It came with white rice. *To settle my stomach.* He closed the menu.

He needed bland. Bringing up the subject of *us* was not going to be easy. *A special dinner for the two of us* is the closest he'd gotten to broaching... What exactly was he broaching? For all he knew, she'd gathered a collection of names from the ice cream social. Guys eager to go out with her. *And that Steve* popped up in his head way too often.

"Everything smells heavenly." Aromas floated over from surrounding tables. Lucy inhaled, her chest expanding, the red top rising. "It's worth it, don't you think? Treating ourselves once in a while?"

Now. The perfect time to remind her he was treating. "A toast." He raised his glass.

"To friendship." Her smile sweet, unsuspecting.

"To friendship." He hesitated. "And more." He gave the *more* a little emphasis as if capitalizing the word. A yearning to make this right, make Lucy take him seriously, engulfed him as they clinked glasses.

If she noticed he tacked on two words, meaningful words, she said nothing.

"So? My question?" She put down the glass, folded her hands in front of her. "What's your passion? Tell me."

"Oh, like you, my students. My private clients, too. Music. But Sara is my real passion." His daughter Sara, *already in grad school, he can't believe it* is at the top of the list, but surely this went without saying.

He took a conscious breath and eased into this most difficult of discussions. "The other night? When Phoebe said that thing?"

"What thing?" Lucy pushed the popover basket out of the way.

"You remember." He flicked his fingers, going for nonchalant. "Us. Being together."

She gazed across the table at him and cackled. Yes, a definite cackle. "Us together? What a joke. Phoebe. She's got her head up her ass, don't you think?"

His face heated up in embarrassment. The one thing he could count on, ever since he was a kid, was his flush-face as his brother called it. Deon wanted to cover his head. Disappear.

"I-I thought we'd...I had this idea we'd...maybe by now..." He stopped, aware Lucy had gone from teasing and bantering to staring at him.

"Oh, Deon." She stared down at her red top while Deon's heart cramped. Two little words with the power to crush his spirit.

"Are you serious?" Her voice held a tinge of regret. "Is that what this is? A romantic dinner?" The word *romantic* lingered in the air, taking on a heavy, ominous meaning, and her face visibly tightened as she digested this possibility. "We've been through this. We've already been through this."

"I thought…thought you'd see what a great time we're having tonight, and you'd…we always have a great time," he finished lamely. Her phone vibrated and she flipped it over, shut it off.

"What? Cancel my date?"

He scratched a nail over the tablecloth. "Yeah, I'll admit it." The lump inside his gut expanded with each word. "I thought you'd cancel your date." Thought you'd send Marcus on his way, he wanted to say. Lucy stared at him, frowning. "See if we…you and I…us…" His voice trailed off as her eyes widened.

"Us? There is no *us*. Beyond a friendship." She blinked and picked up her phone, dropped it in her handbag. There was an almost undetectable quaver in her voice when she spoke. "Deon, we tried. It didn't work."

The feeling of anticipation he'd held onto all evening slid away like bald tires on black ice. Deon shivered, gripping his hands together on his lap.

"Lucy, please, listen to me. I wasn't ready. It was too quick and…my fault…it's all my fault we didn't work." Was he begging? He didn't care, didn't care about anything but making her understand. "I've had time to think. Can't you see that?" *He* was different. He'd had time to agonize, to beat himself up.

She still wouldn't look at him, and from the way her head tilted, he guessed she was measuring her response.

"You're saying a little while ago you felt

different?" Her voice shot up in amazement. "I believed you then. I believed you when you told me…things, intimate things. I trusted you."

"Trust me," he said now, panic coloring his voice, "this isn't sudden." Her gaze pierced him as he leaned forward, hands gripping the table edges. "I've been rethinking us for some time now." The word *us* stuck out in the sentence, calling attention to itself. "From way before that stupid ice cream thing," he hastened to add. "Everything is clear now. It's not too late." He swallowed. "Not too late for us."

"Us? Again with the us?" She registered astonishment as if she hadn't heard him correctly.

"Is that so odd?" He felt helpless in the face of her sarcastic tone.

Her eyes welled up, and he watched as she grabbed a napkin and dabbed at them.

"I'm sorry." His stomach heaved as he fought to explain. "This is a good thing here." He groped for better words. "We'd be good together. It's taken me a long time to—"

"You humiliated me." Her voice shattered the din of the restaurant with the word *humiliated* drawn out, each syllable a different note. All talk and movement on the deck ceased. Deon ignored the silence and reached for her hand. He needed to make contact, show her he didn't mean to hurt her, but she pulled it out of reach. His hand flopped down on the table like a dying fish. With a small tremor, he realized his vision of a romantic evening wasn't materializing.

"I've got to go." She stood, still gripping the napkin, and grabbed her bag. Instead of leaving, she dragged a chair beside Deon, facing him, blocking his view of the other diners. He shrank from her gaze as if retreating would fend her off. Her voice was deadly calm.

"Do you know what it was like for me to go back to being friends—just friends—after that weekend we spent together?"

****

The blood in Lucy's head pulsed hard with the need to straighten Deon out, a bit of unfinished business she should have tackled instead of feeling sorry for him and delaying. The other diners resumed chatting as Lucy inhaled deeply.

Deon's hair fell across his forehead, and he wore the forlorn, collapsed expression of a homeless man on a park bench in the rain.

She poked a finger in his rock-like chest, but he didn't flinch. "You're lucky we're on speaking terms, much less friends. Think about that."

His expression tightened, the underlying hurt noticeable.

"Whatever happened to make you put me on *ignore*?" Her question long overdue. "I never could work it out. Was it a climate change?" A pause to *gird her loins*, Deon's favorite expression when he wanted to lighten the mood. In her case, it served to strengthen her resolve.

"The beach, a great make-out session. Dinner." She sighed a little on the inside, thinking back to the way he'd touched her.

He shifted, hands clasped on the table. "I've done nothing but regret how I handled the whole thing," he said. "Not that—"

"Wait, there's more," she interrupted. "We

practically lived together." She took a long gulp, her throat a puddle. "We had a connection. Three days and we barely came up for air. And then you don't talk to me, don't even text. What was that?"

He swallowed hard. The shadow of his beard growing in since his morning shave made her want to reach over and brush a hand along his chin while driving a fist into his face at the same time.

"I'm an idiot," he stammered. "I couldn't believe all—"

"What you said was *I'm not ready*. Is that an explanation?" The sound of waves collapsing against the deck pilings startled Lucy. She'd almost forgotten they were on the water surrounded by sailboats.

"I was scared," he croaked.

"You ignored me. For five days, you ignored me. How can I forget that? I texted you. Called you once. Or was it twice? Very shitty behavior."

Her wine glass languished next to the bread plate. She reached for it, finished the contents, considered pouring herself another, but decided against it. "Hiding everything from Phoebe, though, that was bad."

Deon's head lowered, and he muttered to the table, afraid to look her in the eye. "You wanted Phoebe kept in the dark."

"True. I was embarrassed. Mortified. I couldn't tell her about…us."

Deon stared at the deck. "I'm so sorry."

They sat in silence, avoiding eye contact.

"I'm such a dick." Deon looked at Lucy, straining to explain. "It was weird. I didn't understand myself what—"

"I should have told Phoebe. She thinks you're a

nice guy." She fixed Deon with a sour glare. "Nice guys don't put their friends on *ignore* and hide behind their widowhood." *Widowerhood?*

Deon's hotness up on that stage at O'Donahue's, blowing that harp and making beautiful music didn't make up for his crappy behavior. Was theirs a true friendship riddled with resentment on her side, and guilt and confusion on Deon's?

"You really hurt me," Lucy said. "It took a long time to get over it, but I did." *Except for those lingering resentments.* "Because guess what? I didn't want to lose my best friend."

"Oh, thank God," he gushed, the relief on his face transparent. "So, you're not cutting—

"I'm not taking a chance this time." She sucked in her stomach. "Remember, we were TWT. Totally Wrong Together. So, leave me alone." Her voice rose, and although she didn't look around, she sensed eyes on her back as the chattering around them ceased once again. "Leave me alone to work on my Instagram and my cakes and my projects, and you do whatever the hell it is you do when you're not working. God knows what that is. Since you're always working." A low blow but she couldn't unsay it.

Lucy stood and slung her bag onto her shoulder. "By the way, I don't care if you tell Phoebe." She paused. "I may tell her myself. It's time."

Outside the restaurant, Lucy trotted to the corner and called for an Uber, glanced back at the crime scene after giving her address to the driver. She settled in for the short drive behind a stone wall of certainty, hardly believing she hurled such horrible things at Deon.

At home, she showered and, as she scrubbed,

thought back to their beach kiss. It started with throwing seaweed and progressed to not believing how good it felt to have Deon's arms wrapped around her. Or how it felt running her hand through his hair for the first time. Such a silly thing. She'd wanted to do that for a long while. Later that night, while making love in his king-size bed, she'd believed he'd somehow passed a milestone in his grieving process.

Only he hadn't.

After her shower, in her favorite place, the kitchen, she pulled out a loaf of bread, raisins, chocolate, and eggs, the ingredients for a New Orleans-style bread pudding. Comfort food. She'd use her basic brown sugar, vanilla pudding recipe with a few flourishes, like rum and a little cream. The movement of the knife soothed, and she sliced the bread, chopped it into squares.

She switched on her phone and noted two texts from dancer Steve awaited her attention. Not tonight. Fumbling with her phone, she switched on her Zydeco playlist and sang along. Her father loved vanilla bread pudding. She'd take a large pan over to her parents' tomorrow morning for breakfast.

A while later, once the delicious rum and pudding scent rose, permeating the whole house, her mind returned to Deon.

What would life be like without him?

Chapter Sixteen

At seven in the morning, Lucy was surrounded by strawberries, blueberries, kiwis and colanders, the makings for three tarts. Baking as therapy, a classic summer *tartfest*. Maybe the blueberry would have a strawberry center, but Lucy hadn't decided.

A whole summer ahead without Deon.

She'd gotten up in the middle of the night and prepared the pie crust for baking later. Tasted the bread pudding. Delicious, she hadn't lost her touch. Her parents would be thrilled, but her mother, always watching her weight, would ask if she'd used cream.

She hadn't gifted them any goodies in a while, so this would be a treat. Plus, it took her mind off…things. Deon things.

Apparently, annihilating her best friend in public disturbed her sleep patterns, even though he deserved every harsh word. Well, didn't he? All that guilty ruminating kept her monkey brain bouncing, remembering the past hurts.

Like his trip to the mall and his plan to ply her with a romantic dinner followed with the *I'm a different person now* speech. Like saying it made it true. Like ordering the Sonoma-Cutrer at forty-five bucks a pop made it a date.

Like toasting to *friendship and more* made the two of them a couple.

Deon's face floated up, voice pleading for understanding, eyes moist. "Lucy, please, listen to me. I wasn't ready. It was too soon, and it's all my fault we didn't work before." Telling her how his feelings had been growing. "Believe me, this isn't sudden. I've been rethinking…us for some time now."

Oh, this *thinking, thinking, thinking* business made her crazy-jittery. Remembering the good parts was the worst. Like that picture-taking jaunt to the beach in March that had been the start of their togetherness. Their first kiss, a teaser of a kiss, tentative, surprising her. Later, after their walk, when he'd rinsed her feet with warm water from the water bottle, she'd almost swooned. How could he be sweet and caring and then so unfeeling?

By nine, she was thinking she should have invoked the "no contact rule" that all the advice columns advocated. Taking him back as a friend after he put her on *ignore* had been a mistake.

The oven beeped signaling it was up to temperature. She placed the crusts in the middle, set the timer. The way things were going, she'd be baking frequently.

She grabbed the sponge and swiped the counter, her eyes moistening. *The reason I'm so mad at Deon is because I want him. I want an us.*

But I don't trust him.

Her phone pinged. She ignored it. See, two could play the *ignore* game. Deon had texted twice since their fiasco of an evening. It pinged again.

—I'm sorry you don't believe there is an us. What I told you is the truth. You can't ignore me forever, but I understand you're ignoring me for now.—

180

She reached for a kiwi. *Us?* The kiwi was fuzzy and perfect and petable, like a small, curled up animal. Her fingers brushed it back and forth a few times as if warming up for the tasks ahead. Deon had a funny name for kiwis, but she couldn't remember it.

The timer dinged and Lucy checked the tarts and placed them on the stove to cool. No worries, plenty of time to finish up, read if she wanted, get on Instagram, nap, shower and then…the date with Marcus. At six. The whole ice cream adventure felt like it happened ages ago. Weird.

Lucy peeled the kiwis and rinsed the blueberries. She wasn't sure about going out with Marcus. At least the baking took her mind off Deon for a little while. Despite the lack of sleep, she was wired.

What if she's wrong about Deon? Another text. She rinsed her hands under the faucet and dried them, reached for the phone.

—*Hey, it's Steve. From O'Donahue's and Macy's, LOL. Hope you are well. Please text back if you'd like to get together one evening.*—

The phone rang in her hand. Who'd call this early? Not a number in her contacts.

"Lucy? This is Marcus." His voice hesitated as if he wasn't sure he was Marcus.

"Hi."

"Uh, how are you doing?"

"I'm baking."

There was a long pause. "I'm so, so sorry."

"Sorry for what?" *What's he talking about?* A few seconds went by and she heard him pacing, the echo of his steps.

"I'm sorry but I have to cancel." Another few

seconds passed before he spoke. "I met someone. Last night. It wouldn't be right for me to go out with you tonight. Will you forgive me?"

It took her a moment to comprehend.

Oh, Marcus! "That's good, you hit it off with Phoebe?" she said without thinking.

"Phoebe…you know Phoebe?" His voice puzzled.

"Look, Phoebe is a friend of mine. I would have canceled anyway, so this is…I'm glad you two hit it off."

"Oh…oh, I—okay then, we're good?"

"We're good." *Was I going to cancel? Probably. Definootley.*

Lucy thanked him for calling. Marcus was turning out to be one of the better guys.

Bolstered by Marcus' honesty, she quick-texted Steve back.

—Thanks for the offer. Yes. Let's meet at the Beinecke in New Haven.—

Why not? She'd meet him in the afternoon. Some afternoon soonish. None of this dinner shit, though. She was done with romantic dinners.

Lucy called Phoebe, who picked up on the fourth ring.

"Marcus cancelled. Isn't that great? How was your date? I'm happy for you. Tell me now and don't leave out a single detail. Where did you go and what did you do?"

Silence from Phoebe's end.

"What did you wear? Did I catch you at a bad time?"

"What's going on with you and Deon?" Phoebe asked.

Now it was Lucy's turn to go silent. "Not up for discussion."

"Don't be ridiculous. I'm coming over there." Pushy. So like Phoebe.

Thank God for Phoebe.

Lucy put the pastry cream in the shells, and was washing dishes when Phoebe rang the doorbell, three times to show she meant business. Lucy raised her chin, huffy and ready for a squabble when she opened the door. Phoebe moved in for a hug. "Are the tarts ready?"

"Almost, I'm tarting them up a little."

"I'll help." They proceeded into the kitchen, where Lucy pointed to the blueberries.

"Can you put them in the pastry cream? You have to be a little pushy."

For a while, they didn't talk. Never mind, the questions would come, but Lucy wouldn't make it easy.

"So. Deon's pretty down."

Lucy glanced over at Phoebe inserting the berries.

"He told me about your fight." Phoebe swung around to face Lucy, but she didn't respond. "You could have knocked me over."

"Me too."

Phoebe's head jerked up. "What do you mean?"

"What do *you* mean?"

"I mean the two of you together—not a clue." Phoebe reached for more berries. "I never would have guessed you uh…got together. This past winter."

For a long moment, Lucy couldn't speak.

"To enjoy a dirty, filthy weekend," Phoebe's voice gravelly with innuendo.

"Not funny." Lucy's throat closed and she glared.

"Nothing wrong with that," Phoebe said. "Except

he backed off and left you hanging. It must have been torture."

"Oh, that Friday night at Humfrey's," Lucy burst out. "I was tempted, so tempted to tell you."

"I'm sorry you went through that by yourself." Phoebe came over, arms outstretched for a hug, and Lucy wrapped her fruit-stained fingers around her back, holding them away so they wouldn't mark Phoebe's top. "So, what are we going to do about our friend Deon?"

"Our *friend*? I'm doing nothing. He's on *ignore*." Lucy wiped her hands on a paper towel. "And don't make any cracks about Three Musketeers. I'm not in the mood."

"His wife died in a horrible crash. To have your loved one leave you suddenly...I wouldn't know how that feels and neither would you." Phoebe's voice was flat, soothing despite the blood rising in Lucy's ears at the mention of *our friend Deon*.

She had every right to reject Deon. To protect herself against the charm that was Deon. "I have feelings too." She wound up the dishtowel and snapped it, catching Phoebe on the leg.

"Ow, stop that." She made a grab, but quicker Lucy sidestepped her.

"He toyed with me and I took him back as a friend." Lucy's voice broke, even though she'd done her best to keep any emotions in check. "That was a very big deal."

"Toyed with you? Seriously?"

A few seconds slid by while she considered what she'd just said. *Did Deon toy with me?*

"Never." Phoebe shook her head. "He wouldn't toy

with you. He's in love with you."

"That's crap," Lucy spat, dismissing this romantic notion. *Deon? In love with me?* A tiny part of her wanted to believe it was true.

Phoebe studied Lucy for a few seconds. "He was dead wrong, freezing you out for five days."

Lucy turned her head away from Phoebe's intense gaze. "I thought Deon was the best thing that ever happened to me."

"Oh, darling," Phoebe soothed, "give it some time."

Time? *What's she talking about?* A tiny quiver of longing overtook Lucy, who wished she'd confided in Phoebe much earlier.

"By the way, I had a great time with Marcus," Phoebe said. "And thanks for being so understanding."

"It's fine." A relief to turn the conversation away from Deon. "Coffee? A maple scone? I've defrosted a couple. Your favorites. From Atticus."

"Oh, I've got to finish the blueberry tart so I can take the pies with me." Phoebe resumed lacing the pastry cream with the berries. "Wasn't the blueberry tart Justin's favorite?" Phoebe asked. "He was a tart man, all the way."

"Justin? Yeah, funny you remember that."

Phoebe lifted the blueberry tart and tilted it toward Lucy to admire. "I was very fond of Justin. Five years. I thought he was a keeper."

Now we're on a Justin walk down Memory Lane?

Phoebe put the pie on the counter and perched at the table. She broke a scone in half and bit into it, making appreciative sounds. "Come on, the guy was outgoing, liked your friends, supported your Instagram obsession."

"You want your scone warmed?" Lucy handed her a cup of coffee.

"One day Justin's part of your life and the next he's gone." Phoebe gulped her coffee and shook her head. "You never talked about it." She gestured with the other piece of scone. "In fact, there's a lot of stuff you don't like talking about."

"I didn't want to live with him." Lucy's too-loud voice stopped Phoebe mid-chew. "Too control-ly."

Now Phoebe wore the same look of irritation she'd had at the ice cream party. "Not everyone is as perfect as you, and Deon isn't control-ly." She broke off a chunk of scone.

"So now we're back to Deon?" *She's right. Deon isn't control-ly at all.*

Phoebe lifted the hand with the scone and flapped it, scattering crumbs on the floor. "Like you've never made a mistake."

"Deon dumped me." Lucy took a gulp of coffee, now tepid. Her comment sat like a bad smell between them. She thought of the long Deonless summer stretching in front of her.

"He didn't dump you," Phoebe said after a moment. "He was confused. Scared. He was buying time. Also, Deon isn't Justin." When Lucy opened her mouth to respond, Phoebe raised a hand to cut her off. "He's not your ex-husband who leaves in the middle of the night. Yes, he made a mistake. We all make mistakes. Just saying. Deon subject closed."

Good. Because Lucy needed to stay away from Deon.

So she wouldn't be tempted.

Chapter Seventeen

Chip Weinstein, in rare form, radiating energy, forced Deon to use all his superpowers to concentrate on his client. He sat on the edge of the fat, cushioned chair, one of several Melinda chose for the office of a proper therapist, as she put it. A makeover she thought necessary and Deon didn't. He's glad she outvoted him.

"Last night was our third date," Chip said. "Guess what we did?" Chip, natty in well-fitted jeans and a sports shirt with the cuffs rolled up, looked at Deon expectantly.

Deon crossed his legs, his ankle bouncing in time to his thoughts. Phoebe and Marcus, the Godzilla guy, hit it off. She sent him texts, detailing their activities, like the sailing, the beaching, cooking together. He'd have to drop the animosity—well, it had been misplaced Lucy jealousy—and make nice with the guy.

His gut contracted. Two weeks and nothing from Lucy, although he'd texted her daily since that blow-up at the restaurant. The whole summer stretched out in front of him, an arid plain of empty time with not a happy hour in sight.

"Deon?"

"Sorry, you serious? Want me to guess?" He'd bet Chip had sex. Third date. Of course, he had sex. For an older dude, Chip was rolling along. Deon should be doing half as well as ol' Chip.

"Claire planned the first part of the evening." Chip's face shone with eagerness and joy. He thought Deon was a hero for getting him into dating, whereas Deon hadn't come close to being anyone's good guy, much less a hero. He couldn't even concentrate, wasn't giving Chip his money's worth.

"Dancing. You went dancing." Deon's mind quickly filled in *and then you had sex*.

Chip's expression changed to surprise mixed with disappointment. "How did you know?"

Instantly sorry, Deon wilted. He should have kept his mouth shut. "Lucky guess. Honest."

"We took a swing dance lesson. Then we went to dinner so we could talk."

"Talking is good." Deon thought back to the ice cream social, wishing he could travel back in time. Cancel out the ice cream and Marcus, a real troublemaker, go back to the three of them, the old days with no worries.

The old days? He was lying to himself.

He wanted the new days, the kissing Lucy days. Minus his big boo-boo of putting Lucy on *ignore*, of course. Deon hunched his shoulders. Who was he kidding, calling his bad behavior a boo-boo?

A discussion of the burden of guilt from his bereavement group waffled through his head. Don't let the guilt hold you back. Embrace the grief. Isn't that what everyone in the grief groups said? Use the tools to move on gradually. Whatever that meant. Deon was never sure. *And you call yourself a therapist.*

Melinda would have reamed him out on that one. So ironic that the one person he needed the most for advice and compassion was no longer available. He leaned forward, forced himself to listen, his brain still concentrated on the new improved Chip, the one with a sex life.

"Claire's easy to talk to. I'm seeing her again tonight."

"Good, good." Sex was on the menu again tonight, lucky bastard. At that moment he decided to call Phoebe. Cut through all the bullshit and get her to help. Make a plan to get Lucy back. "Will you be dating other women?" Deon asked. The look of puzzlement on Chip's face told him the thought hadn't entered his mind. Why should it? Chip's the lucky one. He's got a chance for happiness with the woman of his choice— and the sense to go for it.

Deon was the dummy.

"Dating other…is that what I have to do?" Chip's voice cracked, and he moved forward in the chair as if bracing for the worst.

"No, of course not." Deon's words came out in a staccato, harsh tone. "I was just curious," he amended. "Some people enjoy dating around. It's your choice."

"Date around." Chip worried his lower lip. "That's not me," he said with a finality that Deon appreciated, wished upon himself.

"Go forth and enjoy Lucy's company." Proud of his positive statement, he felt like crowing.

"Claire," Chip corrected, stared at him. "Who's Lucy?"

"Sorry I—" Deon glanced up at the clock.

Although five minutes remained, Chip stood and held out a hand. "You seem preoccupied today. Hope all is well with you."

Deon scolded himself for being unprofessional.

And so obvious. He smiled weakly, hoping this served as an apology. Shook hands. Chip had never before offered him a handshake, so…was this a goodbye shake? Was he done with Deon?

"I already have my appointment for next week. See you then."

Once Deon showed Chip out, he shuffled back to the office and lay down on the couch. This used to be Melinda's study until she offered it to Deon, and they added a small extension for a waiting room. "You're a professional," Melinda said. "I'm fine in the upstairs bedroom." For his office, Melinda wanted the illusion of coziness. She had found and refinished the teacher's desk. "Understated and inviting," Melinda said, arranging two chairs and a bistro table in the corner by the fireplace. "Not everyone wants the couch, honey. Plus, we'll need some plush toys for your young clients."

"You love plush toys," he remembered saying.

Relaxing on the couch reminded him he skipped breakfast. The kitchen was a mere twelve steps away. Oatmeal or scrambled eggs, or even a toaster waffle with real maple syrup. Whatever, he wasn't hungry.

One more client and he was done. At high noon. What will he do all day? What will he do all summer with his daughter in California? And without Lucy?

He couldn't imagine not having Lucy in his life. Life was unbalanced without her. *Unbalanced.* The word stuck in his throat like a walnut eaten too quickly.

He'd told Phoebe about their lost weekend. A sob escaped him and he fought the urge to give in, let all the sobs leak out. The ebb and flow of the grieving process was a concept much discussed in his grief group. He needed to learn to embrace this idea, recognize some days were better than others. Four-plus years should be enough to get over his wife's death, but Deon was aware everyone handled grief differently. "Grief is something that stays with you," a guy in his group said at the last meeting.

Lying down on the couch wasn't working. He rose and checked the clock over his desk. Ten minutes until the last appointment. He went into the bathroom and ran the cold water, splashed his face, went back to his office.

He never did cry after Melinda died, not all out, too busy putting on a brave front for Sara. A zombie-like front, the best he could do at the time. He remembered sitting in meetings, getting familiar with the grief group participants as the weeks went by. Albert, who'd lost his mom, Betty, her son. Noreen, who'd lost a husband only six months earlier.

Another glance at the clock, the need to do something becoming urgent. He'd text Lucy. His hand snaked out as if on its own and plucked up his phone. No. Bad idea. He'd already texted her one of his little news blurbs. Told her he was working out more, got a personal trainer. Mentioned his recent gig with a local band, a first in a long time. Told her he missed her, but erased that part before he sent the text.

Texting Lucy had always been normal, a regular part of his day, and now he was forced to ration his texts, tread lightly in the don't-irritate-Lucy department. Crap, he refused to believe she'd never forgive him, never text him again. Now, right now, he'd give one of his balls—put it on the chopping block—to kiss her.

Stop, stop with the body parts melodrama.

His phone rang in his hand. A familiar ringtone. "Phoebe?" No answer. A butt dial? Quite a coincidence.

What if he called Phoebe back, pumped her for info about Lucy? He'd do whatever it took to get Lucy to listen. Would Phoebe take sides? She'd already told him he was an asshole and had to be patient when it came to Lucy.

That didn't mean she wasn't on his side, did it?

Rustling, the sound of a door opening and closing. His client. No time to call Phoebe.

Lucy. Lucy, Lucy, Lucy.

What would he do without her?

****

The heavenly scent of pancakes, eggs, and bacon drifted up from The Rooster Crows at the mall food court. Quiet on a mid-summer Monday morning, with only a few walkers.

Lucy and Phoebe each lugged two bags of new treasures. "I love this place when it's empty," Phoebe sighed.

Continuing past Forever 21, they turned into Sascha, where Phoebe stopped at a rack of blouses, sexy little wraps with low-cut backs, in turquoise, pink, yellow and white. "These are you."

A total girly day. Early that morning, they'd hit Zumba class, did a few machines, and after a superficial pit cleansing and a change of clothes, came straight to the Westfield Mall in Meriden.

"Marcus is taking me sailing tomorrow. For like the third time." Phoebe's nostrils flared.

"Great." A twinge of jealousy. *Phoebe has a boyfriend.* Lucy concentrated instead on the sale racks, a mishmash of whatever survived the hordes of shoppers who descended on Sascha whenever they cut prices and advertised. Her phone pinged and she dug it out of her bag. Deon.

—*My good morning text is a bit late today. Four clients, a full morning. 5 pm happy hour with the social workers at Humfrey's. Wanna meet me there?*—

Deon texted two or three times a day, but this was her first straight out invitation from him since the falling out. She dropped the phone into her bag.

Five weeks and three days, and she hadn't responded once to Deon's texts. Hadn't seen much of Phoebe either all summer.

Phoebe held up a flamboyant red number with spaghetti straps. Lucy thought of her as more the sporty type. "A datey dress," she said. "For after the sail."

"Try it," Lucy urged. "Datey is good." *I want to dress up for someone special.*

In the changing room, Lucy tried on the tops. *Meh.* Phoebe popped out of her cubicle. "What do you think?" The dress was high-cut enough to be understated, with a twirly skirt.

"You should wear more red. I'm betting Marcus will drool." Phoebe looked pleased and closed the dressing room door.

Lucy hesitated, thinking how to best frame her comment. "Phoebe?"

"Yeah?"

"About…uh Marcus? He isn't what I thought."

"Me too." The swoosh of fabric as she slid off the dress. "You slotted him as a player?"

"I'm sorry."

"Forget it. At the time, I'll admit, I wondered myself." They gathered their bags and hung the unwanted items outside the dressing room, meandered over to Starbucks where they ordered coffee and found seats amid the growing crowd of shoppers.

"Marcus took you sailing, huh? That's great."

Phoebe narrowed her eyes over the rim of her coffee and gave Lucy a knowing smile. "Deon's got a new look. Visible two-day scruff and he's pumped."

"Oh?" Lucy strained to imagine a buff Deon, not that he'd ever been a doughboy. "You saw him?"

"Ran into him on Orange Street a few days ago. Chatted for two minutes. I had a doctor's appointment, and he had a client." She took a sip of her coffee and pulled her new trousers from the Ann Taylor bag, ran her fingers over the material. A little ritual with them, revisiting purchases together, comparing bargains.

"That's it?" *That's all she got in the Deon department?*

Phoebe folded the trousers, put them back in the bag, and fixed Lucy with a half-smile as if she had a secret. "Well, I texted him this morning…um, I asked if…"

Lucy scrunched closer, willing her to hurry up.

"I asked if he had a message for you." She slurped her coffee. "Sorry. He didn't."

Lucy's face fell. What was she expecting after more than a month of silence on her side? A small ache resided somewhere high in her gut.

"It seems he has been texting you all summer." Phoebe's gaze bored into Lucy's head like a termite.

"True." A detail she never got around to telling Phoebe. "He asked me to meet him at his department's happy hour today."

"You going?"

"No."

"So how much longer will you leave him on *ignore?*" Phoebe pulled out her bottom lip, and made a squinty face at Lucy. "You didn't like it when he did it to you."

"It's not the same." Prickles of resentment crawled up Lucy's back. How could Phoebe compare these two *ignores?* They weren't even close to the same.

"Will you forgive him by Halloween?"

"I don't—"

"By Thanksgiving? Or maybe Christmas is the magical time for forgiveness?"

Lucy's known Phoebe a long time. Sure, they've disagreed, but never over an important relationship.

"Wait a minute." Lucy leaned an elbow on her knee. "Is this about my friendship with Deon messing up our little threesome? Or rejecting him because I don't trust him?"

Phoebe grabbed the bag from Lucy's lap and pulled out the sexy little number Lucy paid full price for. The dress came alive in her hand as she held it up, made it skip.

"Who did you have in mind when you bought this, huh? Don't tell me it wasn't Deon."

Lucy flushed. No, she didn't have anyone in mind, did she? No one specific that is…and why was Phoebe being such a bitch?

Awkward. They sat staring at one another, and then Phoebe folded the dress and returned it to the bag. "It's a beautiful dress. Look, I don't want you to get so stuck in making a point with Deon that you lose your chance with him." She stopped as if she'd said too much.

"My chance?" Since the fight with Deon, she'd

relived the scene in the restaurant a thousand times. Her brain rewound, searching for Deon's exact words. Pleading his case, the same old phrases running on a reel through her head. *I wasn't ready. It was too quick, and it's all my fault we didn't work out.*

"He hasn't gone out with anyone else all summer," Phoebe said. "He's waiting…for you."

"He told you?"

"Not directly. Isn't it obvious? You won't even send the man a lousy text, and yet he's kept in touch. Be careful."

"Careful? Of what?"

A middle-aged couple wandered close to the table, the woman in fitted jeans and sandals, and as they passed Lucy caught the scent of perfume drifting in the air as if to remind her that coupledom was still alive and well.

"You don't want to humiliate him. There's only so long he can suck it up and take the freeze-out."

Lucy shivered, her appetite for a cozy, girly lunch gone. "I'm so pissed off." A hollow laugh erupted. "Every time I think of him, I want to punch him in the gut." They slouched, absorbing this bit of oversharing until Phoebe crossed her legs and her expression changed to a smirk.

"So, darling, how often would that be?"

Lucy clutched her hands in front of her chest. "Do you think I've gone too far? That night we went to the beach, the two of us—"

"The night I had the migraine?"

"It was different. He was different. He let go. He was joyful. That's the word. I felt so comfortable with him, but not comfortable like a friend. There was a…"

196

Lucy stopped and looked away. "Lust. A lust factor."

What a relief to unload, to admit even to herself and Phoebe the resentments she'd been carrying around.

"I get it," whispered Phoebe.

"It wasn't that the sex was so great...well, it was." Lucy's voice had a tremor. She continued because telling Phoebe helped sort out the whole thing in her mind. "It was great because I was with Deon. That whole corny friends-first thing is true." She raised her coffee cup in a little toast. Phoebe didn't interrupt, didn't ask questions, an endearing quality in a friend.

"I'm so afraid that if I give him another chance, I'll be waiting the whole time we're together for him to pull back again. I won't be myself. I swore when he kissed me in the closet I'd move on. Date. Seriously look for someone."

"But then you'll always wonder if it would have worked, won't you? And there are no guarantees."

"Maybe. Who knows?" Lucy didn't want to think about Deon as a real possibility, not after going cold turkey all these weeks.

"You could start five relationships in the next five months," Phoebe droned on, "and what are the chances anything will—"

"I get it."

"Testy, are we?"

"Sorry." She cracked a half-smile. "I didn't think I'd miss him so much, but I do. It doesn't make sense. It's not as if we spent that much time together."

"How many times a day did you text him? Like at school?"

Her question surprised Lucy. "Why?"

"Hand over your phone."

"Why?"

Phoebe shot her a stern teacher look and Lucy rooted around in her bag for her phone. Phoebe scrolled, checked dates, scrolled more, her expression intent. "Got it." She regarded Lucy with a twitch of a smile. "A random day back before your torrid weekend—"

Lucy opened her mouth to protest the use of *torrid weekend,* but Phoebe held up a hand. "Let me finish. I'm counting eight, nine," her finger swiped the screen, "twenty-two texts. Students, your lunch, meeting at the gym, some venting, nothing big. Deon responded to every one." She squinted to make her point. "You never text me that much. Not that I want you to."

"Oh." *Does texting count as meaningful communication?* "So, what are you saying here?"

"Don't you see? You two supported each other, like daily. Before your weekend of lust." She exaggerated the word *lust*, dragging it out, and Lucy could see clear down Phoebe's throat to her esophagus.

"Yeah? Well, I'd still like to punch him in the stomach."

A sneer from Phoebe. "Anything else you care to tell me?"

"Then when he's down, I'd jump him and do him."

Chapter Eighteen

Seagull and Wine, at the end of Water Street, was a mad, bustling party with a Friday night wine tasting. A little summer happy hour celebration. Lucy and Phoebe hovered at the bar, hyper-aware that summer was half over. Seagull and Wine offered tasty treats for the happy hour crowd to promote their goodies.

"Hit me again, please. Another taste of that chardonnay." Phoebe chatted up the pourer, probably to get an extra drop or two out of the guy. They waved at their friends, Sunny and Noelle, teachers at the high school, hanging out at a table nearby.

"Me, too." Lucy shoved her glass so it clinked against Phoebe's. White wasn't her favorite, but she was desperate to catch a little of the giddiness that enveloped Phoebe these days. Marcus and Phoebe were an item, almost seven weeks and going strong.

Lucy's phone pinged as she plucked a baby cheese ball from a tray on the bar and gazed out the front window at the dock where dozens of sailboats and double motor jobs were tethered.

A second phone ping. Lucy swiped.

—*Lucy? Hi, it's Steve. I'm here over by the window*—

Steve who? Oh, dancer/Macy's Steve. She looked up from her phone, spotted a waving hand, and made her way deeper into the restaurant where Steve stood at a high top.

"Hey, Lucy."

"Steve."

"Coincidence, huh?"

"Friday night habit. Teacher hangout."

"I'm just discovering places in New Haven." He hesitated. "You're a teacher. That's a tough job at times, huh?"

"Uh, well, it takes stamina." The silence between them grew uncomfortably long, and Lucy's throat contracted with the effort to think of something to say.

"How about that Beinecke?" Steve attempting a joke. When she didn't respond, he added, "I looked it up. Rare books."

"Sorry, Steve. Sorry that Beinecke thing never happened."

He wasn't from New Haven, so of course he didn't know the Beinecke from Louis' Lunch. Anyway, she hadn't been in the mood to meet a new *man* person. Hadn't been in the mood for anything but baking, and baking-related tasks like shopping, testing new recipes, taking photos for Instagram, and delivering to her clients. Quite the summer so far. Lucy knew the staff on a first-name basis in a half-dozen local restaurants.

"Glad I got to see you. I'm leaving in two days. New play. Off Broadway."

"Congrats. I'm happy for you." This was getting awkward.

"How's your friend?" Steve's eyebrows came together and lifted with the question.

"Friend?" Did Steve know a friend of hers?

"You know, the one you were helping with shirts."

"Deon." She shifted from one foot to the other.

Why didn't they provide seats at these high tables? "I don't see him around much anymore." Wasn't that from an old song?

"Well, that's just plain sad."

"Sad? Why?" Now she was glad she hadn't met Steve at the Beinecke or anywhere, for that matter. People complicated things and she didn't need any more hassles in her life.

Steve glanced away and then back at Lucy. "Don't you know?"

A twinge in her chest, faint, a warning. What was he getting at? "Know what?"

"He's in love with you. Clear as monkeys love bananas." His eyes danced with mirth and the good news he was delivering. "Besotted."

"You can't say that." Lucy bristled. "How do you know?"

"The way he looks at you. Any fool can see."

Lucy, aware of standing with her mouth open, backed off with a wave, mumbling pleasantries. She went in search of Phoebe, found her gabbing with Noelle.

"We saw you talking to that cute guy." Phoebe chin-pointed in Steve's direction. "He looks familiar. O'Donahue's?"

Lucy nodded, her head swirling with Steve's words. Silly words. *Monkeys and bananas.* Had he been mocking her?

"Right, right. The Steve guy. Always listening and watching." Phoebe nudged Noelle and turned to Lucy. "Noelle met someone special at the ice cream thingy."

"I did." Noelle tapped her chin with the tip of her index finger. "It's still early days, but the more I hang out with him, the more I like him."

"Well, that's better than the other way around, isn't it?" Lucy smiled in solidarity at this rare occurrence. *I knew it!*

"Deon coming?" Noelle leaned on the bar.

"Probably has a client," Phoebe said. "He'll be along later."

Surely a lie for Lucy's benefit. Although Deon, who'd nicknamed the place Winegull and loved it here, could turn up. He probably wouldn't since... Well, for many reasons, so many. Steve's words floated through her brain. *He's in love with you. Besotted.*

She really missed him. Lucy wanted to tell Deon how much she missed him. Wanted to tell him, well, she had a list in her head, a growing list. "Let's try the pinot noir," she said, looking for a place to perch. She had to get her mind off Deon, and a little wine would be a good start.

A couple at the bar left and Phoebe snagged their stools. "We'll have to order an appetizer if we sit."

Lucy shrugged. "Did Marcus say he's coming?"

"We're meeting here," Phoebe said. "He's coaching, so it'll be a while."

Over the summer, since Lucy had iced all contact with Deon, things between her and Phoebe weren't quite the same. Except for the trip to the mall earlier in July, they'd barely hung out. What a bummer. Giving each other space was too much space. Even though they stayed close friends, the specter of Deon lay like a stuffed buffalo head between them. Or was it Lucy's imagination?

The pourer raised her bottle to show them the label. "This pinot noir has a hint of berries and cocoa, one of our most popular." She poured.

Lucy raised her glass. "Cheers," she sang and sipped, wondering if Phoebe had gotten together with Deon over the summer. Probably, and why shouldn't she?

"Tell me something." Phoebe took a swallow of her wine sample and studied Lucy.

"Sure, what?"

"Halloween," said Phoebe.

"What do you mean, Halloween?" Lucy asked absently, thinking she might order a glass of this one. Cocoa and berries, a sweetheart of a combination.

"You should forgive him by Halloween." She finished the sample. "Definitely. You can trick or treat together."

"You're hilarious." Lucy sipped again to buy a few seconds. Phoebe was such a harpy. The stools had swivel seats, and she took full advantage, swerving away from Phoebe. She wanted to confess, tell Phoebe how much she still missed him, but what good was that? To hear how well he was doing without her? She didn't even like Phoebe bringing his name up.

"I promise I won't nag, but you need a plan."

Lucy rotated around to face Phoebe. "A plan? What do I need a plan for? And you're already nagging."

"You're not the only one involved. The whole situation makes me grossly uncomfortable." Phoebe's scratchy voice was the real giveaway. She had to be down about the breakup too. Friends breaking up was no small thing. "I don't want to be in the middle."

"You're right. I have to…" Not even a glimmer of an idea slithered into Lucy's head. Plus, she was being such a bitch.

"Think about it. Meanwhile, I'm going to the toilet room." Phoebe slid off the stool.

Lucy stared out at the buzzing frenzy that was Seagull and Wine, the queues of wine tasters, the cheery pourers, the front of the store where cashiers racked up sales. The cheesy scent of an appetizer wafted over from a couple at the bar. Sunny and Noelle were still wandering the wine tables.

Her mind reverted to that day at the beach, gathering seaweed and stones and shells to style her photos, the smell of the sea surrounding them. Deon laughing, hugging her—so much more than a friend hug—his hair a wild mess in the wind off the water. Lucy startled as Phoebe's phone buzzed, her body's reaction to the possibility that Deon was on the other end. She reached over, plucked the phone out of her friend's bag, and eyeballed the text. Deon.

—Where are you? Can I join you?—

Her response was light and breezy, exactly how she didn't feel.

—We're at Seagull and Wine. Tasting. Chomping. Come on down.—

She powered off the phone and slid it back into the bag. Maybe Phoebe would think she turned her phone off. Maybe she wouldn't bother checking her messages. *Maybe this, maybe that.*

Lucy straightened up and practiced a nonchalant look for when Deon walked through the door. It had been so long. Too long.

I can't wait.

****

"Hey, dude, you're twitching."

Deon gave Jarrett a twisted grin. Caught by a sixteen-year-old. "Am not," he growled. "And it's Dr. Goldbloom to you, young whippersnapper."

"Have it your way, Dr. Goldbloom." Deon and Jarrett looked out toward the parking lot where a woman was walking her dog, a miniature poodle in a harness. "What's a whippersnapper?" Jarrett asked.

"A polite way of saying smart ass." Should he be talking to Jarrett this way?

"It's a good thing my mom isn't privy to our conversations." Jarrett crossed an ankle over a knee, slouched further down in the chair. "She'd go ballistic."

"Yeah, I doubt that." Deon privately thinking Jarrett was probably correct. The kid was perceptive and articulate, but not much of a talker. It's as if he wanted to melt into the background. Maybe that's what the all-black shoes, shorts, and T-shirt thing were about.

"Doctor, you're still twitching."

"You're right," Deon admitted. "You don't miss a thing." This was the most talkative Jarrett had ever been during their sessions.

"Not much." Jarrett smirked and slouched even further so he was almost lying in the chair.

The side of Deon's brain that concentrated its energy on Lucy was on hyper-alert. As always. Not a single text had arrived since the night of the fight, and yet Deon hung on to the stringy hope that she'd give in one day and text him back.

Earlier that very day he'd texted Lucy. It was the middle of summer for crap sake! How much longer would she keep him in limbo?

His text had been a study in beggary.

—I thought of you today when I got takeout at

Niki's. I got enough for us both, just in case you decide to forgive me and come over for dinner. I'll wait until seven before I dig in. Consider this a standing invitation.—

Like she'll appear at my door? His face heated up remembering what he'd written.

His phone bleated a text, and he tried not to hope. It had been so long he was beginning to lose faith she'd ever speak to him again.

Jarrett sprang to life, raising his arms in a sort of cheer, a surprising burst of enthusiasm. "A text. Go for it," he urged. More enthusiasm than Deon had ever witnessed from the young man. "Check your messages, I don't give a—"

"Now, now." Deon kept his eyes on the boy, faking disinterest in the text. *Jarrett is one tough nut, but after a year there's a tiny glimmer of progress.* The kid was coming around. Today he arrived early, even asked Deon how he was doing. *Unheard of a year ago.*

Deon's gaze swooped to the phone. Phoebe inviting him to a wine tasting at Seagull and Wine. Winegull. But Lucy was there with her, he's sure of this. It must be a mistake.

Or Phoebe didn't ask Lucy.

No way to tell.

Another twenty-five minutes with Jarrett and he'd be free to bolt. No heavy stuff this time. Mostly about Jarrett starting back at school in five weeks and fitting in. *The kid is so smart.*

"Your face, dude. What's wrong?" Jarrett studied him intently, focusing on Deon's hand gripping his phone as if it's a hammer.

The longing is more than he can bear. This text

meant he'd get to see Lucy. She must know about the invitation. Phoebe is the go-between, breaking the ice. *Yes, thank you, Phoebe. I love you.* He couldn't wait to thank her himself, in person. But what about Jarrett?

"I have an emergency." He blurted it out, not daring to look Jarrett in the eye. The kid was way too perceptive for his own good. "I'll have to cut our session short."

"Cool. Someone committing suicide? Some guy murder his wife?"

"I'm well aware you're precocious, you don't need to prove it to me." Deon was careful to enunciate with a pained expression for Jarrett's benefit. "I apologize. We'll make up for it next time. Do you want to call your parents?"

"What for?"

"To pick you up early."

"Nah, I'll hang out here, read the magazines."

"Very funny."

"I've got my phone. You know we're the *phonial* generation, don't you? I'm good."

"Call your parents now, please." To Deon's surprise, Jarrett pulled out his phone without complaint. Deon went over to his little fridge and opened it, listening to the brief conversation. "Coke or Ginger Ale?"

"Coke, thanks. My mom's coming now."

They talked for a few minutes about school and then he ushered Jarrett out the waiting room door and left by the back exit. Flowers, he'd need to bring her an arrangement, a spectacular bunch of long-stemmed roses. Would that be overkill? Too grand a gesture?

In his car he composed a quick text to Phoebe. —

See you there—

The closest florist was on Whitney, five minutes away, and Deon welcomed the errand. Time now to pull himself together head-wise and for that, he's got his playlist. A quick flick of the button, the opening piano chords to Rod Stewart singing "Have I Told You Lately That I Love You?" The corniest, greatest love song ever sung by a guy with a scratchy voice. *Perfect.*

The florist was closer than he thought, and he parked in the small strip to the side of the store. *I'm going to see Lucy.* It's been so long. Too long.

A bell over the door heralded his arrival. Quaint.

"Hello." A middle-aged woman greeted him, dressed in all green, down to the apron and rubber gloves, her hands in a bucket of water.

"About to close. I've got a special on yellow roses and the two arrangements over there. If you're interested." She pointed with her chin to a flurry of purple and lavender and yellow against the refrigerator display cases.

Deon looked with mild interest where she was pointing, unwilling to compromise on his Lucy arrangement. It's got to be perfect, the best. He stood, bewildered, unsure how to explain.

"What's the occasion?" She heaved the contents of the bucket into the sink, rinsed and upended the pail on the counter.

Deon rocked back on his heels. "Uh...we're...we might...someone special. She's more special than the occasion," he managed.

"Sounds like red roses."

"Yes, yes. Red." He couldn't think straight. "Red roses."

He waited patiently while the woman disappeared in back and returned with a bundle of red. At the worktable, she laid the roses down as if preparing them for bed and wrapped twine here and there while Deon stared unseeing out the window. Finally, she held up the bouquet, and waved it in the air to catch his attention. "What do you think?"

"Beautiful, thank you." He reached for the flowers. Twelve perfect roses wrapped in cream and white paper. He fingered one of the petals.

The drive was almost thirty minutes in rush hour, even though he bypassed the downtown area. He pulled into the parking lot, shut off the Corvette and sat, staring ahead at the boats docked along the stretch of wooden planks, all manner of boats and yachts, and what were they called? Ketches. He's ignorant of sailing terminology.

This might turn out not so great for him. Lucy could *ignore* him. She could leave in a huff. She could…he needed to text Phoebe and find out what's going on, find out if Lucy even expected him to show up. A heaviness in his throat and neck at the thought of getting so close only to have her blow him off. What if he got tongue-tied?

Still, he had to take the chance. *I've got to show her I'm not afraid to look stupid in public.*

The flowers sat waiting as if they were winking at him. He hadn't thought this through.

What? He's going to walk into the restaurant with a dozen roses under his arm? Plus, it's the kind of place where he'd likely run into colleagues. What if Lucy blew him off? Where would he be then?

No. He wouldn't think about it. He rested his

forehead on the steering wheel. Wait. He'd check for her car before going inside.

He slid out, leaving the roses behind, his face crimping at the thought of how his splendid buds would fare in the heat with the windows closed. That he'd remedy. He unlocked his car, cracked open the windows. "Is that better?" They hadn't yet had the chance to open their little flower faces.

He peered around to be sure no one heard him, then decided not to search the lot for Lucy's car.

Inside, the air throbbed with the chatter of drinkers under the influence, the pungent aroma of cheese and seafood appetizers blending with the perfume of the wine. He didn't realize Phoebe and Lucy were at the bar until he was almost on top of them.

Phoebe swung her gaze toward him, her mouth widening in a smile. "Hey, Deon."

"Hey, yourself." He lunged in as her arms spread wide for a hug. Lucy had her back to Deon, but she saw him, he's sure of it.

Sunny and Noelle threw their arms around him for a three-way. He's cheered by their presence as if all is right again with the world. His world, anyway.

"Lucy said you might turn up," said Sunny. "Want some wine?"

"Not yet, thanks." *Lucy said he might turn up?* Deon cast a curious look back at Lucy, who was talking to some guy in jeans and an orange T-shirt.

"Here, try this pinot noir." Noelle extended her glass, blotched with her pink lipstick. Deon turned it so the lipstick was on the opposite side and sipped, encouraged. *Things will work out.*

He handed it back. "Nice, let's get a bottle."

The guy in the orange shirt looked as if he couldn't wait to hear the punchline to whatever Lucy was saying, and Deon's belly clenched. Her hand floated onto the guy's arm as she delivered whatever clever remark held him in rapture. In that second or two Deon wondered, *Has she replaced me?*

And then she noticed him, and her eyes widened.

"Deon," she purred, "you're here."

Chapter Nineteen

Deon. Looking good in a short-sleeved chambray shirt. He'd beefed up or was it Lucy's imagination? Not that Deon was ever skinny, but was he putting in a little more chin-up time?

"Lucy, long time."

Not quite ignoring me, but...holding back?

"Phoebe invited me. I hope you're okay with that."

"Sure." *I'm more than okay. And Phoebe didn't invite you.*

He addressed their little circle. "Let's get a table on the deck. Order a couple bottles."

Mr. Take Charge, a bit unusual for Deon.

Everyone migrated to a larger table outdoors. The waitress brought two bottles of the pinot noir and two bottles of pinot grigio.

"This seat taken?" Deon asked. An empty seat beside Lucy. The only vacant seat at the table.

"Of course not." Not exactly warm, but she didn't freeze him out either.

His head swiveled in her direction. "You'll have some wine?"

"Most definitely."

He leaned closer, head bent, eyelids half-closed, and a little tingle pricked the back of Lucy's neck as she took in the heat of him. *This is Deon*, she reminded herself, shifting a tad closer. Texting her every night, little stories, anecdotes, the occasional invitation to meet, which she'd ignored.

She kept every one of those texts, reread them recently. Deon had a great sense of the absurd that meshed with her own, and he kept up with her Instagram feed, posting comments. Compliments, laying them on thick. It had gotten so she was disappointed if he missed a day.

"I won't..." He ran a hand through his hair as if he lost his train of thought in mid-sentence. "I won't bother you, if that's what you're worried about." Lucy shrank back. This wasn't turning out the way she'd hoped.

"Hey, you guys. I made it." Marcus strode up, looking confident in jeans and a black T-shirt. Sliding a hand around Phoebe's shoulder, smooching her.

Lucy did the intros, since Sunny and Noelle hadn't met Marcus. They smiled and looked Marcus over. Noelle turned and winked at Lucy who winked back, an over-the-top wink that mocked Noelle's. Luke, Sunny's honey, turned up a minute after the introductions, and Lucy stood for a hug. "It's been a while."

"Cheers." Deon raised his glass as Marcus poured, and everyone stood and clinked glasses. If Deon still harbored resentments toward Marcus, it didn't show. And it shouldn't. The ice cream social was old news.

"None of you noticed Deon doesn't wear glasses anymore, did you?" Phoebe remarked.

They all looked at Deon. "I knew there was something different," said Luke.

"Sorry. I forgot you were having the procedure." Lucy tilted closer and peered at him.

"Yeah. I had Lasik before the ice cream thing." He

slouched back in his chair and lowered his voice. "I want to tell you something."

Lucy scrunched down and waited, wondering about the big build up.

Deon's face tightened. "I've had a lot of time to think during this long, endless summer," he said, dragging out *long* and *endless*. "More time than I ever wanted." He hesitated, searching her face. "Well." His hand went to his neck and squeezed. "I want to say that—"

"I ordered calamari," Marcus announced in a booming voice. "Meanwhile, I'll go get a couple appetizers. He glanced toward Lucy and Deon. "This is happy hour, so let's get happy."

"I'll get a couple apps too." Deon stood, patted Lucy's hand. "We'll talk later." He moved away quickly, and Lucy gaped after him. *He's leaving now? In the middle of whatever we were in the middle of?*

"Talk about what?" Phoebe called after him. "I heard that. No secrets here." She stared across the table. "He's a little cranky, or am I imagining it?"

"If he finally gets a girlfriend, who will you two hang out with?" joked Noelle. Phoebe and Lucy exchanged if-only-she-knew looks.

The waiter brought two steaming pungent plates of calamari, and before long Marcus returned with appetizers, handed everything around the table. "Help yourselves, folks."

Lucy stabbed a few tentacles and squeezed lemon on them, breathing in the fresh, citrusy aroma. She blinked out at the water where gulls swooped and dived. What would have happened if she and Marcus had clicked instead of Phoebe? No, inwardly she shook her head. Marcus and she wouldn't have worked, not like she and Deon work.

Worked.

The brief flutter of well-being evaporated. After putting Deon on *ignore* for over a month, ever since their fateful disaster of a dinner, Lucy couldn't blame him for not warming up to her more quickly.

Farther out, two sailboats raced in the distance. Although the late afternoon sun glowed a glossy, warm gold, she shivered. Was he ready now? Was she ready? How could she be sure? Dating your best friend was messy business.

"Hey." Phoebe signaled Lucy, gripping her phone. "I'll be right back," she told Marcus, getting up. She slid Lucy's way, gestured with her chin. "Let's hit the restroom."

They skirted the clusters of talkers and wine tasters nibbling at the bar and around the tasting tables, the party atmosphere in full swing. Lucy's mouth watered with the garlic and good onion smells around every corner.

In the ladies' room, Phoebe thrust her phone at Lucy. "I just saw this."

"Yeah. I sent it."

"That was sly of you." Her voice dropped. "Wait," she grabbed Lucy's arm. "He thinks I sent that text. And he's acting kinda strange, don't you think?"

"Not what I expected, yeah."

"Tell him you texted him." Phoebe's eyes were alert, full of hope on Lucy's behalf. "He'll be thrilled."

Lucy frowned. "He wants to talk, and he's been doing a lot of thinking this summer."

They stood off to the side in front of a full-length

mirror, Phoebe in a summer print dress the color of a rose garden, Lucy in white jeans and the metallic silver top she'd worn to the ice cream social. Too showy. A mistake to have worn it. Besides, she didn't know what to say to Deon after all this time. Maybe all the little wine tastings added up to one huge pour and clogged her brain.

"This doesn't have to be a big deal." Phoebe clutched Lucy's arm. "Put your British Red on those full lips and go talk to the man. You know you want to."

****

Deon wasn't on the deck with the group. Lucy continued through the restaurant to the wine tasting area near the lobby, where Deon and a woman in a turquoise shift and flat, glittery sandals stood gripping wine glasses and talking. Confused, she took a step back. Should she approach Deon or retreat to their group on the deck?

Happy customers packing the main dining room ate their way through shrimp and chicken on skewers and mini pizza appetizers. The delicious smell of garlic and toasted sesame seeds wafted up, but Lucy was no longer hungry. *I thought it would be different. Thought he'd be glad to see me, spend time with me.*

She wove around the tables back to the deck, standing just inside the restaurant, reluctant to join the little band gathered at the table. Phoebe held forth, the others leaning in to hear every word. She gestured with a shrimp, and they all burst out laughing.

Maybe she'd relegated Deon to *ignore* for so long he'd gotten used to it. Or he thought she was punishing him. Was this rational thinking or crazy-making?

She turned and threaded her way between the

tables back toward where the woman was now showing Deon something on her phone, his mouth close to her ear. The din of the place hit her, the clanking of forks on plates, people talking over one another.

"Lucy."

She craned her neck, not sure she'd heard her name, and Deon's expression changed shape, a wide grin appearing. "Oh, Lucy." He beckoned her forward. "This is Myra Boswick, a colleague. We ran into each other, and it's been what, twelve years?" Myra held out a hand. "Her husband just got a position at Yale and they're house searching in our neighborhood."

"Lucy? Nice to meet you. Deon says wonderful things about you."

"Oh." Flabbergasted by this piece of news, *wonderful things,* her jaw went slack as she and Deon locked eyes.

"I've got to run. I'll call. We'll have dinner. Lucy, see you soon." The Myra person trotted out the door.

"She'll see me soon? What's that mean?"

"Things."

"Things?" He was being deliberately provocative. She reached out with her index finger and poked him in the bicep. Her finger bounced off muscle.

"What did you tell her?" Curiosity at this newly secretive side. He'd always been transparent, easy to read, the someone she could rely on.

"Never mind. None of your business."

"That's not very nice."

"No, it isn't. I'm done with nice."

She closed her mouth and squinted. *What did he mean he was done with nice?* A few seconds went by while they stared at each other. Deon had those expressive brown eyes with flecks of gold. And dark lashes, like a girl, only not girly, not at all. Laughter erupted from a nearby table, but Deon didn't seem to notice.

"I had it coming." Deon hunched his shoulders to emphasize his point. "You didn't trust me. I get that." He dropped his voice to an intimate, playful purr. "Don't you think enough is enough? Aren't you going to forgive me? Ever?"

Earnest, the only word that fit, an earnest face without a trace of subterfuge behind the teasing. He expected an answer.

"It depends." Lucy kept her face from breaking into a smile by thinking of the grossest thing she could summon to mind. Her niece's newborn baby's poopy diaper, and how it smelled when she changed it a few weeks ago. Who knew little Mitzi could discharge a flapjack with the stink power of a 300-pound hippo?

"Depends, huh?" He scrunched up his cheeks and mouth in a clown-like mask of mockery.

Her face was starting to crack with the effort of not laughing. Hands on hips, she did a little jiggle to the right. "So, what are you saying?"

"You put me on *ignore*. Wasted half our summer when we could have had beach time…" His voice faded and his gaze locked on hers. "And so much more." The innuendo turned her knees to pudding.

Phoebe was right. Enough was enough. She was tired of always being on guard, tired of pushing Deon away, tired of her fear.

He shifted his gaze to the floor for a second, then back up to Lucy. "I know what I want." Deon's gaze remained steady. "Being away from you made me…I realized how I feel about you."

How he feels about me? A tiny tremor ran down her throat to her stomach. Forget anything smacking of glib or clever. "Me too. I want to tell you…"

"Yes?" His expression changed, and Lucy worried he'd put on his silly face and make her laugh when she didn't want to laugh. "Spit it out."

"I missed you." She covered her face with her hands.

"What did you say?"

"You heard me." *I said it, finally told him how I feel.*

"I'd like you to say it again." He gently peeled her hands from her face.

"I missed you," Lucy said, leaning away from him.

"Lucy," Deon warned in a teasing voice. "Don't make me come over there."

****

This is good. Very. Oh, so good. Something knocked around in Deon's chest while his knees squeezed together, or maybe he was squeezing to keep from falling over.

So what were they doing standing here in the lobby of the restaurant? Maybe he'd suggest they go somewhere to catch up. Yes, good idea. Best idea he'd had all day.

"I sent the text," she blurted.

"The text. What text? When?" He knew he was wearing his eager, boyish, kid face, and practically wagging his tail, not that he could help it. "You texted me?"

"That text message asking you to come join us here. Phoebe didn't send it. I sent it."

"From Phoebe's phone? You—?"

"Yeah. I peeked at her phone when she went to the restroom, saw it was you and texted. A spur-of-the-moment decision."

Deon's gaze raked her face and his smile widened. He pulled her to his chest, his arms in a tight hold. Then abruptly, he shoved her away.

"Wait. What? Were you afraid to invite me yourself?"

"Sort of."

He held her at arm's length, his gaze piercing. "I waited half the summer to hear from you, and all I got was that one lousy text way back at the beginning of our vacation. You needed alone time. Without me. You were freakin' damn clear."

He puffed out a breath and closed his eyes for a half second. "It would have been such a relief knowing it was you doing the inviting."

"It was me, okay? Me."

"Okay. There's one thing, though." His gaze never left her face. "I have to be forthright with you."

"Forthright it is."

They stood facing each other for a moment before he spoke. "I don't think I could take, uh, being relegated to friend status."

"No? Friend status is not what you aspire to?"

Deon's mouth twitched. *Is she teasing?* He felt like shaking her.

"Don't you think this is a bit sudden?" she asked.

He frowned. "Now you've done it."

"Very funny." The side of her mouth tilted.

"Wipe that smirk off, Lucy. I'm girding my loins to tell you a hard truth."

"Girding your loins. Are you channeling Stanley Tucci again? From that dancing movie?"

"Stop." A solemn expression clouded Deon's face. "Ever since our fight, I've languished without you." He sliced the air to make his point. "Languished. So, no, this isn't sudden. There's no sudden here. I can't bear any more indecision, not tonight, not tomorrow." He swiped a hand across his forehead. "I want us to be a couple this time. Forget before. Before was a fiasco." He brought Lucy against his chest again, his hands smoothing her hair.

"Before, I wasn't ready," she mumbled against his shirt.

Deon stepped back, his face clenching. "Are you making fun of me? With the not-ready thing? Because I said that to you?"

"No." She grinned up at him. "I was mad at you. Now I'm not." She moved in, and his arms went around her. "Keep hugging me. It's working." Her head rested on his chest like it belonged there. "I was pissed at you for a long time. That's the truth."

His shoulders slumped. "Okay, I get it."

"Hey, before wasn't so awful." She looked up at him. "We had a few good moments."

"That's for sure. A lotta good moments." He couldn't help grinning as his mind slid to that weekend. *Our lost weekend.* Playing Scrabble, cooking, watching movies, walking, making out for hours. And other stuff too. In bed stuff. The muskiness of his aftershave mingled with her special Lucy scent. Oh, he's missed this, getting close, the feel of her body.

He ran a finger along her cheek. "We're good together."

"Yeah?" She eyeballed the lobby where the wine tasting tables were being dismantled. "You picked quite the romantic spot."

A faint smile pulled at the edge of his mouth. His hand found hers and he guided her toward the front door.

"Wait!" Lucy balked. "We have to say goodbye."

They turned as one and headed toward the back deck, paused on the landing overlooking the area where their friends sat. Phoebe spotted them first and nudged Marcus. They both waved. Deon flung an arm around Lucy's shoulder, tugged her close, and smooched her a big one. Hoots and hollers followed as their friends realized what was happening.

"We're scramming," he shouted. Lucy blew air kisses and grabbed Deon's hand as they trotted out through the lobby.

Outside, the light slanted, and a cooling breeze came off the water. Still holding Lucy's hand, Deon guided her to the little boardwalk where all was quiet except for the sound of the water slapping the pilings, a distant foghorn, and the faint laughter from within the restaurant.

"We have a lot of catching up," he said. "I sent you thousands of texts. You owe me."

"I have six thousand Instagram followers," Lucy huffed. "In case you wanted to know."

He jerked her against his chest so quickly she tripped over his feet, and he reached out a hand to steady her. "Sorry, Lucy. Didn't mean to trip you."

"Don't do it again," she teased.

"It's just...never mind followers. Not tonight."

"Six thousand forty-four, last time I checked."

"Good. Now shut up so I can kiss you. I'm overdue for a kiss, a long kiss. It's making me...." His hand under her jaw, he pecked her cheek, the edge of her mouth. They swayed with the rhythm of the dock.

Deon pulled away at the sound of drunken voices and the clumping of feet on wood. "Let's get the hell out of here." He was already steering Lucy off the dock toward the parking lot.

"Where are we going?"

He paused, his hand mussing his hair. "I have an idea. Leave your car here."

"Phoebe drove."

"Good." Deon unlocked his car and opened the door to the cloying scent of overbaked roses. *The roses.* He forgot about the roses. Heat mounted on his neck and face. Would the poor things recover?

Lucy's gaze traveled to the passenger seat where the roses languished like an overdressed prom date.

"It smells like—"

"I'd better get the air going." He started the motor, busying himself with his seatbelt and checking the rearview mirror.

Lucy grabbed the roses and slid in beside Deon. He was instantly transported back to that day at the beach, the day that started their special weekend.

"Deon?"

"Fasten your seatbelt."

"Are these roses for…"

"If you're asking if they're for you, the answer is yes. All for you. I was too chicken to bring them into the restaurant." *Sad sacks, wilting in her lap.*

"How thoughtful." That's all she said, didn't make it into a big deal.

He took off from the parking lot, tires screeching around the corner, Lucy hanging on to the door handle.

"Wherever we're going, can we bring them in, put them in water?"

Deon sent Lucy an evil look. "You're determined to embarrass me, huh?"

"Not at all."

"Kidding. Sure, great idea." He snorted. "This'll be interesting."

This'll be great.

Chapter Twenty

"Surprise. It's oldies night," Deon said. "You'll love it."

Lucy blinked in recognition as Deon pulled up in front of Café Ten, one of their familiar downtown New Haven haunts.

He grabbed the keys. "I'll get your door, dear. This is a do-over date, but it's a real date." He opened the passenger door and snatched the wilting flowers from her hands, cradling them like a newborn baby. "They'll perk up. Shall I carry them for you?"

"No, I'll carry my own flowers." They slipped in the side door past the guy who vetted for minors, and Deon snagged the last two seats at the bar that ran the length of the place.

Lucy lay the flowers on the counter as the bartender wandered over. "Those flowers are in serious need of sustenance," he said.

"Any chance you have a vase?" She was making a minor spectacle of herself. *This isn't a roses-and-vases kind of place.* A few people at surrounding tables looked their way.

"Your man must have messed up big time," called a woman from a nearby table.

Deon shook his head. "Oh, you're so right," he called back, and glanced toward the front of the room. On the small stage, two guys and a woman were setting up. The woman fumbled with the microphone.

"Sorry, no vases." The bartender mustered a sad smile, as if he doubted Lucy's roses would survive the night. "But I can put them in a pot in the kitchen."

"Thanks." Deon extended his hand, and the bartender shook. "Deon."

"I'm Tiger." He lifted the roses from the counter and went through the door that led to the kitchen.

"Give me a second." Deon squeezed Lucy's shoulder. "Be right back." He strolled over to the band. A chorus of "Hey, man, where you been keeping yourself?" and "Long time. Still playing?" followed. *He knows them. It's no coincidence we landed here at Café Ten.* They whispered for a few minutes, and he returned smiling broadly. Something was going on. Lucy didn't much like being out of the info loop.

"Happy your roses were rescued?" He wore a look of satisfaction.

"Yes, very." Lucy waited a few beats for Deon to settle on the barstool before asking the question that had plagued her since their arrival. "Why are we here?" *Too blunt and accusatory.* "I don't mean it as a bad thing." Her voice dropped to an intimate whisper. "Just that we could be at my house. Or yours."

"Ah, I was a little afraid that might come up."

"What do you mean?"

Deon snuggled closer. "I promise I'll tell you." He rubbed his thumb gently on her neck. Would you mind if…I thought I'd sit in with the band."

"Oh— Well, sure."

"One song only."

"Two songs or three. It's fine." Lucy shrugged. She didn't want Deon thinking she couldn't take care of herself.

"Come with me?"

"Where?"

"On stage." He watched for her reaction.

"Me? Sing in front of a crowd?" She swallowed hard.

"We'll be together. It'll be fine."

They remained at the bar as the band began to play, starting with "Wake Up Little Susie," the guitar dipping low in the opening. Lucy chair-danced to the beat, and several folks in the audience sang along.

Tiger stood wiping a glass, and a few more people came through the door and sat at a table near the front.

Deon cleared his throat, exaggerating the effect as if he was about to make a speech. "Two glasses of champagne, please." He kept a straight face.

"Dude," Tiger drawled, drawing the word out like a scratched record. "Are you testing me? We don't cater to the champagne and caviar crowd." Tiger's delivery reminded Lucy of Thomas Haden Church in *Sideways*, that old movie about two guys on a wine tasting road trip. She almost burst out laughing. Instead, she pinched Deon's shirt between two fingers and yanked him closer. "Silly."

"I want to celebrate."

As she planted a kiss on Deon's cheek, Tiger sprang to action. "Why didn't you say so? What are you celebrating?" He looked pointedly at their hands. "No rings. Right. Something else."

Deon and Lucy exchanged looks.

"I get it," Tiger demurred. "None of my bee's wax."

Lucy poked Deon with an elbow. "Bee's wax, huh?

I haven't heard that one since I was a little kid."

"It's not that," Deon hurried to explain. "It's a bit of a sensitive issue is all."

"No problem." Tiger faced the stage where the trio paused. "This is one of my all-time favorites." Then the unmistakable first notes of the beginning to "I Got You Babe."

"I got flowers," Deon sang in Lucy's ear, "in the kit-chen." She punched him lovingly on the arm, and he grabbed her around the waist. "Babe, come with me." He lifted her off the stool and they lurched to the stage, her heart bouncing because she was about to look foolish in front of a bunch of strangers.

"Don't worry, babe. They're professional singers. They'll drown us out."

The woman band member beckoned them onto the stage, and Lucy stood obediently, smiling and joining in on the chorus. It's the best she can do. The old classic was simple and repetitive and brought her back instantly, because she was a sucker for sixties music with a special place in her heart for Sonny and Cher. She stuck to singing "I Got You Babe," bopping and smiling as Deon belted out the lyrics. A rush of claps and hollers followed their performance.

"They're celebrating their anniversary, folks," trilled the band leader, a tall, skinny guy in a vest and jeans.

"Never do that again," Lucy managed, stepping off the stage. "I require at least a two-week warning for guest appearances."

"I suppose you expect to be paid now?" They lounged at the bar. "How about a Stella?"

"Share one with me? I don't really feel like

drinking much."

"One Stella, two glasses, coming up." Tiger winked. "Not bad for amateurs, not bad at all."

When they were ready to leave, Tiger handed Lucy the flowers, wrapped in paper towels. Deon tipped him generously, and they tripped out the door.

Outside, it was cool with the smell of mid-summer in the breeze. Lucy balanced the bouquet on her arm as they trundled across the street to Deon's car. "This was so nice. But you didn't answer my question."

"Why I brought you here?" He unlocked the door and she slid into the passenger seat. He stashed the roses in the back and got behind the wheel.

"I was afraid to bring you home, or to my house."

"Afraid? What are you talking about?"

"The sex thing. I think we should take some time. When you're ready and you give me the word. I don't want to mess anything up. Seduce you too soon."

Lucy laughed, an evil cackle. "You're such a liar," she whispered, hooking a finger in his collar and pulling him toward her. "Admit it. Admit you want to seduce me, you dirty liar."

She kissed him slowly, and he groaned. *Oh, this is better than I thought it would be.* Kissing Deon was like an insta-turn on. She sucked on his lower lip, and her mouth traveled to his neck, below his ear.

"Take me home," she murmured, knowing the subtext was clear as a bright sunrise.

****

Deon planted little kisses around Lucy's mouth. They were parked in her driveway making out like teenagers. Crazy and done for, he might as well give in now before he messed everything up.

We have to go slowly this time. Slowly. What did that mean? At the thought of going slowly, his throat tightened along with his groin and his determination to get this thing with Lucy right.

She pulled back to look at him. "Are you coming in for a nightcap?" To his amazement, she winked. An exaggerated, mocking wink. The kind of wink that says, *Of course you're coming in. Asking is simply a formality.*

He avoided answering, leaned over the middle console of the car and kissed her forehead.

This isn't going to go well. Her playful expression morphed to a frown.

"Look, Lucy." He reached for her hand. "Listen a minute."

The claw in his gut wouldn't let go. How to put her off? Easy-peasy to mosey up the sidewalk, step inside her house. He pictured the living room, the sofa by the fireplace, the kitchen with the panda-cookie jar. The stairs leading up to her bedroom.

He imagined sleeping in her bed. *Too soon.* How to explain so she won't hate him?

"Remember when you kicked me to the curb at the restaurant?" He waited until she gave a quick nod. "I started texting you that day. Every day since then I've worked to figure out why I felt guilty, why I couldn't talk to you after our…that weekend together. I've always been able to talk to you."

"Why do you keep bringing that up? You've got to let it go."

"Let me finish, please."

Lucy stayed very still, but her eyes widened.

"You know guys don't really have friends. Well, I

have guy friends, but it's not the same." He gripped her hand. "I never thought…it scares me how I feel when I'm with you. I didn't think I'd have these feelings for anyone again." The words came in a rush, and he forged on.

"You know what I did for a month?" She squeezed his hand to let him know she was paying attention. "I took on more private clients, got into a big-brother summer program at the high school. "I thought maybe after a week, you know, you'd text. A week seemed reasonable. And then it was two weeks, three. Four and I stopped counting." *I never stopped counting.* He paused and peered out the car window. Left out the six sessions with Erwin, his friend and shrink. Mostly, Erwin listened and drank coffee, a revelation to Deon, who couldn't have pulled through without him.

"You talked to Phoebe?" Lucy asked in a small voice.

Deon gazed down at his hand grasping hers and then back at her. "Phoebe told me I'd be lucky if you ever spoke to me again. That scared the crap out of me. I'm serious. I want us to take it slow."

"Us?" Lucy regarded him curiously. "You mean *we* should take it slow?"

"Us, yes."

Taking it slow wasn't in his original plan. After the wine tasting, and after channeling Sonny and Cher up on stage at Café Ten, it was all about the anticipation of having Lucy back in his life. After a month of no contact, all he could think about was making it up to her. They'd spend the weekend together for starters. Maybe find a cozy beach rental down on the shoreline. Old Saybrook or Madison. Hell, he'd even thought of going as far as Rhode Island for a different vibe. Shack up, just the two of them for a few days. And nights. These precious days of summer…he'd make her forget he'd ever put her on *ignore*.

But something had shifted when he and Lucy were onstage and the words from that corny, old song had taken on a special meaning. Now he wanted to savor every moment.

Lucy was staring at him with an open, vulnerable expression. "Deon? Where are you?"

"Thinking of you on stage singing with me." He leaned over and kissed her on the cheek. "Come on, I'm walking you to the door."

He never thought it would happen to him. Falling in love again after losing his Melinda? He couldn't say it out loud. It was too soon for that.

On her porch, he turned her around and they faced the street. It was quiet with the faint scent of charcoal and steak or chicken grilling nearby. A few doors away, a neighbor appeared with his dog.

"We've never dated." Deon tightened his hold around her waist. "I want that experience, all the experiences…I want them with you. Beaches, dinners, hikes, bike riding, slow dancing. We have a month of vacation left and all the time in the world after that to, you know." He nuzzled her neck.

"Do the dirty deed?"

"I wouldn't put it like that."

"We've done the dirty. It's not like—I feel so silly. It's like I'm begging for sex." A playful tone crept into her voice. "We can just sleep together, not fool around."

Deon groaned. "I couldn't. I don't have it in me."

"All right, all right. I get it. I should be flattered."

Deon held her close and breathed in her scent, freshly washed shampoo mixed with a little perspiration, probably from her stage debut. Nerves.

He kissed her cheek, and yanked himself away, gripping the railing. "If I don't leave now..." He bounded down the steps. "Tomorrow let's do the beach and a picnic. Hammonasset. I'll call you."

I'm either a fool or a wise man. I'm not sure which.

Chapter Twenty-One

The scent of Lucy's Honey Perfume roses, planted last spring, floated on the breeze through the open windows of Deon's car.

His beloved Corvette wasn't ideal for kissing, and petting was pretty much impossible. *Petting.* Lucy loved the word. It deserved a comeback. They couldn't do much in the Corvette where Deon had barely enough room to bend his elbow and fondle her breast.

Yeah, she was complaining. He was taking it slow. Way too slow. Why were they in Lucy's driveway, at the tail end of yet another date, when they could be inside on her couch? Or God forbid in her bed.

"You okay?" Concern in his voice. *He knew.*

"Fine." A smooch on his neck to reassure him. "You coming in tonight?"

His face stiffened.

Playing kissy face with Deon was the thing Lucy looked forward to so, so much. Lucy and Deon up in a tree, k-i-s-s-i-n-g. Like the old nursery rhyme.

Only not in a tree. Not in her driveway squished in a race car either. Lucy had a much better idea. How about Deon's king size bed, big and comfy, where they'd spent a big chunk of *that* weekend?

These days, though, Deon was relentless in his pursuit of outdoor activity. Tonight, they'd gone dancing, hamming up the moves. Dinner and a bluegrass band in Hamden developed into almost more fun than humans should have.

She'd been hoping.

Judging by the stricken look on his face when she asked if he was coming in, it wasn't happening.

The truth? She was *sick and tired* of all the dates. So much activity and no action.

She squirmed in his arms. Not that she didn't love kissing Deon. Lucy loved the way he planted little kisses all down her neck, stopped at her cleavage, and detoured to the inside of her elbow. PG rated, but delicious, nevertheless.

The effort he put into avoiding…intimacy…well, it bordered on an athletic endeavor. One chilly evening after a downpour, they'd gone to the East Haven beach for a walk and a bottle of wine, armed with a blanket and mosquito repellent. Deon groping for ideas.

How romantic was that?

They'd ended up taking a short stroll in the drizzle, and popped into The Stork, a cozy little place with a guitarist. And plenty of wine. She'd sucked down two glasses of a very passable pinot noir.

A tightness gripped Lucy's back and traveled down her spine. Deon was reaching for ways not to be indoors near a bedroom.

"Don't tell me you're not coming in. Just for a little bit." Lucy pouted, sticking out her lower lip.

Deon kissed her, another full-on smackeroo that curled her toes. Then he kissed the tip of her nose. Cute. His kisses were meant to be gentle and spirit-calming. Instead, a bubble of doubt rose up. What was Deon trying to prove with all this frantic activity?

Yeah, yeah, all that hooey about taking it slow.

Slow was one thing but this was ridiculous. Lucy pushed against Deon's chest, a gentle shove. She needed to get out of the car. Think this through. Talk to someone. A shrink? Was sex-obsession normal? *I want a full relationship. Not too much to ask.*

Phoebe. Nothing wrong with her that Phoebe couldn't cure. She'd call her. Or dash over there for a dose of emotional support. Maybe she knew something Lucy didn't. Phoebe reframed; that was her special talent.

Lucy slid toward the car door, her butt against it.

"Aren't you kissing me goodnight?" Deon's smile tickled in all the right places, and she changed course, moved closer. He lifted her chin. "Be patient with me. A little longer."

"Summer doesn't last forever," Lucy blurted. "Let's go away for a weekend and sleep in the same bed." *Four stinkin' weeks left until school starts. How long is this celibacy thing going to drag on?*

"Our next date..." His tongue teased the edges of her mouth. "Tomorrow. How about dinner at this non-touristy place in Old Saybrook? We'll have wine on the beach. Then hit the restaurant. Soft-shell crabs. Their specialty." Prickles as his tongue and lips skimmed her shoulder. He bared his teeth, took hold of her sleeveless top, and yanked it off her shoulder.

She groaned. *Torturing her on purpose?*

He straightened and kissed her on both cheeks, his interpretation of French kissing these days. *I sound bitter.* Deon was the greatest kisser, but cheek kissing was his signal their date was ending.

"I'll pick you up at seven?"

"Seven, eight, nine." Lucy's tone reflected her

plummeting mood as she slid back against the door, resigned to sleeping alone. "Whatever."

"Lucy." His voice, soft and soothing, rankled her.

"What?" she barked.

"Are you miffed?" His tone was faultless.

No matter what she said or how she said it, Deon continued to be the master of patience and understanding.

Shouting aloud "Stop entertaining me and get real!" would get his attention but wouldn't make a difference. Ahh, what she wanted was smooching, kissy-face, and canoodling, whatever that was. Snogging, and cuddling, and full-on lovey-dovey. But only if Deon wanted the same.

"Nighty night." Lucy opened the car door and almost fell out on her bottom in her haste to make a quick exit. She stomped up the sidewalk to the porch, heard the car door open and turned, waved, and blew him a kiss. He was still standing by his car when she let herself into the house.

A healthy dose of Lucky Duck, the Australian shiraz she'd opened last night was called for and pronto. Lucy poured herself a glass, settled on the couch and quick-dialed Phoebe.

"What is it now?" Phoebe groaned. "More whining about Deon?"

"Deon still won't come into my house and isn't inviting me to his house either."

"Wait. Let me get this straight." For a few seconds dead air circulated through the ethernet. Phoebe preparing to lambast her. "Hasn't he spent every day with you since you hooked up at the wine tasting?"

"We never hooked up," Lucy protested, offended.

"That's my problem."

Another weighted silence. She squeezed the phone as if it were a snake.

"Let me outline a few things," Phoebe snapped with an undertone of forced patience Lucy knew too well.

"I can't wait to hear about my criminal record," Lucy giggled.

"When you finally forgave his ass at the wine tasting, you did yourself a favor. Think about it."

Her reasoning was lost to Lucy. "Yeah, but—"

"Hasn't he stepped up to the plate and a dozen other clichés? I know you love a good cliché."

"Rolled up his sleeves?" Lucy quipped. "Knuckled down. He's in it for the long haul, huh?"

Phoebe didn't miss a beat. "Escorted you to beaches and concerts and dinners, and at least two sunset picnics?"

"Sure, but—"

"You're both into wine so he hauls around that huge picnic basket on wheels you said he bought special."

"What about—"

"Not to mention canoeing with Sara and Lily. The man goes out of his way to get the two girls together. Makes a special day for the four of you. You know, last week, that town with the funny name. Moo—"

"Moodus."

"Moodus, yeah. I went to Girl Scout camp near there."

"You never told me that."

"Never mind, and don't try and change the topic." Phoebe was all business. "First you moon over Deon.

Now you complain. Make up your mind."

She had a point. And yet Lucy had imagined a different scenario the last few weeks before school started. A train ride into New York for a little overnighter. Or hanging out for a dirty weekend at her place. Not all this contrived activity. She couldn't take much more of this…wooing.

Lucy jerked up to a seated position and planted her feet on the floor. What if Deon was still undecided? What if he was going through the romantic motions? What if all the frantic showboating meant he was still riddled with doubt? Her neck tightened with this notion, and she got up to pace from the living room into the kitchen as Phoebe thought out loud into the phone.

"Honey, the guy is a romantic. And we both know he loves rom coms. Let him take his time." Phoebe plowed ahead, as if she knew Deon more intimately than Lucy did. "He's making up for—he's got a lot to make up for, or he thinks he does. He wants you to know he's serious."

Silence for a moment, and then Lucy sighed. "I know." *I don't know.*

Phoebe's voice softened, the better to lull Lucy into letting go of the Deon sex obsession. As if that bothered her.

This whole super romantic thing with Deon was weird. She couldn't help but feel there was something closed off and unreachable about Deon. No way was she sharing those thoughts with Phoebe, ideas she didn't fully understand herself.

She scratched an elbow. A mosquito bite from a sunset picnic, and a free performance of *A Midsummer Night's Dream* at Edgerton Park a couple nights back.

Wine and food and flowers and sex weren't all that defined her and Deon. The proof was in their lost weekend. She wanted all of that weekend magic back, but how? What could she do to get through to him when he covered his fear with a romantic comedy illusion of romance?

She refused to settle for the plastic version of love.

"I've got to go, but I have an idea," Phoebe chuckled. "Remember that episode of *Sex and the City*? The Bunny? That's what you need. Get on Amazon or go to that big sex store off the Merritt Parkway. Order a vibrator."

"Not funny." *Phoebs doesn't get what I'm going through.* "And it's Rabbit, not Bunny."

Ut oh. Phoebe had gone quiet. Probably making her irked face, eyes narrowed and lips tight.

Phoebe fired back in a lower register. "Life is good. Shut up and enjoy. Don't call me again unless you're bleeding."

****

This is the night.

Deon backed out of the garage. Despite the cool flow of air conditioning, he was sweating.

This was definitely the night.

He couldn't take it anymore. Every time he kissed Lucy goodnight and walked her to the door knowing he wouldn't be sleeping over, disappointment ragged his spirit.

He glanced at the daisies nestled on the seat beside him. Fun flowers, a far cry from red roses and all the romantic hoopla they represented.

"Hi," he recited out loud. "Change of plans. Forget Old Saybrook." He'd grab her around the waist, lift her

240

off the ground. Or something equally dramatic and manly. "Would you like to come for dinner at my house?" What a dork, practicing what he'd say. But he wouldn't mess this up by taking Lucy for granted ever again.

When he pulled in front of her house, she was waiting on the porch swing holding a beach bag and wearing a short, flowery turquoise and yellow dress. Obviously expecting an evening of sitting by the water, feet dangling in those low- slung chairs, sipping zinfandel and nibbling appetizers.

This was all wrong. Lucy was supposed to be inside so he'd ring the bell and surprise her with the daisies and a change of plans. He had it all worked out in his mind.

She stood, threw the bag over her shoulder, and galloped down the sidewalk, hands in puffy little pockets, dress twirling around her thighs.

He plucked the flowers from the seat and slipped out of the car, holding them behind his back.

She stopped short. "You're not dressed for the beach."

"Change of plans," he blurted.

She tilted her head, smirking. "What's up, Deon?"

The hand behind his back holding the flowers appeared. "These are for you." The flowers sagged as if swooning, and he groaned inwardly. Leaving flowers in the car was getting to be a bad habit. Plus, he'd held them so tightly, he crushed the life out of them.

Her eyes crinkled up. "Thank you." She reached for the bouquet. "Poor things."

Deon blushed, realizing what he'd done. Lucy can probably read his mortification. The woman in the flower shop had dressed up the daisies with long green and yellow stalks, a bouquet within a bouquet, impressive as crap when he left the store, more like garbage now.

"Let's put them in water." Lucy's attempt to mollify him. "So they'll perk up."

He took Lucy's beach bag. They walked up the stairs, and Deon held the screen door open as Lucy turned the key in the lock. He followed her into the kitchen where she stood on tiptoe and pulled out a vase from a corner cabinet.

Deon slouched awkwardly holding her bag. *Why am I always worrying? She'll love my change of plans.*

Lucy laid the limp flowers on the counter and filled the vase with water.

"There's a little envelope with the secret ingredient. Flower food. The lady at the shop said..." His thoughts drifted away as Lucy tilted her head back and fixed him with a strange look.

"Deon." Her voice cranky and out of sorts.

Deon startled. "What's wrong?"

"Nothing." She folded her arms across her chest. "Does everything have to be so...perfect?"

"Perfect?" The question befuddled him.

"Never mind."

Lucy went quiet, and now Deon twitched. He searched the bouquet, found the envelope, ripped it open and handed it to Lucy. She added the powder to the water and stirred it with a long-handled spoon. He slid the flowers into the vase, imagining them reviving. "Soon, they'll wake up smiling."

His attempt to sound playful came off all wrong. He looked over his shoulder to find Lucy watching him.

He felt the atmosphere in the room tilt, and for a millisecond he couldn't catch his breath. Things weren't going the way he'd envisioned them.

"So, no beach."

"No." He hesitated. "I planned a surprise."

Lucy shrugged and said nothing.

"The thing is…in order for it to be a surprise, you've got to…" He fished the sleep mask from his pocket. "Will you wear this in the car? Intrinsic. To the surprise. So you won't know where I'm taking you."

She grasped it and twirled it on her finger. "Seriously? I have to wear a mask?" Her mouth turned into a pout. "Let's get this over with."

Maybe he'd gone too far with the mask, but too late now. He was committed to the whole enterprise, even though he hadn't thought this through.

What about driving with a masked woman in the passenger seat? If someone from the neighborhood caught sight of him, he'd probably get arrested. Thank God the Corvette wasn't a convertible.

A sideways glance at Lucy, slouching deep in her seat, convinced him his whole idea was indeed ridiculous. Nevertheless, he drove a few blocks in the wrong direction and hopped on the parkway by the high school for one exit. That would throw her off. Damn it, he was determined to surprise her. When he finally pulled up in front of his house and killed the motor, she yanked off the mask and looked around.

"Your house? Really? Was all this subterfuge necessary?"

He stiffened like a cardboard cutout. "I just wanted everything to be good for you."

"It's like you're trying for the perfect rom com.

You don't have to do that." Twisting in her seat, she faced him, her eyes like little swords piercing his protective shell, seeing through to his vulnerable inner workings, his obsessive need to plan for fear of making a mistake. "Did you do that with Melinda because I can guarantee you didn't."

"What are you talking about?" His shoulders hunched around his ears.

"You. Trying too hard." Her eyes widened as if to punctuate her point.

"I'm not—"

"You were in a real relationship with Melinda, and sometimes you had fights and sometimes she hated you, and maybe you even hated her for like an hour. But you didn't fake it and neither did she."

Fake it? His mind wavered putting the pieces together. Lucy—his Lucy—had the wrong idea about him. About them. *She thinks I have doubts.*

He twitched, wanting to explain a few things just as she relaunched.

"You don't have to buy me flowers every five minutes and take me on sunset beach walks. You don't have to prove anything."

She opened the car door. "I need to think about things. I'm—I'll see you later."

She's leaving me? No, this isn't happening again!

Before he could stop himself, Deon reached over with a crooked forefinger and hooked Lucy's pocket as she moved forward.

The pocket ripped, a long ungainly tear that exposed an expanse of thigh and left him sprawled across the front seat, his mouth open in wonder and shock.

Chapter Twenty-Two

Lucy almost burst out laughing as Deon let his crooked finger go slack and sprang out of the car. He stomped around to confront her.

"You can't go. Not now." He flung his arms up in frustration. "I've got so much to talk to you about. I have things to show you. Explain. Make plans."

"I thought we were going out," she said through clenched teeth. *Who was he to tell her what to do?*

They stared at one another.

"Are you punishing me for trying too hard?" He rubbed the sweat from his face. Without another word he picked Lucy up and headed toward the porch.

"Put me down. This is ridiculous." She thrashed her feet in the air and pushed against his chest.

"There, there, pumpkin seed." He squeezed her closer, breathing hard. No surprise since she wriggled like an octopus. "You'll come inside, my Lucy. We'll talk." His voice calming, soft. "I have dinner," he murmured. "And everything."

They were at eye level. He was strong but for how many more minutes…seconds could he hold her before he dropped her on the pavement? "Give me a sign, quick before I drop you. Not on purpose."

"Yes, yes, fine."

He loosened his grip, and Lucy slid to the ground. One of her shoes slipped off and she hung onto him while she shoved her foot back into it.

"I have to pee," Lucy said once they were in the house. Taking the stairs two at a time, she escaped to the upstairs bathroom and slammed the door. Why was everything such a big deal? The trip on the highway, the deflated flowers, the whole big surprise idea. She peered into the mirror, eyes tearing. That sad, smashed bouquet…trying so hard, too hard. Pathetic.

Wasn't she just as pathetic hiding in the bathroom? Lucy opened the door and tramped into the loft separating the bedrooms, squinted down into the kitchen. No sign of him.

She hadn't been in Deon's house since…that weekend.

Carried away by sheer curiosity, she drifted toward Deon's bedroom, crossed the threshold and looked around, at first confused. Nothing was as she remembered it. The bureaus, the paintings, the floating shelves crammed with Melinda's collection of frogs— all gone. Including that frilly old comforter. Instead, two huge silver pillows, one purple pillow, the spread a tasteful, textured white.

The silver pillows? She loved them so much she could marry them.

The setting sun slanted in through the slats in the blinds and birds sang on the tree outside the window.

Two controls sat on the new end tables, and Lucy did a double take. Deon had bought a new bed, one of those fancy sit-up jobs that support the back and even raise your legs. On impulse, she grabbed the remote and pressed a button. The foot of the bed rose, and she laughed out loud. *Deon bought a new bed*. Was it part of the surprise he'd been talking about?

She ambled over to the window and peeked at a little brown finch singing his heart out. When she was around twelve, she'd gone birding with her father almost every weekend. "A bad singer can have trouble finding a mate if his singing doesn't measure up," her dad told her at the time.

As she made her way down the stairs, Deon came into view, clinging to the railing, waiting for her. At the bottom, she glimpsed the semi-empty living room, strangely barren with most of the furniture gone, no pillows or knickknacks. Not a frog in sight.

She moved closer, bumped his chest with her head and his arms went around her. *Oh geez, to think I almost messed things up.*

"I thought I'd lost you," his cheek against her hair.

"Shh." She leaned into the warmth of him. The crushed daisies, the mask, Deon putting her on *ignore*, her mistrust, cutting him off. "You'll never lose me." That was true. *No more time wasted listening to our fear talking. We need to talk to each other.*

Phoebe was right. Underneath all the roses and the sunsets, Deon was actually invested.

He started with tiny pecks on her forehead and cheeks, down her neck and back up to her mouth. Sucking on Lucy's bottom lip, nipping her neck. The feel of him clenching her close sent a few vibrations to the right places. He steered her backwards, leaning her against the wall, bracing his hands to support himself as she stretched up to taste him, her arms around his neck, pulling his head down.

His body reacted as she lifted onto her toes to grind into his pelvis at crotch level. *God, this is great, better than great.* So not what she expected while pouting in the bathroom.

"I've always wanted to do this," she panted. "Like in the movies. You know, when two characters can't wait to—"

"Shut up, sweetie," Deon mumbled. Lucy unbuttoned his shirt and he tilted forward, his hand in her hair, pushing back against the hard surface and kissing her more deeply this time. She stopped thinking and analyzing. The feeling was so good, his mouth, his hands under her ripped dress caressing her thigh. She wrestled off his shirt and let it drop, her mouth and tongue wending their way to his neck, down his chest to his nipple. He groaned, and his mouth found hers again, hot, amazingly hot. She smiled inwardly, thinking of how everything changed when he was aroused. *I need to arouse him more often, let the alpha Deon come out to play.*

"The couch," he groaned. Lucy giggled as they trundled over to the sofa, Deon guiding her with his body, his arms supporting her almost dead weight. They dropped onto the cushions, entwined, her legs wrapping his waist, her hands traveling over his chest and up to his neck where she buried her mouth. He began the kissing all over again as her eyes closed. This time he moaned, a sound she'd never tire of hearing. He kissed her, the pressure so slight she trembled, and then he was kissing her harder, his hand cupping her chin. She was still straddling him. *Oh, this is good, I've missed this, missed all this.*

She pulled gently away. "Tell me again how you feel about me," she murmured, pausing.

Her mouth was a centimeter from his and he kissed her in between words. "I crave you." Little kisses. "All those weeks I craved you." More kisses. "I couldn't stand being without you."

His hands smoothed her thighs, and he heaved himself up, Lucy clinging like a monkey, and he walked them back out to the hallway.

"Where are we going?" she asked, laughing. "I want to try out the new bed."

"You do?" He unwrapped her legs from his waist, and she glided down, wobbling, and leaning into him. "You sure?"

She nodded. They stumbled upstairs to the bedroom where he tossed the giant pillows onto the floor and lay down, his head on the bed pillow. "Come cuddle with me." She settled into him, one thigh sprawled over his hip, her head on his shoulder.

After a few minutes, he kissed her, his hands fumbling for the zipper on her dress. He adjusted her position on the bed for better access, unzipped slowly.

"We'll talk about that rip in your dress later," he mumbled. It took like three days of kissing and another day went by before he peeled off her dress. His eyes roamed over her scarlet bra and matching lace panties. "Nice. But I'd like you better without them."

I bought them with you in mind, Deon. "My turn." Her voice was firm.

He peered down at her, his forehead crinkled.

"Stand up," she said. "I want to undress you."

One side of his mouth rose in a half-smile, his movements languid as if going slow were all part of a game. "I was crazy."

"Crazy?" *What's he getting at?*

"To think I could resist...to think we wouldn't..." His voice faded into a low groan.

"Wouldn't what?" Anticipation as part of the turn-on, but nothing was better than teasing and going slow.

He stood and Lucy unbuckled his belt and unzipped his jeans. They fell to the floor. She urged him back on the bed, caressing his chest and neck, her gaze never leaving his face.

"Oh, I missed you," he said. "So bad." His voice dropped to a purr. "I was afraid you'd disappear in a haze of self-righteous, pissed-offedness."

She giggled. "Are you ever…?"

His head dipped back and one side of his mouth lifted in amusement. "Am I ever what?"

Her arms encircled his neck and as he kissed her, she felt his smile widening. Silly kisses counted as much as serious kisses. "Are you ever going to stop talking?"

"No, no I'm not." The Elvis drawl. "I'm a talker."

She narrowed her eyes.

"Yes, yes, I am," he amended, kissing the corner of her mouth before planting little soft kisses all down her neck and back up. "Except for the *I love you* part. Am I allowed to say those three words?"

"Show me," she breathed. "Show me what you mean."

****

Much later, and only because they were both woozy and starving, they pulled on T-shirts and toddled down to the kitchen. Deon languidly opened the bottle of zinfandel while Lucy leaned on his shoulder, her arms wrapped around him.

"Sit, relax, I'll pour the wine," he said. "And I'll be your server for the evening." He gave her a cockeyed grin, and she could almost feel the zinger coming before it landed. "You must be exhausted from being so pissed off at me."

"I'll never be pissed off at you again," she blurted, laughing.

"I look forward to it." He turned to the three large takeout bags on the counter, their aroma of basil and oregano wafting toward up in heady, mouthwatering clouds of deliciousness.

Lucy swallowed hard. "You made me so hungry." She leered at him, leaning on the word *hungry*.

"I *knows* what you *likes*."

"You certainly do."

"Are you leering at me?" he asked, waggling his eyebrows.

"Me?" *Oh, yeah.* "You went to Niki's?" She was wide awake now. "Is this a do-over or something?"

Deon took a few seconds before responding. "I'll do you over if you don't watch yourself."

"I look forward to it. I'm not afraid of you."

He approached, his stare unwavering. "You're afraid in a good way. Because I'm a shape shifter. With alpha male capabilities." He hunkered down, his gaze wandering to her mouth, and kissed her, a sweet, lingering kiss. "What about when I bend notes on the harp, make all the women swoon? Are you afraid then?"

"Hardly. You know why?"

"Nope. You gonna tell me?"

"I'm the only woman who counts."

"That's true. And you're a little smarty panty."

"Smarty panty? Is that different from smarty pants?"

"You bet." He lowered his voice to a growl. "I love

your panties, by the way. Love removing them." He kissed her cheek, his mouth wandering down to Lucy's neck. "Wanna hear the specials?" he whispered, his breath tickling.

"I forgot how you tend to over-order," she said in a low voice that matched his sexy tone. "I love that about you."

Still smiling, he went over to the counter and lifted a container.

"Watcha got there?" she asked.

He opened the first carton. "Chicken Florentine. And this here's sausage and broccoli rabe...eggplant parm, and two meatballs just in case. And salad. I'll make a salad. Um, if you insist."

"Not insisting. This is plenty."

Deon warmed the food and they sat close together in the booth of the Happy Days kitchen, thighs and occasionally shoulders touching. Deon started by giving her a morsel of eggplant parmigiana from his fork and the whole meal went like that, silly and sappy and lovey-dovey. Lucy finally leaned back and groaned. "It's a good thing we had sex before we ate. Planning ahead is a wonderful thing."

Deon chuckled.

"Did you...do you still have the movies?"

He closed his eyes for a second. "Ahh, I could never get rid of those movies. They remind me of Melinda. And you. They remind me of the best weekend of my life in a long, long time."

A little tremor ran up Lucy's spine to her neck and back down. Deon would never have to hide memories or thoughts about Melinda. She was part of him. Someone to share.

"By the way, have I told you I'm so glad you finally, finally texted me on Phoebe's phone?"

"Well, I'm glad you're glad I texted you on Phoebe's phone, too," she mumbled, wondering where this was going.

"Melinda would be happy for me," he said, offering her his hand. "Come with me, pumpkin seed."

I'm his pumpkin seed.

They moved to the couch and sat in comfortable silence for a few moments. When Lucy's eyelids grew heavy, she slouched down and rested her head on his lap. Deon stroked her hair, and she closed her eyes.

"I didn't think I could be good with anyone again," he said.

She turned slightly to look up at him and smiled, the air inside her lungs tugging. "You needed some time. You and me both. Except in my case—"

He stopped her words with a slow kiss. "I know what you could use about now."

"Do you? Who says?"

"I'm saying." Two words, gentle yet voiced with heat, which made his hidden intention all the more potent. "Sit up, will you? It won't work with your head in my lap."

She sat up lazily, her eyes half-closed. "Another surprise?"

"I've been working on it all week. A harp serenade finally texted me on Phoebe's phone?"

The warmth was there, nestled in his voice like a cat's purr. Whatever he was up to, he was serious. "You would do that for me?"

"I would and I will." He reached for his harmonica on the side table. "I have them all over the house these days. Encouragement."

The first notes of "When a Man Loves a Woman" cut through the quiet, full and round, rich with longing. Lucy tensed and after a few moments, relaxed, watched his mouth on the instrument.

This was what life would hold for them together.

This was their beginning.

Chapter Twenty-Three

One Year Later

"Is that the doorbell?" Lucy burrowed deep under the covers seeking Deon's warmth.

"They'll go away." Deon spooned her against his body and tightened his hold.

She jerked up in a haze of confusion. "Oh, no, did we fall asleep? What time is it?"

"Oh crap." Deon sat up and grabbed his boxers. "You take a shower first," he said, ever the gentleman. "I'll get the door."

"Like that's going to work."

"Go, go." Deon pulled on his pants and shirt and ran a hand through his hair. "Whose idea was this pizza thing?"

Lucy raced into the bathroom. "Fix your hair," she shouted over her shoulder.

Another ring, this time two short and one long. A signal.

Through the open bathroom window, voices wafted up from the porch. Lucy peered down at Phoebe hoisting a Tupperware container against her hip. Marcus set a thermal bag on the stoop. Thank God it wasn't the girls.

"We could be here a while," Marcus groused.

"Maybe they forgot we're coming." This from

Phoebe.

Lucy heard every word, their voices loud and carefree, since they had no idea she was there spying.

"Love in the afternoon," Marcus added.

For a moment Lucy was taken aback. Were she and Deon that obvious?

"You're right," Phoebe laugh-hooted. "They're totally doing it. *Love in the Afternoon*. With Audrey."

Of course, Phoebe knew it was one of Lucy's favorite movies. Audrey Hepburn and an older, but never more appealing Gary Cooper. Billy Wilder directing. Instantly, Lucy wanted to watch it with Deon. Tonight, no matter what.

"Hi, you guys," she called from the window, and they glanced up and waved. "Just a minute."

A car pulled up and honked, and Sara and Lily got out. Artemis, Phoebe's daughter, who worked the ice cream event last year, wouldn't make it today as she was in Crete visiting relatives.

Lucy leaned out and waved, but no one noticed. Their voices grew louder when Deon finally opened the door, and then there was quiet. Lucy stepped into the shower.

Under the spray, she took her time, breathed in the patchouli-scented soap Deon kept especially for her visits although she practically lived here. He'd bought the soap and a treasure trove of girly goodies on a fall weekend trip to Massachusetts. They'd toured the Norman Rockwell museum and stayed at the old Red Lion, the sort of inn featured in Hallmark movies. Deon loved weekend trips.

He also loved that they were getting the girls together—no easy feat with their grad school schedules.

By the time Lucy took a tour of her walk-in closet and decided what to wear, Deon had started the grill and taken his shower. He popped upstairs to assure her everyone was rolling out the dough. "Take your time, pumpkin seed," he said, pecking her cheek. "I've got it all under control."

"I'll be down in a few minutes." Dawdling was so relaxing, but she needed to put on some speed. She dried her hair, laced it with defrizzer, and pulled on jean shorts and a red top to disguise the inevitable pizza sauce stains.

Downstairs in the kitchen, everyone was fussing over their mini pizzas.

"Hey, Mom, it's about time," Lily said. "I rolled out your pizza. Deon's got it on the grill."

Deon tripped in from the deck with two pizzas. "Get crackin' with toppings for these," he instructed, taking the last of the crusts out to the grill.

"Dad loves evenings like this," Sara remarked as they put the finishing touches on the pizzas. "Making dinner together. He loves cutting up veggies and grilling and—" She gave a wan smile. "Like when Mom was around."

Everyone quieted for a moment.

Sara glanced out at her father on the deck and lowered her voice. "All this homey stuff is really good for him." She paused, holding a slice of red pepper, and contemplated Lucy fussing with her pizza. "You're so good for my dad," she drawled in a gravelly voice. "He really loves you. You know that, don't you?"

Lucy's mouth went slack with wonder at Sara's comment.

"I'll always miss my mom but…you're nothing

like her. I'm so glad things turned out the way they did, you know. You and my dad found each other. And you and my mom—such opposites. A happy coincidence."

"Well, that's one way to put it," Lucy mumbled, unsure what to make of *happy coincidence* then decided it was a good thing.

Deon ambled in from the deck. "Twenty minutes, and we're ready to go." He gazed around the room. "Why's it so quiet in here?" He set the timer on the stove and came over, hung an arm around Lucy and nuzzled her neck. "Did you make mine extra garlicky?"

"Nope."

"Why not?"

She kissed him. "No pesto for you, dear. Not tonight." She leaned close and whispered, "You know why."

****

For a while there was little talk as they devoured the pizza, but soon Marcus and Deon launched into a Yankees versus the Red Sox discussion, and Lily mentioned a new Zac Efron movie. Phoebe and Marcus talked in low voices while the girls chattered, happy to see one another. Finally, Lily wiped a pizza-saucy finger on her napkin. Her gaze floated around the table and came to rest on Lucy. "I have a question."

Lucy sipped her wine and looked at her expectantly. The air above the table vibrated with Lily's big build-up.

"Are you two getting married or something?" Lily barked, startling Lucy.

Sara cleared her throat and nudged Lily with an elbow. "Spill," they said in unison.

Deon leaned close, resting a hand on Lucy's arm.

"Very perceptive of you, but no cigar."

"You mean no marriage cigar?" Sara asked.

Lucy and Deon grinned at the group. "We're moving in together," they laugh-yelled.

"Oh, yeah!" Sara hooted and everyone joined her. "Your house? Or ours?" Sara probed.

Lucy and Deon paused, exchanged a look.

"We're looking for a house," Deon said.

Sara teared up. "I'm so happy for you." She wobbled over to hug Deon, overcome by emotion.

"Both of you," Lily murmured, coming over and squeezing Lucy.

"So happy for you, Daddy," Sara sniffled. "I was getting sort of worried for a while there."

"You were?" Deon was at a loss for words. "Don't you worry about me."

"House hunting is a pretty fun thing to do," Lily said, handing Sara a tissue. "Checking out strangers' homes, rifling through personal papers."

"Yes." Lucy sprang off the stool and clapped. "Will you help us look? If you have the time. Both of you."

"I love visiting other people's houses," Lily laughed through sniffles.

"Good." Deon looked ruffled. "That's settled. And for dessert, Lucy has three flavors of ice cream and Phoebe brought toppings."

"It's Phoebe and Marcus' anniversary," Lucy added.

Phoebe smiled as Marcus pulled her in for a kiss. "We met a year ago." He hesitated. "At that ice cream thing, you know."

"What thing?" Lily asked, and they were off,

Phoebe and Marcus and Deon, holding Lucy's hand in the telling. The story of that year-ago event.

"I thought for sure she was going to meet some guy and forget all about me." Deon pulled Lucy into a hug.

Lucy listened contentedly, warmed by the feeling you get when you've learned something about yourself that allows you to bend, makes life a little easier, and all the good things even better. She'd call it happiness, but you don't have to name feelings, you can just sit back and let them wash over you.

Lucy's Recipes

Lucy's recipes have been created especially for this book. The character made an effort to bake using healthy ingredients. They're all original creations from my young friend and entrepreneur, Eva Papadogiorgaki. Please scroll down for more information. All comments are Eva's.

****

Healthy-ish Blondies

This recipe is packed with fiber, minerals and protein from the chickpeas, tahini, oats, and flaxseeds, and gets some of its sweetness from applesauce. Walnuts are optional but highly recommended.

Ingredients:

½ cup applesauce

2 cups chickpeas (from 540ml can, approximately), drained

½ cup coconut oil, melted

¼ cup tahini

2 tsp vanilla

1 flax egg (1 Tbsp ground flax seeds + 3 Tbsp water, let sit 10 minutes)

1 1/3 cup rolled oats

1 ½ tsp baking powder

1/8 tsp salt

½ cup sugar

1 cup walnuts, roughly chopped

2/3 cups white chocolate chips, or use a chocolate bar and chop into chunks

Instructions:

Pre-heat oven to 350 degrees F. Place applesauce,

chickpeas, coconut oil, tahini and vanilla in a blender or food processor and blend until smooth, about 1 – 2 minutes.

Pour into a bowl and add all the remaining ingredients. Stir well until incorporated.

Pour in a baking pan about 9x9" lined with parchment paper and spread evenly and press down.

Bake for 30-40 minutes, or until toothpick inserted into center comes out clean. Let cool for 10 minutes, remove from pan and allow to cool completely.

Optional: drizzle with melted white chocolate and once it's cool and hardened, cut into squares.

Store in airtight container, in the fridge, for 5-7 days.

****

Strawberry Cheesecake Surprise

This is a summery dessert. The recipe was given to me by my aunt, so I don't know the origins of it, but I have tweaked it a little to my liking. For strawberry lovers, this dish is heaven on earth!

Ingredients:
1 ½ cups plain pretzels, broken into small pieces
¼ cup plus 1 cup sugar
½ cup softened butter or coconut oil
1 8-oz package plain cream cheese
1 small package strawberry or berry flavored Jello
1 pound/ 500 gr frozen or fresh strawberries
Approximately 1 cup whipped cream
Instructions:
Preheat oven to 350 degrees F. In a bowl, mix pretzels, ¼ cup sugar and butter until incorporated and spread in a 9 x 13" pan. Bake for 5 – 10 minutes and let

cool.

In the same bowl, beat the cream cheese and 1 cup sugar. Fold in the whipped cream and spread on top of cooled pretzels.

Dissolve the Jello in 2 cups boiling water and add the strawberries. Spread over the pretzels and chill.

Keep in the freezer and remove 10-20 minutes prior to serving.

****

Brown Sugar Vanilla Pudding

A classic old-school vanilla pudding with a caramel hint given by the brown sugar. Best of all, it's versatile. True pudding lovers eat it plain. Or use it to top a cake, as filling in a pie or jelly roll, or even as a layer in a trifle. Add bread and rum or chocolate for a tasty bread pudding as Lucy did in the novel.

Ingredients:

2/3 cup brown sugar
2 Tbsp cornstarch or 4 Tbsp all-purpose flour
Pinch of salt
2 cups cashew milk (or regular dairy milk)
2 egg yolks, lightly beaten
2 Tbsp butter
1 tsp vanilla

Instructions:

In a saucepan on low heat mix cornstarch or flour, sugar and salt.

Gradually stir in the milk and cook over medium-low heat stirring constantly, until thick and boiling. Boil and stir for 1 minute. Pour a little mixture into the eggs while stirring and then pour that back into the pot. Boil and stir for 1 more minute. Remove from the heat, stir in butter and vanilla and pour into individual bowls. Once cooled, keep refrigerated.

****

Classic Cheesecake

Rich and creamy. My Greek aunt used to make it regularly when I was growing up, and now I make it for my father as a special treat we both enjoy. Top it with a berry sauce or whole fruit jam.

Ingredients:

1 cup digestive cookies (or similar type) crushed, finely but not to a powder

1 cup finely chopped roasted and unsalted almonds

¼ cup granulated sugar

½ cup melted butter

1/8 tsp salt

2 x 8-oz packages plain cream cheese

¾ cups full fat cream

¾ cups ricotta cheese

1/3 cup confectioners' sugar

2 tsp lemon juice

½ tsp vanilla

Instructions:

Pre-heat oven to 350 degrees F. If your cookies and almonds aren't pre-bought finely crushed, you can use a processor and pulse the cookies and almonds until desired consistency. Stir together with salt, sugar, and melted butter. Pour into a pie plate or a springform pan and pack tightly on the bottom and a little up the sides. Bake for 10-12 minutes or until edges are very slightly golden.

Whip the cream in a chilled bowl until stiff peaks form. Place cream cheese and ricotta cheese in a separate bowl and using a hand mixer or a stand mixer whip until incorporated and soft. Add confectioners' sugar, lemon juice and vanilla and mix again. Using a spatula, fold the whipped cream into the cheese mixture by hand.

Pour into cooled crust and spread out evenly. Cover with plastic wrap and place in fridge to set for at least 6 hours.

Serve plain for the full flavor effect or top with berry compote, fresh berries or jam.

****

Chocolate Macaroon Cookies

These macaroons are a similar version of the favorite little gem but since it's a healthier version, it's perfect eaten as part of breakfast or better yet, for an afternoon energy pick-me-up.

Ingredients:
1 cup shredded coconut, sweetened
1 cup oats
1 cup milk of choice
1 Tbsp honey
3 Tbsp coconut oil, melted or very soft
½ cup chocolate chips
2 Tbsp flour

Instructions:
Pre-heat oven to 375 degrees F. Mix coconut, oats, milk, and honey together in a bowl. Stir in melted coconut oil and chocolate chips. Add flour 1 Tbsp at a time until you form a dough. Spoon tablespoon sizes of dough on a parchment lined cookie sheet. Bake for 20-25 minutes.

****

Chocolate Orange Brownies

While the combination of chocolate and orange might still be under debate, this recipe is not. Easy to make, impressive to serve and super tasty!

Ingredients:

½ cup melted butter
¼ cup cocoa powder
2 eggs
¾ cup sugar
¾ cup all-purpose flour
½ cup chopped walnuts
2 Tbsp orange juice
1 Tbsp orange zest
1/8 tsp salt
Frosting:
1 ½ cups confectioners' sugar
3 Tbsp soft butter
2 Tbsp orange juice
2 tsp orange zest

Instructions:

Pre-heat oven to 350 degrees F. Stir cocoa into melted butter until incorporated. In a separate bowl beat eggs and add the cocoa mixture. Add. sugar, flour, walnuts, orange juice and zest and salt. Stir with a spatula just until incorporated. Grease and flour an 8x8" baking pan and pour the mixture in. Bake for 25-30 minutes and cool.

Make the frosting by stirring all ingredients together well with a hand mixer or a whisk.

Spread frosting over the cooled brownies and serve. Garnish with more orange zest if you like.

****

Pizza

Ingredients for dough or purchase ready-made
2 ½ cups white flour
2 packages dry yeast (about 4 ½ tsp)
1 tsp salt
1 tsp sugar
2 Tbsp oil of choice (I use olive oil)
1 cup water
Instructions:

Combine flour, yeast, salt, and sugar. Add the oil and water and stir with a wooden spoon until incorporated. Once dough starts to come together, knead by hand for 5 minutes. Kneading the dough by hand brings out the flavor!

Shape the dough into a ball, place in a bowl lightly coated with oil so the dough doesn't stick and cover with a tea towel or plastic wrap. Leave in a warm place (not somewhere cool or drafty) and let rise until double in size, approximately 2 hours.

Punch down, knead again for a few seconds and roll out on a floured surface with rolling pin.

This dough makes one very large pizza, or 2 medium pizzas.

Ingredients for Sauce:
1 cup tomato sauce from a jar or can**
1 tsp dried oregano
1 tsp dried basil
½ tsp black pepper
½ tsp garlic powder
½ tsp onion powder
**Or you can use half a cup tomato puree and ½ cup tomato sauce, or for a more potent sauce, use only

tomato puree and add your spices
Toppings:
Top the pizza with your favorite ingredients. Some of my favorites include:
Lightly grilled zucchini
Sun-dried tomato
Pre steamed or roasted broccoli
Anchovies
Purple potato or sweet potato (pre-cooked)
Pine Nuts
Arugula, basil or spinach (best added after your pizza is cooked)
Cheese of your choice, such as mozzarella, parmesan, or vegan cheese sauce
It's a great opportunity to use up any leftovers!
Instructions:
Stir all your sauce ingredients in a small bowl. All spices are optional but add a lot of flavor. You can also add thyme, garlic, or minced onion.

Pre-heat your oven at 500 F, unless you use a pizza stone. Note: Some pizza lovers prefer to pre-bake the crust. Your choice.

Once your dough is rolled out and placed on a baking sheet with parchment paper, start the fun part!

Spread your sauce on your pizza as thick or thin as you like

Next spread the cheese around and go close to the edge. I like to leave about ½ inch. Then add your toppings.

Bake pizza for about 20-25 minutes.

As soon as you remove from the oven, add any fresh greens such as arugula, and drizzle with a little olive oil.

Let cool for a few minutes and slice into triangles or squares.

Option to use pesto instead of tomato sauce. I love the flavor combination of pesto, broccoli, and anchovies on a pizza!

These are all original recipes contributed by Eva Papadogiorgaki, The Cretan Nutritionist. Find her on Instagram and Facebook @thecretannutritionist. Thank you so much, Eva, for your hard work and support.

A message from the author…

Follow me on your favorite socials:
https://www.facebook.com/midagedating
https://www.instagram.com/shirleygoldbergauthor/
https://twitter.com/mylifeasadate

Thanks so much for reading *A Little Bit of Lust*. Please take four minutes to write a short review if you enjoyed the book or leave a rating. We authors need readers to pass the good word to their friends, and I speak for writers everywhere when I say, "Thanks so much. Your kind words are appreciated."

A word about the author…

Shirley Goldberg is a writer, novelist, and former ESL and French teacher who's lived in Paris, Crete, and Casablanca. She writes about men and women of a certain age starting over.

Her website at http://midagedating.com offers a humorous look into dating in mid-life, and her friends like to guess which stories are true. *A Little Bit of Lust* is her third book in the series *Starting Over*, although all her books are standalone. Her characters believe you should never leave home without your sense of humor and Shirley agrees.

A Readers Guide to *A Little Bit of Lust*
Warning: contains spoilers!

1. Lucy, Deon, and Phoebe are friends. Whom do you consider to be the lynchpin of the friendship? Why?

2. The characters want different things at the beginning of the story. What does Deon want? What does Lucy want? How will this difference cause problems?

3. What do you think of the concept of eight-minute dating? What do Phoebe, Lucy, and Deon think of the experience?

4. What could explain Deon's backing away from Lucy after their intense but loving weekend together?

5. What does this quote from Chapter 13 tell us about Deon and how difficult he's finding moving on after the death of his wife? "He loved being married and the idea of dating filled him with a subdued hysteria."

6. Why do you think Lucy is interested in Marcus? What dampens her enthusiasm for him and what does this say about her friendship with Phoebe?

7. After Deon puts Lucy on *ignore*, he reverses himself and tells her he is "ready." Do you think her strong reaction to this news is warranted? In your opinion, why does she have such antipathy for him at this moment?

8. Lucy and Deon shop for clothes together at the mall, where Steve, a salesman-actor flirts with her. How do you think this might have prompted Deon to rethink and escalate his efforts to win Lucy back?

9. How do Lucy's early pregnancy, marriage, and her husband's desertion color her view of relationships?

10. How do you think Phoebe plays an important role in getting Lucy to take Deon seriously and to move on from his past bad behavior?

11. Why does Lucy have last-minute doubts about Deon? How does he quell those doubts?

12. Why do you think the author included an epilogue showing the characters a year later? What does this add to the story?

An excerpt from *Middle Ageish*, Shirley Goldberg's first book in the Starting Over series.

Luke touched my shoulder, his fingers lingering for a moment. Heat spread from my shoulder in a wave down my chest to my belly.

"I don't know how you say mosquito in French but the candles are dying down and I'm feeling the pinch. Come, I'll make you comfortable inside." He stood, still holding his glass, pulled me up very gently, walked me to the back door, and opened it. I stepped into a dimly lit room with two huge couches and a fireplace. He had built a fire.

"A springtime fire," I said. A huge painting above the fireplace and bookshelves to the ceiling. More bookshelves than I'd seen in a long time.

His hands massaged my shoulders. "Yes." He was touching my neck. "Any excuse for a fire will do." He kissed me, a gentle touch, more of a brush with his lips.

"Nice. I've had quite a lot of wine and everything is so nice." I looked behind me at the couch and my eyes closed.

"Do you need a nap?" His mouth was moving on my neck so slowly I felt breathless. Did he mean a nap for two? Not yet, *not yet*, the kissing was going so hummingly, like a little hummingbird. Half my mind, the practical part, focused on cleaning up all the fishes, carrying in plates, rinsing. The other half jumped up and down. This kissing was going really well, and I knew it was going well because I felt the tingle of it all the way down my back to my toes.

"Ah, yes." Luke took my hand and led me to the couch, eased me down, careful to leave a cushion's space between us. He reached out and touched my face, so gentle, his hand lingering a few moments. "I couldn't stop thinking about you. That was a big clue. Everything in my big, dumb brain kept coming back to that."

I leaned away from him to get a better look at his face in the darkening room.

He swayed closer and there were kisses, the faintest of kisses, his voice soft and low. "I hope it's the right time for you. I hope you're not dating anyone, but I'm not asking any questions. Not yet." More kisses, delicate as breath, slow, deliberate, until all thinking dissolved.

Enough. I had thought and planned in the past, asked questions, analyzed, searched for red flags, discussed, telephoned, and emailed. This time I was doing what I felt like doing, and what I felt like doing was…this.

And a little of that.